Mary Cowden Clarke

Honey from the weed

Mary Cowden Clarke

Honey from the weed

ISBN/EAN: 9783743333901

Manufactured in Europe, USA, Canada, Australia, Japa

Cover: Foto ©Andreas Hilbeck / pixelio.de

Manufactured and distributed by brebook publishing software (www.brebook.com)

Mary Cowden Clarke

Honey from the weed

HONEY FROM THE WEED

VERSES

BY

MARY COWDEN-CLARKE

AUTHOR OF "THE CONCORDANCE TO SHAKESPEARE,"
"THE GIRLHOOD OF SHAKESPEARE'S HEROINES,"
"THE IRON COUSIN," ETC., ETC., ETC.

"Thus may we gather honey from the weed."—*Shakespeare.*

LONDON:
C. KEGAN PAUL & CO., 1, PATERNOSTER SQUARE.
1881.

PREFACE

As one who wanders in a stately wood
Amid the glories of the grand old trees,
Stoops here and there to cull a wayside weed,
A spray of fern, a white anemone,
A blade of feathery grass, or harebell blue,
Until a simple nosegay grows, brought home
In token of the pleasant way gone through—
So I, long traversing the sunny glades,
The verdant depths, and lofty forest growths
Of Shakespeare's verse, have happed at intervals
On waifs and strays of fancy, here tied up
In likeness of a handful of wild flowers;
Collected for the sake of that which they
Record, and for the sake of those who crush
Not under foot the smallest weed that may
Possess one grace of shape or fragrance sweet.

VILLA NOVELLO, GENOA.

1881.

CONTENTS.

A PARLOUR ROMANCE.

Four months ago I thought him lost:
  I strove to think I did not care:
But deep, deep down within my heart
  Was something very like despair.

He often used to come and stay
  At brother William's pretty place,
When I was on a visit there
  To see the famous boating-race.

He, laughing, said, he'd " pull us out,"
  To see how well the oarsmen wrought
In practising ; but took us where
  We passed the time in doing naught.

He used to row us out beneath
  The trees that overhung the stream ;
Where, gliding on in cool, green light,
  We felt as if in pleasant dream.

He talked with her—not much with me—
  With Alice, brother William's wife ;
They kept up lively, sportive talk,
  A kind of amicable strife.

B

Sometimes he'd make us sing to him ;
  And Alice, after some demur,
Would join her sweet-toned voice with mine ;
  And then he thanked—not me, but her.

I liked that best : I liked he should
  Not take much notice of so shy
A mortal as myself ; that she
  Should have to answer him, not I.

And next she would insist that he
  Must make the harmony complete ;
And so we found that he likewise
  Possessed a voice both full and sweet.

We sang a dozen charming things ;
  Stray bits and pieces, in three parts,
Remembered from our favourite stores,
  Gounod's, or Weber's, or Mozart's.

And while he sang, his eyes would rest
  Upon the spot beneath my feet ;
But sometimes suddenly upraised
  His glance, and mine unwares would meet.

I did my best to look away,
  And not allow myself to note
The droop or raising of his eyes ;
  But mine had learned the trick by rote

Of watching—when 'twas turned from me—
  His face : and, do whate'er I could,
My wayward eyes still followed his ;
  Yes, though I did my best, they would.

I felt myself grow hot and cold,
  I told myself I would not do it ;
And yet, the very next time, did—
  However sharply I might rue it.

I took myself to task, and thought,
  I'm sure I care not whether down
Or up he cast his eyes, or if
  He smile, as lost in thought, or frown.

His gaze is fixed upon one spot,
  Perhaps because he's thinking how
The next bar comes : or, p'rhaps, because
  He does not feel inclined just now

To banter Alice with quick wit
  Like hers ; or else, perchance, he may
Be musing on some others who
  Might sing with him some former day.

Who knows ?   Our music may recall
  Some better music to his thought ;
Some softer, dearer voice than ours ;
  Some singing to which ours is naught.

His look seems often inward bent
  On some remembered face and voice :
And yet, when upward it is raised,
  It seems to thoroughly rejoice ;

As if it took delight in what
  It gazes on ; and yet—how's this ?
I'm pondering again upon his looks :
  What matters if I guess or miss

Their meaning ?   What is it to me ?
But still—they're interesting looks—
Expressive eyes—the sort of eyes
   One reads enigmas in, like books.

The sort of eyes that draw one on
   To speculate upon their soft
Intensity : and that, no doubt,
   Is why I watch his eyes so oft.

I reasoned thus within myself,
   And fancied I was " fancy free " ;
But all the while was fancying
   If fancy 'twere he fancied me.

One afternoon, it chanced that he,
   And I, and Alice snugly sat
Ensconced in parlour window-seat ;
   And had a quiet sober chat.

At least, *they* had : I silent kept,
   And listened to their talk sedate ;
Unusual in this lively pair,
   So fond of rallying debate.

But now they held a grave discourse
   On subjects high and nobly good ;
And well did Howard West—his name—
   Maintain the grounds on which he stood.

I found how lofty was his creed,
   How firm his principles and pure :
I learned to value, to esteem,
   Where first I—What ? Well, I'm not sure

What 'twas I felt for Howard West :
  'Twas interest, 'twas quite above
A common liking ; yet, I think—
  I think—it could not have been—love !

And still they earnestly talked on,
  Until a servant came to say
Some visitors were come ; and so
  My sister Alice went away.

He stayed : I plied my needle, mute :
  He took my scissors up, and clipped
Small morsels off my reels of thread :
  I quietly worked on, but slipped

Some stitches, though I tried to keep
  My hands from trembling ; for I felt
His eyes upon me : but no word
  Fell from his lips.   At last, I smelt

The fragrant whiff of Will's cigar
  Outside the open window where
We sat : he loungingly approach'd,
  And asked his friend to come and share

His smoking in the elm-tree walk :
  But Howard shook his head and smiled
Refusal : William leaned against
  The sill, and said to me, " Why, child,

" How notably you're working ! if
  You had to earn your bread, you could
Not work more diligently ; come,
  Put by your stitchery ; be good,

" And pleasantly play lazy, when
    We want you to amuse us, West
And I : we like to have your looks ;
    Not that bent head, which I detest.

" It don't allow the comment of
    The eye ; a man can't be aware
If what he's said has pleased or not ;
    It isn't right, it isn't fair."

" Not fair ?" said Howard.   Then he stopped,
    Significantly laughing.   " No,
Not fair;" retorted brother Will,
    In his blunt, headlong way ; " and so,

" I hate to see a woman work
    As if her life depended on't ;
Especially when rich, like you,
    Miss Nell, who from the very font

" Were mistress of a good round sum ;
    Our Indian uncle leaving you—
Not me—his sixty thousand pounds :
    What made the good old fellow do

" So wise a trick, I wonder ?   P'rhaps
    He knew that sister Nell would take
Far better care of it than I,
    And work and stitch and drudge to make

" It up a hundred thousand pounds !
    A plum !   An actual money plum !
Now what would sister Nelly do
    With it, if she had such a sum ? "

And brother William pulled my curl
That hung provokingly below
His hand: I smiled at him, and looked
A moment up: in doing so,

I caught a glimpse of Howard's face:
'Twas deadly pale; his very lips
Were white; but brother William goes
Still rattling on, and lightly flips

The ash from end of his cigar.
" And, by-the-by," he said; " you come
Of age next month, child; don't you, Nell?
I hope a feast, not ' kettle-drum,'

" Will celebrate the grand event.
What does my father say? Does he
Intend to have us all to spend
The day? What is the thing to be?

" A morning in the garden grounds?
Their modest limits set ablaze
At night with lamps among the trees,
And rockets sent up to amaze

" The country-folk? How have you planned?"
" We mean to have a quiet day;
But hope you'll come, with Alice, Will;"
Was all I mustered voice to say.

" A quiet day! What, when you come
Of age! That memorable date
Which sees you your own mistress, Nell,
The mistress of your future fate!"

" But, brother mine, I do not wish
   My daughterhood to kill ;
I would not have my father feel
   I'm independent of his will.

" I like to know and him to feel
   I'd rather be his guided child,
Than have my own free mistress-ship ;
   So gentle has he been and mild."

" You little goose, I do believe
   You would !" laughed brother William ; " still
'Tis glorious to be the sole
   And thorough master of one's will."

" The master, yes ; the mistress, no ;"
   I answered·: " Women mostly fear
Responsibility, and wish
   The help and counsel they revere."

To my relief, our Alice then
   Returned ; and I, upgathering
My needlework, the parlour left,
   Attempting some slight tune to sing.

But when I crept to my own room,
   I threw myself upon the bed ;
And lying dumbly there, as stunned,
   I thought o'er all that had been said.

And still more all that had been *looked :*
   I thought of that pale face, those white
And firm-set lips, as if he would
   Not let them quiver, held so tight.

I thought of that sad stricken look
  His eyes had in the moment when
I raised my head to answer Will:
  It was but for an instant then,

But now it dwelt upon my sight
  Like some strange haunting portrait-face,
That follows with persisting eyes
  Where'er one moves from place to place.

My fortune! Yes—'twas hearing that
  Which caused the sudden change I'd seen:
But why? Why? Could it be because—
  Because—whatever might have been

He felt must now be given up?
  Oh, could it be because his sense
Of honour told him he was poor
  And I was rich? He has intense

Abhorrence—that I know, I heard
  Him say so—of a man who makes
A woman's wealth the means of his
  Advancement; of a man who takes

A wife as so much stock in trade
  To help him to begin the world
And set him up in business
  For life; or worse, to keep him curled

In soft luxurious idleness,
  Not needing then to work for bread:
As well, he said, and better, that
  A fellow starved or dropped down dead,

Than be so base.   He said as much,
   I well remember, on that day
When we were by the river-side
   And fed the swans with bread: "We may—

Who knows?"—half laughing, Alice said;
   " We some of us may come to want
This bit of bread that now we throw
   Away to birds : 'tis waste, I grant."

" I do not grant 'tis waste ;" said he :
   " It pleases us, and more the birds ;
And therefore it has had its use :
   But this I'll grant, you've said true words

" In saying we may come to want
   A piece of bread : in some remote
Excursion 'mong the Alps, or some
   Delicious ramble in a boat

" Along the shores of lonely lake,
   Where food is hard to find, and where
The most fastidious might be glad
   To have a crust, the sorriest fare.

" The richest of us may feel this ;
   Then well may I that am not rich
At all !" he laughing said.   " And we,"
   Said Alice, " know the relish which

" Belongs to moderate means ; for Will
   And I have not too much ; and you,
You know, have not a sixpence yet,
   Poor church-mouse Nell ! the very few

" You have are what your father gives
   You for your pocket-money, dear!"
She nodded at me archly, with
   An irony to me quite clear,

But which I saw, was lost on him,
   Who took her in good faith, and deemed
Me penniless, as she implied ;
   A thought he rather liked, it seemed,

For he went on, in sprightly mood,
   To speak more freely of himself
Than usual ; and 'twas then we fell
   Into that talk of worldly pelf,

Of seeking dower in a wife,
   As chief inducement, not free choice :
And I remember well the tone
   Of scorn and loathing in his voice,

As he denounced those men who act
   The fortune-hunter ; those who make
A mercenary marriage ; those
   Who give up love for money's sake ;

Who forfeit the divinest boon
   On earth, and of their own accord
Renounce God's dearest gift, to make
   Secure of lodging and of board.

And then he drew a pleasant sketch
   Of union where the two had dared
To face together poverty ;
   And simply dressed and humbly fared,

Until the man's exertions earned
    Position, competence, and ease ;
The woman's cheerful care the while
    Conducing—busiest of bees !—

To garner up the honey in
    Their hive of home and life :
And as he drew that picture of
    The little busy cheerful wife,

I fancied—was it fancy ?—that
    His eyes had rested tenderly
On me : or had I built in air
    My castles all too slenderly ?

However that might be, 'twas past :
    For now he found I was not poor,
He never would confess he loved—
    E'en if he loved—I felt quite sure.

And did he love ?   That, that was still
    The question throbbing to and fro
Within me, pulsing in my veins,
    And beating on my heart its blow

Of passionate demand.   At length
    I stifled its appeal, and would
Not listen to its urgency ;
    But soon as possibly I could,

I rose, and bathed my swollen lids,
    Arranged my ruffled hair, and cooled
My burning temples with my palms ;
    And then I resolutely schooled

Myself to wear the wonted mien
  Of quietude that often won
Me from my stalwart brother Will
  The names of silent little one,

And placid chit that nothing moves.
  And when I told myself my look
Was just as usual, I went down
  Into the parlour and betook

Me to my needlework again.
  There William found me when, with shrill
Short whistle, in he peeped, and cried :
  " Why, Nell, you're here, and stitching still !

" I could not think where you had gone :
  I hunted for you everywhere,
In library, in music-room ;
  Beneath the tree in open air ;

" Down by the shady river-side,
  Your favourite seat ; but no, in none
Of your own usual haunts could I
  Or Alice find you, Nell, not one ;

" And we were wanting you to tell
  The news : a telegram has come
To summon West to town at once.
  I told him I was sure 'twas some

" Announcement of good news, its words
  Were so mysterious ; but he
Appears to think it rather a
  Forewarning hint of bad to be,

" He looks so thoughtful and cast down :
    A right good chap is West," said Will,
" And most sincerely sorry I
    Should be, if aught befell him ill.

" He's gone to put his traps to rights,
    And means to start by earliest train ;
I don't half like to part with him
    So soon ; I thought he would remain

" At least till you, Nell, went back home ;
    And as for Alice, she is quite
Upset because he's going away
    So suddenly ; she says he might

" Have waited till he had a more
    Precise intelligence ; for in
The telegram, they said they'd tell
    More details soon : we could not win,

" However, from him his consent
    To stay one hour longer than
Was need ; he would insist he ought
    To go, and he's a steadfast man

" Where principle and duty are
    Concerned : a sturdy fellow's West :
There's naught can move him when he's sure
    He's doing what is right and best."

And then Will bustled off again
    To help his friend, and bring him down
A moment ere he left : and then
    Came sister Alice, in a brown,

Brown study ; she was deep in thought
   On what could be the cause of this
Abrupt recall ; and seemed to fear
   It augured somewhat much amiss.

For she was fond of William's friend ;
   Esteemed him highly, though a jest
Was ever bandying between
   Herself and lively Howard West.

But grave, not lively, looked he now
   When he came with Will to say
" Good-bye ! "   He said it briefly, but
   With fervour, in the manly way

That Englishmen are wont to use
   When feeling much : he said it first
To them : and then he came to me :
   Ah, that was hardest task, the worst

To bear with quiet seeming ; but
   I bore it firmly, wondering at
Myself for standing there so calm—
   As if I felt not even that.

He stood an instant there, and made
   As if he'd take my hand ; but did
Not touch it, after all ; and mine,
   With sudden drop, beside me slid :

He uttered nothing ; not as much
   To me as to the others ; said
Not e'en the simple phrase, " Good-bye " ;
   But silently that instant staid.

Yet though he spoke no single word,
  His eyes were not without their speech ;
They had their own mute eloquence
  That to my heart of heart did reach.

From that one look I learned the truth :
  I saw it clearly, he loved me ;
But saw, as clearly, that his love
  For ever undeclared would be.

Another instant—he was gone :
  And Alice followed him, and Will
Drove with him to the station ; I
  Remaining there, dead-cold and still

As stone.   Before a week was past,
  I begged my brother and his wife
To let me go to my dear father.
  I longed to be at home: my life

Seemed smitten into listlessness ;
  I only felt a constant dull
And dreary pain, that nothing else
  But father-love could help to lull.

I had that father-love ; I had
  It amply, fondly, as of old ;
But though it soothed me as I hoped,
  It left me with that deadly cold

Oppression which benumbed my frame ;
  And which with paralysing weight
Deprived me of all strength to live.
  I battled hard against this state :

But ever more and more it crushed
  Me down, until I sank at last
Beneath its heavy load ; and lay,
  While many, many weeks went past,

On what to all appeared my bed
  Of death. But, no ; I did not die :
My youth, my father's care, the will
  Of God, prevented that ; and I

Recovered. If, indeed, it might
  Be called recovery, which was
But a return to that dull sense
  Of loss, that knew no moment's pause.

I felt that he was lost to me ;
  And though I had no right to grieve,
And would not own I grieved, yet still
  That feeling nothing could relieve.

I sat one evening upon
  The hassock at my father's feet :
My eyes were fixed in dreamy gaze
  Upon the fire ; a host of sweet

Yet bitter recollections thronged
  Upon me ; when my father bent
Down towards me with a whisper that,
  For all its gentleness, quick sent

The blood in torrents to my brow :
  " A silver penny for your thoughts,
My quiet Nelly ; " were his words ;
  " You can't attempt to say that naught's

C

" The sum of them ; I've watched your face,
   And know its every line too well
To doubt there's something troubling you.
   I long have thought that you could tell

" Me, if you would, a story of
   Some secret fret : alas, my child,
You know you have no mother now
   To counsel and console with mild

" Benignant wisdom ; but, my dear,
   If you could summon courage to
Confide your griefs, as though he were
   A woman, to your father, you

" Would find him no less eager to
   Give comfort and advice than she.
Come, Nelly, darling, trust me, love :
   Ay, lay your head upon my knee,

" Just so, and then your tell-tale face
   Will hidden be, and you can speak
Unfearingly." He put his hand
   Upon my hair, and smoothed my cheek;

And somehow in my spirit rose
   A strength, a calm, it had not known
For months : it let me talk to my
   Kind father now as if I'd grown

A little child again ; and so
   I said : " Dear father, I will tell
You something I've been thinking of ;
   A fancy that your daughter Nell

" Has lately had : you know I came
  Of age when I was ill; and while
I lay upon my sick-bed, I
  Remembered with a sort of smile

" How rich I had become, and how
  My riches were of little good
To me, but might be made of use
  To those who almost surely would

" Survive me ; so I thought I'd lose
  No time, if I recovered, in
Consulting you how I might make
  My will; but never could begin

" To speak to you, till you yourself,
  Kind father, gave me courage for
The task. I wanted to explain
  What are my wishes, father, or

" I rather ought to say, what are
  My hopes; my hopes that you will see
As I do in the three bequests
  I wish to make ; that you'll agree

" They're right and fitting." Here I paused
  A moment, and my father said :
" But why, my Nelly, should you think
  About your will ? You've left your bed

" Of sickness now, and ought to think
  Of nothing just at present but
How soonest to get well." He tried
  To speak in sprightly tone and put

Some playfulness in what he said,
    Although his voice was trembling : I
Replied with steadier voice than he :
    " I do not feel afraid to die,

" And think I have not long to live ;
    So, father, I had better not
Put off what should be done at once :
    And therefore let me tell you what

" I wish to do with uncle's gift.
    First, I should like to leave a third
To you, my father, for your deeds
    Of charity ; I've often heard

" You long for somewhat more to give
    Away in help to your own poor :
Next, I should like to leave a third
    To William and his wife ; I'm sure

" They would not sorry be to have
    A larger income, when the joy
That Alice looks for comes to them :
    I know they hope 'twill be a boy,

" And asked me to be godmother ;
    But I shall leave my christening gift
For them to give him, shall I not,
    My father ?"   Suddenly the lift

Of his soft hand from off my hair
    Bespoke him moved : but soon, his mild
Serenity regained, he said :
    " Go on, my dear ; go on, my child."

I nerved myself, and hurried on :
" Dear father, as regards the rest—
The last third of my wealth, I mean—
I wish it left to Howard West."

A silence followed, during which
I heard the beating of my heart ;
But presently my father said—
His very quiet made me start—

" And who is Howard West, my dear ? "
I mustered breath to low reply :
" He's William's friend, I met him there ;
He is not rich ; and, father, I

Should like to make him so, for he
Would make a noble use of gold.
It was my brother showed me this,
When he of Howard's virtues told."

My father answered nothing for
A while ; but stooped and fondly kissed
Me. I lay still and comforted ;
And stole my hand around his wrist

To hold the clasping smoothness 'gainst
My throbbing forehead, which it seemed
To calm. We sat for some time thus :
A sense of peace fell on me, streamed

Upon my heart, so long the seat
Of secret trouble and unrest ;
I felt that now I even could
Think tranquilly of Howard West.

The being able to speak out
  His name to my dear father had
Itself brought ease ; that dull dead weight
  Of aching dreariness and sad

Depression left me, seeming raised
  As by a spell of magic power—
The spell of parent's tenderness,
  Soft thrown around me in that hour

Of fireside confidence. And who
  So fit to be the confidant
Of daughter's heart-perplexities
  As a loved parent ? Why, for want

Of parents' sympathy, should girls
  So often driven be to seek
In so-called " bosom-friend " the help
  They fain would have from counsel meek

Yet firm of their own mother ; or,
  If she be lost, from father's wise
Experience and care ? It is
  Because too often parents' eyes

Are apt to be unlenient, and
  To view unfavouringly those
Their children think perfection ; which,
  If harshly shown, is sure to close

The lips of the confider. But
  My father's kiss had softly told
Me he approved—at least, that he
  Would give no disapproval cold

To my strong wish regarding
  The recipients I had chosen for
That money I should never live to use—
  My Indian uncle's well-earned store.

Thus musing placidly, I leaned
  In motionless content : until
My father gently stirred, and said :
  " Come, Nelly mine, we've had our fill

" Of quiet talk and quiet thought ;
  And now we'll prudently retire
To rest : my invalid has had
  Enough of gazing in the fire.

" To-morrow she and I will take
  An early drive to see our Will
And Alice : we'll go slowly ; by
  The coppice lane and water-mill."

But on the morrow I was not,
  My father thought, so strong and well
As he had hoped ; and would not let
  Me go with him.   He said he'd tell

My sister Alice, that he'd played
  The tyrant, and forbidden me
To venture out, but promised that
  He'd bring me with him next time he

Drove over to their house.   When he
  Was gone, I made our faithful Stoke
Warm wrap me up in shawls and let
  Me go and sit beneath the oak.

At first she shook her head, my good
  Old nurse ; but when I showed how bright
The sun fell near the tree, and yet
  That there was shade, she said I might

Sit out for just an hour or so,
  If I would promise to be good,
And honestly confess if I
  Felt chill : I promised that I would.

And then the dear old woman brought
  Me out my work-basket, and I
Luxuriated in the sense
  Of being once again in my

Accustomed ways ere I fell ill—
  My garden-seat, my needle plying
In dreamy fashion, as of old,
  That measured pace with sweet thoughts
    flying

Like flitter-wingèd butterflies,
  Now here, now there, across my brain.
I had not known for many a day,
  So peaceful—almost happy—train

Of musings as the one that now
  Possessed me ; and I let it take
Its way. I let it lead me on
  To when he (women always make

The little pronoun " he " the name
  Of him they chiefly think of!), when
He would be poor no more, but rich
  From Nelly's legacy ; and then

I wondered whether any thought
   Of her who once had sung to him
With Alice in the boat, and fed
   The swans, and listened to the whim

Of jesting at the thought we might
   All come to want a piece of bread,
Would e'er recur to him? Or his
   Own picture of the couple wed

In poverty and happiness?
   Or whether, even, he might glance
At that fair sketch he'd drawn
   Of busy cheerful wife, perchance?

I fancy 'twas because my nurse,
   Whenever she approached me, found
Me looking quietly content,
   That she consented, when came round

The more than "hour or so" agreed,
   To let me stay beneath the oak;
But when three hours had passed, and still
   I lingered, then good careful Stoke

Insisted I should come back to
   The parlour. There I found a book
That held me deep entranced until
   The shades of evening fairly took

Me by surprise, in casting o'er
   The page a tint of grey. I laid
Aside the volume then; and while
   The twilight veiled the room, I played

Some wandering chords of harmony,
  By snatches murmuring to myself
In lowest tones the words and tune.
  At last came lights, and Stoke herself,

To tell me that our dinner-time
  Was near, but that my father had
Not yet come back; and did I think
  He meant to stay the night? A lad

Had brought a note from him, it seemed;
  Which now she gave to me to read,
As very likely it would tell
  If master stayed—quite sure, indeed.

Thus nursey talked apace, to break
  The startle of bad news, should such
Await me when I oped the note:
  But no; it only said thus much:

" I don't return to-night, dear child;
  Because there happens to be here
A guest, with whom I want to make
  Acquaintance: I may not, I fear,

" Be home again just yet; so bid
  Good Stoke put up what I shall need
And send it by the messenger.
  Both William and his Alice plead

" For me to make my visit not
  Too short; but we shall see: I now
Already long to be at home
  With Nelly mine, who well knows how

" I truly sign myself her own
  Affectionately faithful friend
And father, Alexander Bruce."
  I had not nearly reached the end

Of what I quickly read, before
  I found myself repeating, " Guest!
A guest my father wants to know :
  What if it should be Howard West!"

And all the while I tried to dine,
  And all the while good nursey talked,
And all the while I tried to sleep—
  When, lastly, I had slowly walked

Upstairs and gone to bed—my thought
  Was still, " What if 'twere Howard West!"
The mere idea it might be he
  Sufficed to banish sleep and rest.

Next morning nursey scolded me
  For having lain awake all night;
As she could see, she said, I had,
  By heavy eyes and cheeks too bright

With their pink spot on either side.
  I only laughed, and told her they
Were trying to get colour while
  My father was detained away,

That I might look less ghostly than
  I lately had, when he returned :
But nursey still looked grave, and put
  Her hand against the spots that burned,

And muttered something vexedly,
 The while she helped me as I dressed :
But I was once more thinking, " If
 It really should be Howard West ! "

Another day, another night
 Went by, and nursey now spoke out ;
She said, " My master's very wrong,
 And doesn't know what he's about

" To stay away so long : but that
 Is so like men ; they never see
What's close before their eyes : his child
 Might actually dying be

" Of thousand foolish fancies, of
 Suspense and inward fret, he'd not
Perceive it : no, not he !"   " Hush, nurse ;"
 I said ; "be sure he's doing what

" He thinks and knows is right ; I know
 My father always acts for best :"
I thought within myself : " What if
 He should be judging Howard West ?

" What if he should be staying but
 To learn his worth and excellence ?
To see if really he possess
 The principle and true good sense

" That daughter Nelly said he had,
 And made her want to leave him some
Of her dead uncle's money ?"   Then
 Aloud I said : " You'll see, he'll come

" Now very soon ; you know how hard
  It is to get from them away ;
My brother William and his wife
  Are always sure to make him stay."

Despotic nursey only gave
  A half-assenting grunt to this ;
As she stooped over my arm-chair,
  And pressed upon my cheek a kiss.

" It's just like you, my dove, to speak
  Up bravely, think and hope the best ;
But now, lean back, and try and put
  A stop to thinking ; try and rest."

She left me quiet, by myself,
  Beside the parlour-window, where
I watched the sunset golden glow
  Amid long streaks of cloudlet fair.

A ripple of encrimsoned lines
  Across a sky of pearly green,
And dazzling radiance centred there
  That cast abroad its glorious sheen.

The hills were steeped in purple gloom
  Beneath the brilliant upper light ;
They looked the darker for the near
  Excess of that effulgence bright.

So seemed my life, that had been near
  To happiness supremely bright ;
But now seemed left in cold and gloom
  By the withdrawal of that light.

Yet, still, the hills had had their hour
  Of revelling in sunshine rife ;
So I had been the better for
  The love which beamed upon my life.

What though it had been brief ? what though
  It had been silently withheld ?
It only had been kept unsaid
  By reticence that I beheld

And knew for what it was ; that made
  Me but the more respect and love
The man who thus could act, and let
  Right principle take place above

E'en love itself. What though I'd lost
  Him from my earthly life, perchance
In other and more perfect life—
  But who were those I saw advance ?

Two figures yonder, coming on,
  Amid the golden halo shed
Around them from the western sky,
  Now soft suffused with rosy red ;

Two figures—surely, they—how came
  It that my heart so quickly guessed ?
I knew that one my father was,
  The other none but Howard West.

They came on, on : and by the time
  They reached the window where I sat,
I'd bid my heart be still and calm.
  " I told you we should find her at

" The window in her favourite seat ; "
  My father said. " And how's my child ?
How is she, quiet Nelly mine ?
  Prepared to welcome, with her mild

" Low voice, her loving father and
  His hard-to-be-persuaded guest ?
I had some difficulty, I
  Assure you, child, with Howard West ;

" He had some scruples, when he found
  You were not well, to come and pay
A visit to us now : but I
  Would make him come ; I'd have my way.

" It is not often that I find
  A fellow so congenial to
My old-world notions of what should
  Make up a manly man, one who

" At once becomes a valued friend,
  A cherished intimate : I ask
His pardon for outsaying this
  Before his face ; but I can't mask

" My liking for a man because
  He happens to be modest and
Abashed when blunter men are frank
  And speak their mind." My father's hand

Gave cordial grasp to Howard's, as
  He led him in, and brought him to
The parlour where I sat. I saw
  That he was deeply moved, and knew

It was because he found me changed
　So much—so thin, and wanly pale ;
He pressed the wasted hand, and *looked*
　This, when he found his voice *would* fail.

" I told you, West," my father said,
　" This wilful little Nelly means
To slip away from us, and leave
　Behind her something that she weens

" Will comfort us for losing her :
　I look to you to prove to her
That thinking thus she makes mistake ;
　We want herself; and much prefer

" Her to her kindly meant bequests."
　My father bent a moment close
Beside me, saying softly in
　My ear : " Dear quiet Nelly knows

" He's worthy of all trust : I think
　So too : but, darling, mind you *give*
Not *leave* your money to him.   Mind !
　I want my little Nell to live."

My father left us.   Howard's hand
　Had never loosed its folding clasp
Upon the wasted hand it held ;
　And now I felt a closer grasp,

With tender yet compulsive force,
　Take firm possession of the poor ,
Thin thing that he upgathered to
　His lips and breast, as making sure

It was his own : his eyes asked mine
  If 'twere not so : and mine told his
He knew it well—as well he did.
  What need was there of words ? Our bliss

Was perfect : ne'ertheless he said—
  He said—no matter what he said ;
The gist of it, I think, was this—
  He asked me when we should be wed.

Four months ago I thought him lost,
  I thought him lost to me for life :
But now I know he is my own,
  And I'm to be his happy wife.

THE YULE LOG.

The evening was cloudless : but there hung
A cloud upon the hearts of those who sat
Beneath the moss-grown apple-tree in midst
Of their small cottage garden ; for that night
Must sailor Charley leave them all to go
To sea.

" 'Tis old," the grey-haired father said,
As 'mong the almost leafless boughs he gaz'd ;
" Time was when May beheld it full of bloom,
With clusters flushing pink and white against
The tender green ; and autumn brought a crop
Of ruddy fruit that bent the branches down—
So laden was the tree.   But now 'tis old
And fit for naught : ay, ay, we all must come
To uselessness, old age, and then to death.
'Tis well if while we have our youth and strength
We put forth blossoms good and fruit."   " Say not
'Tis fit for naught ! " exclaimed the cheery voice
Of Charley.   " See its mossy arms, how broad
They spread, how soft and sheltering extend
Above our heads, as if to gather us
Beneath their loving canopy, and make
Us feel the more together here at home.
At home ! where still my ev'ry thought returns
And nestles happily while I'm away !
I see you all, in thought, assembled here
And sending out your thoughts to me across
The sea: say not 'tis fit for naught, the dear
Old apple-tree !   And more, besides the screen

It makes above our rustic seat, yon clump
Of gnarlèd canker'd wood, which grows apart,
A burly limb excrescent, just will serve
For our next Christmas log, our good Yule log!"
" But you will not be here to fell it down,"
The wrinkl'd mother sighing said : " Ah, son !
How many ways shall we your absence feel ! "
" If I'm not here to fell the clump, at least
I will return for when 'tis burnt ! " he cried ;
" I cannot be away at Christmas-tide ;
I must be back among you all by then ;
I must, I will be with you all, be sure !
Now, mind my words, you'll see me, I will come !"
His wrinkl'd mother smil'd to hear his tone
Of confidence ; his sister Peggy, with
Her merry eyes, look'd gladly up ; and Ben,
His younger brother, gave a joyful shout ;
While gentle Mary Gray, his sweetheart and
His promis'd wife, drew closer to his side
And press'd his arm with both her clasping hands.
" You will ? you will be sure to come ? you will
Get leave of absence, then, you think ? I fear'd
It would not be till after New Year's Day ; "
She whisper'd, with a tremble in her voice.
" Nay, that is when we shall be wedded, dear,
I trust ; " he answered low ; " so, judge if I
Will not strain ev'ry nerve to come back here
Before the time ; besides, I feel I must
Spend Christmas Day among you all at home ;
I must, I will ; so, mark my words, I'll come !
You'll see me here ! " He gather'd her within
His strong right arm, and held her to his breast
With grasp as firm as were his tone and words ;
And she felt hope and comfort fill her soul.
But gravely then the grey-hair'd father spoke :

" My son, ' If God be willing,' pr'ythee add ;
Your words of cheer and confidence are right ;
But say ' If God be willing,' too, my lad."
" 'Twas in my thought, I had it in my heart,
My father ; " Charley said ; " 'tis so much part
Of all I think and hope, I speak it not
Aloud ; but none the less I breathe it still
Within myself 'neath all I say and do.
When our good ship, the Antelope, in stress
Of weather, drives amain upon some stern
Lee-shore, begirt with cliffs and frowning bluffs
Forbidding access, threat'ning death, my cry
Of ' Courage, messmates ! We will keep her off ! '
Is ever follow'd by a deep ' Please God ! '
That echoes in my soul : or when, 'mid rocks
That bristle 'neath the surging breakers white,
Rough cresting the wide waste of waters dark,
She glides with dang'rous swiftness, and I shout :
' 'Ware rocks ahead ! We'll get her through, my lads ! '
' If God be willing ' bases still the loud
Shrill tone wherewith I labour to outpierce
The screams of whistling winds and din of weather :
Believe it, father ; earnest faith and trust
Are ever in my heart, though not mayhap
Upon my lips ; and so, if God doth will,
I'll surely come.   But now, farewell ; 'tis time
I should be gone ; farewell, my mother ; bear
My absence well by thinking of the day
When I shall back return ; farewell, my dear
Ones all ; take care of one another till
I come again to thank you for your love
Of each I love."   He grasped his father by
The hand ; his mother kissed ; his sister and
His brother Ben he hugg'd ; then snatch'd in haste
His gentle Mary to his breast, as though

He dar'd not trust himself or her with long
Last words : a look ineffable—but one—
One rapid passionately stifled sob,
And he had darted off full speed ; was gone.

Was gone !   A world of blank forlornness lay
In those two words, which day by day were felt
By Charley's dear ones, left to understand
The full and bitter force of all involv'd
Therein ; to try and hide from all the rest
The pain at heart of each, the loneliness,
The sense of loss and vacancy that ached
Within. ˙ But then there came a letter, said
He'd sailed ; was well ; look'd forward to the time
Of hop'd-for home return ; bade them be sure
To do the like ; and finished with his own
Bright cheerful tone of confidence and trust.

The days went by; the weeks ; they swelled to
    months ;   .
Then came the Autumn winds, that swept the trees
And bar'd them of their leaves ; that sobb'd and
    moan'd,
And filled the throbbing hearts of those at home
With fears for him they loved at sea ; and yet
Withal a hope, a growing hope, a hope
Expectant, yearning, day by day more strong,
That he might any moment be at home ;
Might take them by surprise, and come at once.
December with its frosty sun set in ;
No rain, no snow, but bracing, clear, and sharp.
" High time," thought Ben, "to hew the Christmas
    log !
Since Charley cannot get away, and be
At home to fell the clump himself, I must ;

That it may dry and season, ready for
The Christmas blaze upon our cottage hearth.
That ruddy glow and sparkle of the good
Yule log ! How cheerily it looks ! How well
Our Charley loves it ! And how like himself !
So full of warmth and brightness, comfort, life,
And joyousness ! My spirits always rise
Beside the Christmas fire and when I'm near
My brother Charley ; both inspire a glad
Courageous trust." As thus the lad ran on
Within himself, he struck and chopp'd amain ;
And dealt the gnarlèd branch such sturdy blows
With well-directed axe, that soon he cleft
A wide division 'twixt the bole and it ;
Another stroke, and then it fell to earth :
But as it fell, the dull deep heavy thud
Of fallen wood was blended with a low
Strange sound, a sound as of a human cry,
A cry half forc'd from lips by deadly pain,
A moan, a gasp, an anguish-utter'd tone.
It startled Ben, who sharp look'd round, as if
Some wounded creature needs must be close by.
No one he saw : the little orchard ground
Was still and peaceful in the frosty air ;
The sparkling rime was glistening on the trees
And grass; had one white fragment dropped, it
    might
Almost be heard, so silent was the spot ;
And then, with shrilly softness, there trill'd forth
The few clear notes of sudden-singing robin,
That made the silence but the surer seem.
The boy drew breath ; for he had held it check'd
As listening whence that smother'd cry should
    come :
What could it be ? Or had he really heard

A cry at all?   For now 'twas gone, he scarce
Believ'd 'twas aught beyond a fancied sound:
And yet it had been wonderfully like
A human tone, and even strangely like—
Or so he for a moment thought—the voice
Of Charley: but he drew a lengthen'd breath,
And laugh'd that notion from him, as he stoop'd
And rais'd the sever'd branch, and bore it on
His shoulders to the wood-house; where he sang
A blithe old Christmas carol while he shap'd
The clump into a goodly sizèd log
For burning when the time should come.

                                    And soon
It came: the time of peace, goodwill, and joy:
The starry eve, the Christmas Eve, the eve
Of eves: and yet no news of sailor Charley!
" He will not come to-night, he'll come to-morrow; "
They said with ill-assumèd smile and look
Of confidence: for still they would not let
Themselves admit they felt a doubt he would
Return for Christmas-tide as he had said
He should.   And Peggy stole away, and went
Alone to lay the fire upon the hearth
In their bright parlour-room, where twice or thrice
A year the cottage party met to keep
Their rarely holden festivals in state.
Already she had deck'd it with green boughs
Of shining holly, beaded coral-red;
With wreaths of ivy, dark and glossy leaf'd;
With clusters of arbutus and white tufts
Of laurustinus, interwining sprays
Of fanlike arbor-vitæ; while 'mid all
There hung aloft a certain mystic branch,
Its rounded-ended leaves begemm'd between

By berry pearls; 'neath which, if maiden pass,
Her lips pay toll: but Peggy hurried on,
Nor glanc'd once up, nor shyly smil'd at it;
Her mouth was grave, her eyes were downward
    bent,
As straight she walk'd towards the lowly hearth,
And knelt beside the heap of sticks plac'd there
By Ben, together with the goodly log
Of Yule, all ready to her hand: she laid
The slender sticks and twigs across, a light
And well-built mass; then turn'd to lift the log;
And as she turn'd, the thought swept through her
    mind:
" Ah, if but Charley now were here, he'd lift
It for me with that strong right arm of his,
That always seems beside me at a need
When he's at home": and as the thought arose,
There seem'd to rise beside her in the dusk
A stalwart form, that stoop'd towards the log
And aided her to raise it.   Was she sure?
She look'd with straining eyes: ay, there it was:
The figure of her brother Charley, dark,
And dimly seen, but yet none else than his;
His sailor shoulders, broad and manly back,
His curly hair and firmly well-set head:
She could have heard the beating of her heart,
While still she kept her fixèd look upon
The form so near her yet so far, so real
And yet so insubstantial; for it thus
Appear'd to her: but even while she gaz'd,
It faded, grew more indistinct, became
A part of all the objects round it, lost
Its shape and substance, and she felt and knew
It to be naught but her own aching fancy
That yearn'd for sight of him who absent still

Remain'd : she gave a little shrug, half smile
Half sigh, and chid herself for giving way
To whimsies of the brain, and set herself
In earnest to fulfil her task : " To-night
We will not light our Christmas fire, but leave
It till to-morrow," murmured she ; " when he,
We trust, will be among us here to keep
Our Christmas Eve and Day in one:" and so
Withdrew, and clos'd the door, and left the room
In sacred silence, darkness, solitude,
Until the morning, which she hop'd would see
The place illum'd by Charley's presence there
No less than by the Yule log set ablaze.

The morning came, and with it Mary Gray :
She walk'd in quietly ; she ask'd no word
Of news ; but in her eyes there sat a world
Of soul-assur'd expectance ; greeted all
With loving Christmas wishes : then she took
Her part with Peggy in the busy work
Of household preparation, festive cheer
Of good old English beef with pudding crown'd ;
And, while engag'd in tending on the roast,
Brisk Peggy ask'd her friend to set alight
The Christmas fire that she had ready laid :
And Mary went into the parlour-room,
So silent and so tranquil, with its shade
Of verdant boughs, its altar-hearth ; a shrine
It look'd of peace and blessed Christmas joy ;
A hallow'd temple, consecrate to home
And happy gladness for the time supreme.
She touch'd with flame the heap'd-up wood, and
  watched
It burn : and as the lambent brightness rose
And rose, and play'd around the good Yule log,

And finally enkindled it to warmth
And glow, and tower'd up a steady spire
Of candent strength, there seem'd to glide
A strong right arm around the waist of Mary,
And 'neath her gentle head a shoulder firm ;
So palpably she felt them there, she could
Have cried " He's come!" And yet she knew it was
But image of her heart's desire—a shape—
A something—mere embodying of her thought :
Those eyes that seem'd to look into her own—
That breath that crept among her hair and swept
Her cheek—were they but reflex of her thought ?
That touch of balmy softness on her lips—
Could that be only fancy ?   Surely not !
Th' impression was so absolute, she gave
Her spirit up entirely to the sweet
Beatitude, and breath'd aloud his name.
The loving earnest eyes withdrew from hers,
Grew dim, and seemed to melt away: the arm
Receded, and the shoulder was no more
Beneath her leaning head.   She rous'd herself
With effort from the dreamy bliss of strange
And actual presence that possess'd her : went
To find his parents old, to cheer them with
Her talk, and help them pass the hours away
Without too restless looking forth for him.
Yet, spite of all, their glances constantly
Would wander up the path by which he should
Appear ; and still they spoke in idle phrase
Of aught beside the one thing that engross'd
Their thought : until the wrinkl'd mother sigh'd,
And murmur'd low: "Not come, not come ; my boy's
Not come ;" and shook her aged head down-bent.
" He'll come ; be sure, he'll come ; he will be here ;
He said it, mother ; and you know he keeps

His word ; " soft whisper'd in her ear the voice
Of Mary ; " trust in him, have patient hope :
Before the day is out, you'll see him here,
If God permit."

             But dinner-time arriv'd,
And yet no Charley. " Come, we will begin ; "
The grey-hair'd father said, with trial at
A smiling jest ; " who knows but he will come
In pudding-time ?   In time to drink the toast
Of ' Merry Christmas and a good New Year '? "
But dinner pass'd, and still no Charley came.
Before they drew their chairs around the hearth,
The grey-hair'd father solemnly arose,
And filled his glass, and said : " God bless my son !
I would it had been His good will to let
My agèd eyes behold him here at home
On this blest day, to cheer our hearts and bring
Us prospects of a surely happy year
With him beside us : but God's will be done ! "
He reverently rais'd his glass in act
To drink, but stood suspended, motionless :
" Great Heaven ! he's there ! I see him there ! my
    son ! "
His gaze was fix'd upon the hearth, where, in
The rich red light thrown by the Christmas fire,
He saw a form, the very figure of
His sailor son : the old man mov'd a step
Towards it ; but 'twas gone ; 'twas there no longer :
" 'Tis strange," the old lips muttered ; " sure, I saw
Him there, my Charley, my own sailor lad ! "
He pass'd his hand across his brows, and sank
Into his chair. " I saw him too," low said
The wrinkl'd mother ; " saw him standing there,
With smiling lips and eyes brimful of love ;

I saw him clearly as I see you all :
Alas ! 'twas only for a second ! Gone !
He's gone ! And we shall never see him more !
I know ; I'm sure ; it was his spirit sent,
To let us understand he's dead ! My boy !
My Charley ! Oh, my brave, my darling boy ! "
An awe fell on them all, a deep, deep awe ;
And very sad and silently they sat
Around their Christmas fire, and watch'd the log
Of Yule to embers red and then to dusk
White ash die out : with heavy hearts they bade
Good-night : but gentle Mary Gray soft spoke,
And said : " His word was kept ; God granted him
To come ; he said we all should see him here ;
And God vouchsaf'd him to our sight : Thank God ! "
She press'd her lover's parents in her arms,
And look'd them in the face with a strange calm
Of faith and trust. And ever from that night
She wore the same serene regard, and came
And went, and made his parents her chief care,
And sooth'd them with her placid words, and gave
The cottage light with her sweet patient look
And loving ways. But deadly pale she was,
And thin and shrunk ; scarce half her former self
She seem'd in bulk, so shadowy spare she grew ;
A wasted figure, hollow cheek that made
Her eyes look large, unearthly, and a step
Of gliding weightlessness : a maiden ghost,
Far rather than a living girl, she mov'd ;
And once when Charley's mother notic'd it,
And said she must not grow so thin and pale,
She look'd more like a spirit than a lass
Of flesh and blood, she smiled within herself
And thought : " The more like him ! " But said
Some cheering playful words to draw away
The mother's mind from sadness.

So, the weeks
Lagg'd by, till the New Year was well-nigh two
Months old: and yet no news. The sky was clear
One afternoon : the February rains
And churlish flaws had yielded to the bland
First touch of mildness: Mary stood beside
The cottage casement, looking forth upon
The moss-grown apple-tree, 'neath which she last
Had seen her sailor love ere he took leave :
His sister Peggy crept close to her, and
The two kept silent sympathetic gaze ;
Each thinking of the same unspoken theme.
At length fair Peggy, once so brisk and blithe,
Said whisperingly : " Mary, if you fade
Into a slender spectre thus, you'll not
Be long with us ; and we can not afford
To lose you, dear ; you must remain on earth ;
My poor old father and my mother both
Sore need you now, and more than ever, dear ;
You must remain to comfort them ; you must !"
" I'm going to him !" was Mary's low-breath'd soft
Reply ; " you will not grudge me going to him,
Dear Peggy, will you ? " Peggy answer'd not ;
And both the girls stood hand in hand, with eyes
Still bent upon the leafless apple-tree.
" When its first budding green appears, you'll
    know
Me gone to meet him, never more to part ; "
Said Mary with a tender inward voice
Of deep content: she paus'd ; and then said, "Hush !
Look there ! Do you see what I often see ?
His figure, there, beneath the apple-tree ;
Look, Peggy, look ! and tell me if you see
It too ; it seems to me so plain this time,
I cannot think but you must see it too."
The face of Peggy flush'd to flame, her breath

Was held, her hands were clasp'd and rais'd,
stretch'd forth
In eagerness of doubt and hope and joy
At what she saw. "'Tis he!" she cried, "tis he!
Dear Mary, it is he himself come back!"
She flung the casement wide, and call'd aloud:
And then sprang forward Charley; darted in;
And caught his Mary in his arms before
She fell to earth: "My darling! she has swoon'd!
I fear'd it would be thus; I hung about
The garden ere I'd enter, lest you might
Have heard the tidings of my death, and sight
Of me thus suddenly should startle your
Dear mourning hearts. My Mary! sweet, look up!
Look up, my dear one! see, your sailor is
Return'd, unharm'd, unchang'd! Return'd to you,
To all his dear ones! Sweet, revive!" At sound
Of his lov'd voice, her senses, like a flight
Of scatter'd doves, came fluttering back, and took
Their rest within his close embrace; while Peggy
Quick ran to tell the joyful news, and fetch
Her father, mother, brother Ben. And when
They came, and fulness of first happiness
Had calm'd a little, Charley told them how
His messmate, brave Will Hardy, had been cause
That he still liv'd and safely had return'd:
"My friend," he added, "is at hand; he did
But stay to let my mad impatience have
Its way; had his advice been taken, he
Would first have come, and broken the glad news;
But I could not restrain my eagerness,
And dear I might have paid for my"—he look'd
At Mary, stopp'd, and then went on: "Will's here;
I'll hail him; he shall tell you all the yarn
Of our adventures." Saying this, he gave

A seaman's shout; and through the porch there
   came
A bronz'd young mariner, with aspect frank,
And handsome open face, who made himself
At once at home, and took his seat among
The cottage circle as he'd been a part
Of it from childhood : willingly he told
The story of his friend's and his own last
Sea-voyage ; how the good ship Antelope
Had sail'd to distant unfrequented regions ;
'Mid spicy islands, grov'd with lofty trees
Of palmy foliage, thick with jungle wood
And rampant climbing plants that flung their arms
In wanton lush luxuriance around
The tallest barks, festooning all the space
With garlands, drooping blossoms, pendent fruits
Of gorgeous hue ; high stems behung with nuts
Colossal, rough of rind with milky core ;
Stiff spiky leaves with thorny edge, in midst
Of which rose stately pine-apples, brown gold ;
And store of roots delicious, yielding food
Abundant, succulent : and told them how
In one of these far islands it bechanc'd
That Charley and himself with certain of
Their crew were sent ashore for water fresh :
" The springs," said Will, " lay up a little way
Beyond the beach, among green slopes that show'd
In emerald brightness 'gainst a dark thick wood ;
And straight for these we made : we had been there
Before, though no one had we seen; the place
Seem'd uninhabited ; no creature save
The birds, who flew about in myriads,
With jewell'd wings and throats of amethyst,
Of ruby, topaz, sapphire ; living gems
They glanc'd amid the trees. We'd fill'd our casks,

And were returning to our ship, when pounc'd
Upon us, like a swoop of hawks, a horde
Of savage creatures, wild, and scarcely men ;
So brutish were their motions, glaring eyes,
And spring ferocious, leaping at our throats
And dashing with their clubs abrupt assault.
We kept them off as stoutly as we could,
With knives and cutlasses drawn forth at haste ;
But numbers made them more than match for us.
Pell-mell they drove our messmates to their boats,
While Charley and myself were left behind :
For he had been the foremost in the fray,
And now lay senseless on the earth ; a blow
Had struck him, and with dull, deep heavy thud
He fell, uttering a single sharp-forc'd cry."

    Here Ben half broke into some question ; but
Suppress'd it, held his breath, and Will went on :
" I rais'd him in my arms and bore him tow'rds
The shadow of the wood to screen him from
The burning sun and hide him from the horde,
Who might come back ; but they return'd no more,
And solitude the most profound was mine
Within the deep recesses of the dark
Green forest, gloom'd with thickly woven roof,
Of overarching giant trees : and one
There was so huge, so agèd and decay'd,
Its trunk was hollow as a cave ; and this
I made our hut : I heap'd a bed of leaves,
And laid my friend thereon, and search'd his wound :
'Twas on his head, a ghastly bruising dint,
That stunn'd him into deathlike torpor ; pulse
There seem'd none ; breath unheard ; all colour
    gone:
I thought his life extinct, and could have wept

Hot woman's tears upon his marble face.
But near at hand I found a freshet clear,
And lav'd his temples with the crystal cold
Until a merest flitter stirr'd his lids,
That made my heart leap up ; it show'd me that
He liv'd.

        He liv'd, indeed, but hardly liv'd ;
So slender was the thread mysterious
That held vitality within him : long
He lay in that condition, corpselike white
And motionless: but when at length he woke
To consciousness, fierce fever seiz'd him, and
He rav'd in wild distraction ; to and fro
His head turn'd ceaselessly; his arms, flung wide,
Were toss'd in vain endeavour : madly tried
To throw himself from off his couch of leaves,
And struggl'd with me to be up, away,
Away to England, home, and you: for so
His ravings ever ran : ' I must be back !
I promis'd ! They expect me ! Hold me not,
I say ! I must, I will be back !' Then chang'd
His tone to gentlest deprecation, low
And plaintive, humbly suppliant: ' Dear God,
Deny me not ! Vouchsafe me to return !
O let me see them there at home ! I said
I would be there, if such were Thy good will !
And let it be Thy will, dear God ! O let
It be Thy will ! I cannot stay away !'
And then his earnestness would ramble off
Into faint mutterings of ' Mary's hair '—
' Those gentle wistful eyes that soft beseech
Me to return '—of ' Peggy's merry glance
And witching smile that beckon me to come '—
And so would sigh and shiver tremblingly,

E

Sink down despondent, only to fling forth
Again his arms, and start into fresh raves
Of wandering delirium.

                        And so
The dreary time went by, until one day—
'Twas Christmas Eve—he laps'd into a state
Akin to that first dreadful torpor : stretch'd
He lay, in lethargy so absolute,
His senses steep'd in such profound oblivion,
The spirit seem'd indeed to have left its cage
Of flesh, and wing'd its flight far, far away :
I knew he was not dead, for still I felt
At intervals the dull, deep sluggish beat
Of his slow-toiling heart, like muffled boom
Of minute-gun from some distressèd ship
At sea : but as I watch'd him through those long,
Long six-and-thirty hours of trance, I ask'd
Myself the question, o'er and o'er again :
' His spirit is not here, 't has passed its bars
And flown ; but whither flown ?   Unto the skies
Not yet 'tis gone.   Then where?   On earth?   O'er
   sea ?
Can God have gifted it with power to soar
With dove-like instinct to the distant nest
Where dwell its dear ones ?   Hath it found its way,
Mysteriously endow'd, to that lov'd home
Where centres all its wishes, fondest hopes ?
Hath strong desire prevailed ?   Doth sympathy
Exist with such intensity of might,
It can convey with magic potency
The spirit where it listeth ?   'Tis not here :
Then whither, whither hath it flown ? ' ''   " It came
To us," in low-breath'd whisper Peggy said ;
" God sent it here ; we saw him, felt him here ;

His spirit was permitted to return
To us, while absent from its fleshly bounds :
But tell us more ; go on ; how he reviv'd,
How both of you surviv'd that time ; go on,
Go on." " I've little more to tell ;" said Will ;
" For, strange to say, from that same deadly trance
He woke to life, to health, to energy :
He told me he had seen his cottage home,
Its Christmas hearth, around it those he loved ;
And seem'd restor'd to his old cheery strength
Of spirit by the dream, or vision, or
Whate'er it was : how may we know ?   Suffice
Us to adore the Power that doth create
Such miracles of sympathy in love.
Soon after Charley was his own strong self
Again, we had the fortune good to spy
A ship not too far out in offing to
Perceive our hoisted signals : she put in :
Took us aboard : and brought us straight to port,
To England, where we hasten'd hither that
Our safe arrival might precede whate'er
Bad tidings should perchance have got afloat,
That Charley and Will Hardy had been kill'd
In an affray with savage islanders.
But here we are, return'd in health and life ;
Prepared to be receiv'd as heroes of
Adventure, made the most of, cherish'd and
Caress'd : mate Charley has, I see, secur'd
Already some of his earn'd welcome home ;"
Said Will, with archness in the glance he cast
To where his friend sat leaning o'er the back
Of Mary's chair ; " and as for me, he knew
I had no friends, no sweetheart, no dear home
To go to ; so he brought me here with him ;
And you have ta'en me in with such a frank

And hospitable warmth, I ne'er shall feel
Again I have no friends or home : perhaps—
Who knows ?—I may here find a sweetheart too."
He said no more just then ; but on the morrow,
As Ben was showing him their cottage-garden,
And telling him of what bechanc'd while he
Was hewing down the Christmas log, Will saw
Fair Peggy gathering some snowdrops and
Some golden crocuses to deck their room,
Their parlour-room, in honour of their guests.
He went, with sailor promptness, to her side ;
And, off'ring help, he linger'd near : " I learn'd,"
He said, " from Charley how to picture to
Myself the merry eyes and witching smile
Of Peggy ; and I dwelt upon their image
Until I grew to long to see them : now
I see, I find them more than true to his
Description : and beyond their beauty, they
Possess the charm of eloquence in mute
Expression, saying how her brother's friend
And fellow-wanderer is welcome, for
His sake, to Peggy. Is it so ? " " Indeed
It is ; " she earnestly replied ; " for his
Dear sake you're dear, most dear, to all of us."
" And for my own, I would be dear to you
Yourself, sweet Peggy, " he rejoined ; " I know
I must seem strangely sudden and abrupt ;
But not to me is this a sudden thought :
I've ponder'd on it, brooded o'er it in
The watches of the night, the hours of eve ;
I felt, before I saw you, I should love ;
And love you, Peggy, I most surely do,
With all my sailor heart ; say, can you take
That heart and all its faithful honest love ? "
Fair Peggy answer'd by no words ; but eyes

And smile, with eloquence their own, said what
Look'd very like a cordial " Yes." Howe'er
That was, 'tis very certain, when the bells
Rang out the wedding-peal for Charley and
His bride, they rang besides for Will and his
Sweet Peggy. Cottage annals farther say,
That when the log of Yule next time was burnt,
Two-christenings enhanced the festival.

MINNIE'S MUSINGS.

PART I.

He speaks but little when he's here ;
  A grave and peaceful look he wears ;
His voice is easy, even, clear;
      And yet, I think he loves!

He talks with me, as with the rest ;
  Not more with me than them, and yet
I sometimes think he likes it best ;
      I'm almost sure he loves !

But sister Annie's sprightly, gay,
  Her laugh is like the rippling rill,
She's lovely as the flowers in May—
      Ah, *whom* is it he loves ?

I see him watch her sunny smile,
  I see him note her airy form,
And see his charmèd gaze the while ;
      No wonder, if he love !

She's graceful, slender, shapely, tall ;
  She's very beautiful and bright ;
I'm little, quiet, shy—that's all—
      Not one that *he* can love !

*   *   *   *   *

Last evening, in the shrubb'ry walk,
 I saw them, though they saw not me,
They pass'd along in low-toned talk—
  The very tone of love!

Not many seem'd their words—he deals
 In sparing speech—but smiling, sweet,
Yet earnest; just the words one feels,
  Must be the words of love!

They pass'd; he took her hand in his;
 A light was in her shining eyes,
A light of sparkling heartfelt bliss;
  The light of happy love!

Oh, Annie! Dearest sister mine!
 Thy happiness shall be to me
Instead of that which I resign—
  All thought henceforth of love!

To see thee bless'd shall be my joy;
 For thy dear sake I'll never wed;
For thee my life I will employ
  In solely sister love!

*   *   *   *   *

Just now, she came to me in glee,
 In breathless state of ecstasy,
A rapture beautiful to see—
  A rapture of pure love.

"You mouselike quiet little thing,"
 She said, "how 'lone you're sitting here!
Do rouse yourself, and come and sing
  Some ballad of true love.

" He's waiting in the music-room,
    And made me promise I would send
You there to let him know his doom
        Of hope, or hopeless love."

"Of hope—of love?"   I falter'd ; stopp'd :
    Then wicked Annie laugh'd, and peep'd
Beneath my tell-tale eyelids, dropp'd
        In mute revealèd love.

" I guess'd it, dear," she said, with fold
    Of arms about me ; " guess, in turn,
How danc'd my heart when I was told
        That Walter is in love.

" I guess'd his secret too, and made
    Him half confess it as we walk'd
Last night beneath the shrubb'ry shade.
        Dear Minnie, he's in love!"

Another clasp, with cheeks that burn'd ;
    And then—and then—she made me go :
I went : and now I too have learn'd
        He loves, and *whom* he loves.

PART II.

My Walter—he's my husband now—
    My Walter said to me one day,
" I wonder why it is and how
        Our Annie does not love.

" So sympathetic, fair withal,
    So cordially affectionate,
I cannot think it natural
        That Annie should not love.

" And yet she turns indifferent ear
 To all advances, one by one,
She will not for a moment hear
   A hint of offer'd love.

" There's Blandford of Northaughton Glen,
 Sir Edwin Leigh of Ash-Tree Hurst ;
Good fellows both, and manly men,
   Men whom I trust and love.

" Will Blandford's heart is hers, I've heard,
 If she'd encourage him to speak ;
Sir Edwin wants but half a word
   To make him own his love.

" How is it, Minnie mine, that she
 Thus resolutely shuns my friends ?
Dost think, my mouse, that it can be
   Bright Annie will not love ?

" Can it be true that she is cold ?
 I mean, is cold to love itself;
That she is warm, I know of old,
   In friend and sister love.

" So happy am I with my wife,
 My darling little quiet mouse,
I'd fain see Annie's daily life
   Of happy wedded love."

" Dear Walter," I replied, " I've thought,
 With thee, 'tis strange our Annie shows
No sign of preference, when sought
   By those who'd win her love.

" She's full of tenderness for all ;
    For me, for thee, for parents, friends ;
For every prattling toddler small
        She kisses has, and love.

" Her eyes so beaming, yet so kind,
    Her mouth so mischievous, yet sweet,
Her voice that round one's heart doth wind,
      . Proclaim her form'd for love.

" It is that she has not yet found
    The very man she could prefer ;
'Tis that prevents her, I'll be bound,
        From listening to love."

Herewith I nodded my wise head,
    In such a final little way,
That Walter laugh'd, and bant'ring said,
        " An oracle of love !"

But that same evening he ask'd
    Our Annie which of his two friends
She thought the pleasanter ; and task'd
        Her closely as to love.

His brother fondness gave him right
    To question her ; and she replied
With just her own sweet look of bright
        Sincerely open love.

" Sir Edwin Leigh, and Blandford, both,
    Are gentlemen of merit, true ;
But, brother Walter, by my troth,
        That is not cause for love.

" Unless you'd have me have the two,
The merit of that one is wrong'd
Whose left; but what should poor I do
With such a dual love?

" If merit be a ground of love,
Why, all the meritorious men
· I ought to take, and be above
Slight scruples in my love."

" Come, come," said Walter, " I suspect,
For all your saucy merriment,
You cannot seriously object
To either man, my love."

" To either? Nay, to neither, I ;
They're both the very best of men,
The men to treat respectfully,
To anything but love.

" The one's too good, the other just
As bad ; the one's a sort of man
So excellent, he gives disgust
To all idea of love.

" The other has the world's esteem,
And that's enough, at least in my
Opinion it doth surely seem
Enough, without my love.

" I know no jot against them, I ;
But Walter, this you'll own is true ;
They're irreproachable, that's why
I cannot give them love."

" But Annie, have you made a vow,
　To give up thoughts of marriage, dear ?
Are you resolv'd, come, tell us now,
　　T' abjure for ever love ?"

" Why, as to whether I will marry,
　I've not decided yet the point ;
I only know that ' hateful Harry '
　　I'd love as soon as them."

" Who's ' hateful Harry ' ? " Walter said.
" Oh, he," said I, and laugh'd aloud,
" Is one she nam'd so, when a lad ;
　　A lad to loathe, not love."

" Just so," said she ; " an odious boy
　A neighbour's son, who from a child
Unto the age of hob'dehoy,
　　Had none but mother's love.

" None but a mother could descry
　A quality to like in him ;
A mischief-loving imp that I
　　Detested—couldn't love.

" A wilful peremptory way
　He had, that teas'd my very soul ;
A way of having his own say
　　In spite of law or love.

" He contradicted bluntly, flat ;
　He plagu'd me constantly at play,
Though I a girl and he a brat,
　　A brat no one could love.

" I named him ' hateful Hal ' or ' Harry,'
I hated him most heartily ;
So fancy whether him I'd marry,
   Or give to him my love !

" And yet I'd marry ' hateful Hal '
Far rather than the one or other ;
This shows you that I never shall
   Give love to one of them."

So saying, Annie off did flee,
 And caroll'd blithely as she went,
" ' My heart's my own, my will is free,'
   My love's still mine to give."

PART III.

Next day—the sun had not a cloud—
 Beneath the old oak-tree we sat
At work, while Walter read aloud
   The love of fair Elaine.

Then came a stranger bounding through
 The trees of skirting copse, and rais'd
His cap, and smiling at us two,
   Said, " Ladies, neighbour love

" Of old may warrant this address ;
 You have forgotten me, I fear ;
But I remember you ; yes, yes ;
   The little girls so lov'd

" By my dear mother ; " there he paus'd
 And then went on ; " my playmates once,
And now "—he glanc'd at us, and caus'd
   A smile of love from Walter.

" 'Tis hateful Hal ! " exclaimed our Annie.
" Precisely so ; " he laughing said ;
" You know me well ; there are not many
          Can boast that name of love

" You gave me formerly ; so call
     Me by it still ; I like it best."
She redden'd ; bit her lip ; let fall
          Some words of aught but love.

" The very same, that hateful way
     Of his ; so masterful, so bluff! "
I heard her mutteringly say,
          With eyes that flash'd no love.

My Walter ask'd him courteously
     Of all his many wanderings ;
" You are a sailor, sir, I see ;
          A calling that I love.

" Your banded cap, your jacket blue,
     Your epaulette, and sunburnt cheek,
All show me by these tokens true,
          You love a seaman's life."

" Ay, that I do ! " frank Harry said ;
     " And yet, when I return at length,
And see the happy life you've led—
          The life of home and love—

" I feel that life on land may be,
     With books and women by your side,
As nearly good as life at sea ;
          A life to lead and love."

My Walter smil'd and look'd at me,
 While Annie bit her lip again,
And knit her brow, and tried to be
  Unlovely in a frown.

" The same imperious lordly style !
 So ! ' *Women,*' truly ! Likely he
Should ever find one to beguile
  With needlework and love

" His home on land, or bring him books,
 Or listen while he read aloud,
Or tend upon him with her looks
  Of fond and happy love ! "

She murmur'd this with flushing face,
 As Walter led his guest away,
To show him o'er our pleasant place,
  Our home of happy love.

Then seeing me still sitting there,
 She broke into a trilling laugh,
And said, " Why, Minnie, do you care
  For stitching, still, my love ?

" Can you remain so quiet, mouse,
 While Walter is with ' hateful Hal,'
And making welcome to his house
  A man we cannot love ?

" You know his hospitable way,
 His friendly, kindly, earnestness :
If ' hateful Harry,' now, should stay ;
  Oh, think of that, my love ! "

" We'll try and bear it, dear, if so ; "
    I answered quietly : then rose :
" I think I'll fold my work and go
        And see to it, my love."

We went : she would my basket carry,
    And ran before : and soon we join'd
The gentlemen—that ' hateful Harry '
        And Walter, my belov'd.

It prov'd as she had said ; he had
    Been ask'd, and he had gladly stay'd.
" Come, Annie," whisper'd I, " it's bad ;
        But never mind, my love ;

" We'll make the best of it, and treat
    Him so politely that he can't
Be churlish, rude, and bluffly meet
        With roughness so much love."

Bright Annie gave a careless look,
    A careless toss of head, and smil'd ;
Then pencil and her sketching took,
        Amusement that she loves.

While I my needle closely plied ;
    And Walter ask'd, and Harry told
Of countries distant, far and wide,
        That he had seen and lov'd.

" And have you never chanc'd to meet
    In any of those foreign lands
A woman 'bove all others sweet,
        A woman you could love ? "

" In none ; " said bluntly " hateful Hal " ;
" Abroad I never once set eyes
On any, and I never shall
      On any I could love.

" The only woman in my life
  I could have lov'd, deep hated me ;
So never shall I take a wife,
      And never shall I love."

There came a silence on us all ;
  And shortly after took his leave
Our guest ; but in the outer hall,
      He said to Walter, " Love,

" Such love as you have shown to me,
  A manly love of friend to friend,
A welcome home to one from sea,
      Brings hearty love in turn.

" Believe a sailor rough who says
  In his rough way, I love you, friend ;
I'll love you truly all my days
      In gratitude for love."

He turned away, and darted out,
  Out in the balmy night of June ;
And presently we heard a shout,
      A loving cheer, " Hurrah ! "

F

PART IV

Next morning Walter went to him ;
And took him out a rambling walk,
A walk among the birch-trees slim,
        The slender trees we love.

The silver-stemmèd birch-trees green,
    That cluster in our hill-side wood ;
With pendent branches, boles of sheen,
        The graceful trees we love.

And soon the sailor, hateful Harry,
    Came in and out, just as he pleas'd ;
A moment only, or he'd tarry
        Like one at home and lov'd.

And Walter lov'd him, and I grew
    To tolerate him for his sake ;
And then, I think, I loved him too,
        Because my husband lov'd.

Though still I called him by his name
    Of ' hateful Hal' ; in part because
He lik'd to have it still the same,
        For mockery of love ;

In part because our Annie us'd
    It always, with an emphasis
And energy, that oft I mus'd
        How she, so full of love

For all beside, could have for one
   A hate so strong. Well, time went on :
The summer season past and gone—
      The season of ripe love

In fruit and flower, leaf and tree—
   One day that hateful Hal declar'd
He must be off again to sea,
      And leave the friends he lov'd.

I saw him give a sharp quick look
   At Annie as he spoke the words ;
But she was buried in her book :
      Some tale of antique love.

That look of his, in one swift flash
   Reveal'd to me his secret heart ;
I saw 'twas Annie's self this rash
      Young sailor deeply lov'd.

He said there was one whom he could
   Have lov'd, but that she hated him ;
I saw now who it was ; but would
      She e'er change hate for love ?

" Impossible ! " I thought, as soft
   I crept away : and since I've learn'd
What pass'd while I revolvèd oft
      The fate of Harry's love.

He drew more near to where she sat
   Absorb'd in reading, as it seem'd,
And then abruptly said, " What's that
      You're studying of love ? "

" You hateful Hal ! " retorted she,
 Yet with a little break of voice,
" Why come you thus disturbing me
        In story of true love ? "

" Ay, ' hateful Hal ' ! " he said, and turn'd
 His face away ; " that same old name !
You always hated me ; I learn'd
        That long ago from love."

" From love ! " she echoed, "surely never ! "
 " From love," he said vehemently,
" From love in boyhood, manhood, ever ;
        From love that taught me fear.

" I fear'd your bright blue laughing eyes,
 I fear'd your roguish smiling mouth ;
I fear'd you did too sure despise
        My boyish ardent love.

" I took to hiding it in rough
 Rude ways, that made you hate yet more
A lad so peremptory, bluff;
        A lad you couldn't love.

"And still you hate, I see it clear,
 You hate me worse than you did then ;
Rough hateful Hal, who loves you dear,
        With all the strength of love.

" Well, be it so, I'm going away,
 To bear it bravely if I can ;
But, Annie, to my dying day,
        My love is yours for hate.

" For hate I give you love in turn ;
   Say ' hateful Hal,' then, once again ;
That name still somehow makes me burn—
       'Twas giv'n by her I love.

" From your dear lips it has a charm,
   It thrills me strangely through and through,
It sounds as if it meant no harm,
       And still increas'd my love."

" I thought your roughness was dislike ;
   How could I fancy it aught else ?
It seem'd so very, very like ;
       I couldn't think it love."

Her voice was low as she said this ;
   And then she tried to rally it ;
" Well, ' hateful Hal,' sir, there it is,
       Since that's the name you love."

" You hated when you gave it me,
   You hate me now, you'll hate me ever,
Is it not so ?   Or can it be,
       Oh, can it be, that love "—

He stopp'd, breath'd short, then hurried on ;
   " Dear Annie—speak—do let me hear
Your voice ; if but one word, but one,
       Forbids me not to love."

He look'd at her with searching eyes,
   As if he'd read her very soul,
Her soul of truth without disguise,
       Her soul of inward love.

Beneath his eyes her eyes did sink;
    In tones half arch, half sweet, she said,
" I almost now begin to think,
            Perhaps my hate was love."

He trembled; caught her hand in his;
    He snatched it to his breast, his lips;
He gave it a quick fervent kiss
            Of eager hoping love.

" Ay, ' hateful Hal ' you still shall be,
    I'll always call you by that name;
For ' hateful Hal ' you are to me,
            The ' hateful Hal ' I love!"

He took her in his arms so strong,
    He press'd her to his beating heart,
And held her there full soft and long:
            Between them there was love.

THE TRUST.

"Wilt thou make a trust a transgression?"—SHAKESPEARE.

Ay, from my very boyhood I had seen
And known her: Clarice Merton of the Hall;
A fine old stately mansion that had been
The seat of all the Mertons since the time
When Tudors reigned. As niece and heiress to
Sir Horace Merton, she was mistress there
Already: for the portly gentleman,
Her uncle, loved the tall fair slender girl
With all a father's fondness; and she queened
It with right royal dignity and grace.
She looked the well-born lady that she was—
The representative of ancient blood
And birth: her every movement was instinct
With native self-possession, high-bred ease.
Her beauty was imperial, and made
For sway. I well remember, when a lad,
How it subdued myself: I used to see
Her pass on horseback, with her uncle, through
The lane that led from Merton Hall, and oft
I lingered by the way to watch for her.
There was a roadside stile, half hidden by
The thickly clustered hedge that shaded it;
And this was frequently my resting-place.
Time after time I saw her passing by,
Until her face and form were graven on
My mind, and they became thenceforth to me
The sole embodiment of womanhood's

Perfection : by the roadside stile again
And yet again I stood, and gazed my fill.
She ne'er saw me : or saw me as one sees
A pebble, twig, or blade of grass, that lies
Upon the path one treads ; a thing of naught ;
A thing unheeded, unremarked ; a thing
That merely makes a part of all around.
I knew full well both who and what she was ;
But who and what was I ?   Poor Edward Helme :
Of humble origin : an orphan left
In earliest years, and bound apprentice to
The village stonemason, who thought the lad
Gave token of intelligence and power
To learn, so took to him, and taught him skill
In carving, modelling—the more refined,
Artistic portions of his trade, for which
The boy showed aptitude and special taste.
    I reached to early manhood thus, absorbed
In two main sources of pursuit and thought :
One—quiet, steady labour at my work,
Whereat I earned an honest livelihood
And gained my master's still-increased goodwill ;
The other—evening rambles through the fields
And lanes, where I might chance to see at times
The object of my worshipping regard.
If blessed with sight of her, my heart was filled
For days with secret sense of deep content.
I question whether Clarice Merton knew
Of even my existence : but I knew
Of hers ; and that made mine a gladdened one.
    It happened that Sir Horace Merton wished
To have some vases for the terrace steps
And balustrade, above the grassy slope
On which the mansion stood : he sent to my
Employer, who despatched me to the Hall

To take instructions. In a tremor of
Excitement I set forth : but none of it
Appeared beneath my usual quiet mien
And sober aspect : I was always known
Among our village folk for gravity
And thoughtful look beyond my years : and they
Would sometimes nickname me " Young Serious."
That.day my outward grave composure served
Me well to hide the inward hurry of
My spirits, as I found myself within
Her very presence. She was standing with
Her uncle on the terrace, where they both
Received me : tall and stately even in
Her girlish slenderness and grace, she leaned
Against the marble balustrade and smoothed
Caressingly the gorgeous throat of a
Tame peacock, that with coy reluctance stooped
Its neck to her familiar hand alone.
The while Sir Horace spoke to me about
The vases ; and I listened to his words
Through all the mist of wilderment in which
My thoughts were wrapped by consciousness of her
And her proximity. Sir Horace talked
With fluent dictate, affable command,
The sort of kindly condescension used
By one who gives his orders to a man
He finds to be proficient in his trade,
A clever artisan and competent.
    " A well-informed, intelligent young man,"
I heard Sir Horace say, as he dismissed
Me and rejoined his niece : " Indeed ?   I did
Not mark him," she replied with negligence.
    They spoke in but a half-low tone, with just
That carelessness of being overheard
Which people sometimes use when only their

Inferiors are by.   I felt it to
The core : I was to her no more but simply
The stonecutter, the mason's man, the clerk
Sent by his master to receive and note
The orders of Sir Horace Merton for
The vases on the terrace balustrade ;
And of no more account than was the stone,
The marble, or the granite that he wrought.
Yet, after all, what more could I expect ?
.What more was natural ?   She knew no jot
Of me but what she saw ; and that was naught—
Naught of the inner self, which p'rhaps contained
A something worthy in its quality ;
A certain sturdy manfulness and strong
Reliability : at least, my good
And constant friend, my master, used to give
Me credit for possessing these, and I
Believe I had them.
                              Time went on ; and there
Was coming blankness at the Hall.   'Twas said
Sir Horace Merton's health was far from good,
And that a long sea-voyage was prescribed ;
'Twas added that his niece was going with
Him ; that she would not let him go alone,
Although she dreaded leaving her old home ;
Disliked the sea, and cared not for new scenes ;
Was sure there was no place like Merton Hall,
But told her uncle playfully, 'twas true
She loved it more than any house or lands,
Yet loved him more than house or lands or aught.
    All this reached village ears, as doings of
The great are sure to reach their neighbours' ears,
And form the theme of gossip comment : thus
I learned the day was fixed for their departure,
And pictured to myself the void that then
Would yawn around my daily life.

Meantime,
It chanced that my employer had to send
Abroad on confidential business ;
And he chose me to execute the charge.
I willingly obeyed ; for change of scene
And action were the things I could have wished,
To take me from the dull, dead, dreary round
Of days and nights beset with aching sense
Of loss, and absence, and soul's want, that would
Be mine when Clarice Merton once was gone.
   A distant colony my mission had
For goal ; I took my passage in a ship
Was thither bound ; when who should prove to be
My fellow-passengers but Clarice and
Her uncle ! My intense surprise to learn
They were on board leaped up like sudden fire
Within my heart, and kindled into blaze
A thousand embers of deep-smouldering joy
That I had thought had been well nigh extinct.
To find myself thus near her, thus in reach
Of seeing her and hearing her, while I
Remained unnoted, seemed renewal, ay,
And more than a renewal of the old
Enchanted times, when I beheld her pass
Through Merton lanes, a vision pure and fair.
My passage had been taken in the fore
Part of the ship ; while they, of course, were aft,
And had commodious cabins to themselves.
So that I saw them as they walked the deck,
Engaged in chat, and pacing to and fro.
Sometimes she leaned upon his arm ; sometimes
She gave him hers, when he seemed feeble, or
Less well than usual ; always she appeared
The gentle, graceful, and devoted child
Attending on a parent's steps, alive
To all that could alleviate and cheer.

No wonder that he loved her as he did,
Indulging her and making her his all.
   One day I heard Sir Horace say to her—
" Who do you think I fancy that I saw
On board this ship an hour ago?"   " I can't
Imagine," answered she ; " how should I guess ?
Some one we know?"   " Well, not exactly *know ;*
Some one that we have seen—a Merton man ;
No other than that well-informed young man
Sent up by White, the mason, to the Hall
To take my orders for the vases.   You
Remember him ? "   " Why—scarcely," she replied :
" Oh, yes—I think I do : a quiet, grave
Young man, that you thought well of, did you not ? "
" He seemed to me intelligent and skilled,"
Sir Horace said ; " moreover, struck me as
Remarkably trustworthy, and to be
Relied upon in matters that required
Attention.   He impressed me favourably."
" He did," returned she, with an absent air ;
" I recollect it now ; he did."   " I wonder what
Has brought him here," replied her uncle ; " I
Suppose that White has sent him out on some
Commission to the colony ; I heard
He had some dealings there."   " Most likely," she
Responded in a final way, as if
No farther interest attached to what
They talked of.   After a short pause, she said,
With animation—" Uncle, do you know
What I've been thinking of ? "   " Of Merton Hall,
Of course," Sir Horace smiling said ; "your
   thoughts
Are always hovering there, like doves around
A dove-cot."   " I was thinking," she resumed,
" Of how the dear old place must now be bathed

In sunset light, and looking at its best.
And yet I know not why I say ' its best ' ;
It always looks its best—*the* best—to me."
She laughed at her own sally, and went on
To talk of their return to their loved home.
I saw Sir Horace Merton's face assume
A sudden sad expression : but it cleared
Away again, when she looked up at him.
    Some mornings after this I noticed him
Upon the deck alone. As he caught sight
Of me, he beckoned me to join him where
He stood. He spoke most courteously—nay, with
A kindly, almost friendly tone : he said
It gave him pleasure to have met with one
Who came from Merton village, seeming like
A neighbour—one long known : he asked my name,
And told me that he took a liking to
Me when I came that time to Merton Hall ;
That I inspired him with belief in my
True faithfulness and manly character.
I bowed my thanks, but nothing said ; I was
So taken by surprise at this address.
" Away from home," he said, " I feel the want
Of some one I can talk to as a friend,
To whom I may confide the fear that stings
Me now acutely, for my niece's sake.
I feel my health is failing fast, and should
I die, she will be left in foreign lands
Alone and unprotected. Helme, if so,
I look to you to guard her, think for her,
Watch over her unceasingly, and see
Her safely home again to Merton Hall.
Remember, Helme, I trust her to your care
When I am gone, if go I must, while we
Are far from home. It may seem strange to place

Such confidence in one of whom I know
So little; but there's something in your look
That tells me I may safely trust to you,
That you'll be faithful to the trust.   Do you
Accept it, Helme?"   "I do," was all I said,
With earnest firmness.   What was in my heart
Myself and my Creator only knew.
"And now," Sir Horace said, "we'll speak no more
Of this; 'tis understood between us two.
I would not have my niece suspect that I
Have any present cause to fear my death;
'Twould serve no purpose, and disquiet her."
He turned to speak of other things; and when
His niece approached, she found him cheerfully
In talk with one of the ship's company,
A sailor, whose long yarns amused him oft.
    I kept aloof, thenceforward as before;
Because I thought I could perceive, for all
Sir Horace thus had spoken to me, that
He cared not I should join him when his niece
Was with him.   Whether it was from dread
That Clarice should discover what he feared,
Or whether it proceeded from a sense
That she shared not his good opinion of
Myself, I do not know; but certain 'tis
I felt that he was better pleased I should
Not speak to him when she was by.   Content
It should be thus, I fell again into
My way of watching her from distance, and
Unseen, unnoticed, making her the one
Bright jewel of my life.
                        One night there was
Alarm of fire aboard the ship: upon
The instant all was noise, confusion, and
Distress.   I started up, threw on my clothes,

And hurried upon deck. Already had
The flames advanced, and now were licking their
Dread way aloft, among the shrouds and rigging.
Amid the burning glare I sudden saw
Sir Horace and his niece—a ghastly group.
Half dead with terror, she had sunk down at
His feet, and held her face within her hands.
He called to me aloud from where he stood :
"For God's sake help her if you can, good friend!
Remember, Helme, the charge, the trust, I gave ! "
He reeled and fell, the moment after, crushed
By falling fragments of a blazing mast.
I snatched her from the spot and drew her towards
A spar I saw, and knew would float ; to which
I fastened her : she made attempt to free
Herself from my endeavour ; but I said :
"Your uncle charged me take care of you ;
He trusted you to me, and bade me try
To save you." Then she yielded, and allowed
Me do whate'er I would that I thought best.
    I hardly know how afterwards I found
Myself upon the red-reflected waves,
My precious spar in tow, held by one hand,
While with the other I struck out and swam
For life, for very life—my own, and one
Far dearer than my own. I made some way :
When all at once there came a noise that seemed
To rend the air asunder, split the sky.
The flames had reached the gunpowder : the ship
Blew up : and not a soul survived the wreck.
But—crowning horror of the whole to me—
The roughness of the surge, the heave, the swell,
At moment when the ship blew up, had wrenched
My spar away, had torn it from my grasp,
And borne it out of sight. A long loud cry

Of anguish and despair broke from me, and
I wept aloud in agony of heart.
The roaring waters dashed in mockery
Against my face, and swept my tears away
As fast as they welled forth.   Instinctively
I struggled on ; but now had lost my wish
For safety.   What was life henceforth to me ?
Why should I try to save it if I could
Not save the one was life of life to me ?
The bitter misery of that lone hour
When, toiling on through buffet of the waves,
The fierce emotions raging in my soul
Were wilder than the horrors of the night,
I shudder to recall : but after I
Had swum a weary space, and felt upon
The point of sinking, I became aware
That I was now in smoother water, where
My feet touched ground.   Another stroke or two
Soon brought me to the shore.   A scene it was
Of almost magic beauty and repose :
A tropic moon shed broad effulgence o'er
A stretch of wooded sward that skirted round
A sheltered bay : tall palm-trees rose against
A starry sky of deep and cloudless blue ;
Unbroken silence reigned : but all this peace
And harmony of loveliness extern
Contrasted with the war within myself.
" Why did I escape when she is lost ? "
Was still the cry of my distracted heart.
I wrung my hands, and flung myself full length ;
Then started up, and wandered madly on,
I knew not, cared not whither, in my grief.
Along the margin of the moonlit bay
My steps conveyed me, till I saw before
Me on the ground a prostrate form : I sprang

To it : oh, joy of joy ! 'Twas hers, 'twas hers !
Borne onward by the influx of the tide,
The spar had drifted safely towards the shore,
And landed on the bay's smooth shelving sand.
She senseless lay ; her eyes were closed ; her hair
Hung loose in tangled masses, scattered wide.
A piteous sight : but, still, she breathed, she lived !
I gently disengaged her from the spar ;
I raised her tenderly from off the sand,
And carried her to where the green-sward made
A better resting-place. I chafed her hands ;
And soon I had the comfort of a change :
A flutter of the breath, a quiver of
The eyelids : then the eyes were opened with
A dreamy wandering look that finally
Met mine. "You know me?" whispered I; "you do?"
" Yes—yes ; I think you are the person that
My uncle liked." She sighed and closed her eyes ;
As though 'twere too much effort yet to think.
Just near to where we were there was a knoll
Of rocky moss-grown ground, in which I saw
A deep recess, a hollow, like a cave :
To this I bore her ; placed her on a couch
Of soft dry leaves I piled up high, and left
Her to the healing balm of sleep.
                              I kept
Incessant watch that night around the cave,
But naught approached to frighten or molest.
The place seemed desert, perfect solitude ;
But whether it were continent or isle
I knew not. It abounded with wild fruits ;
Among the bluffs and cliffs beyond the bay
A multitude of sea-birds laid their eggs ;
Innumerable shell-fish swarmed the beach,
And clustered on dwarf rocks beneath the cliffs :

So, food there lacked not in this land of fair
Seclusion.
            After the first violence
Of grief had passed for her loved uncle's loss,
Sweet Clarice drooped into an apathy,
A languor of indifference to all
Around, the most pathetic ; she took note
Of nothing, interest in nothing, cared
For nothing, ate the meals I brought, arranged
The flowers I culled, accepted all I did,
And acquiesced in all I ventured to
Suggest for her behoof; but, listlessly,
And with a perfect quietude, she showed
That she did not intend to rouse herself;
She meant to be her own sole guide ; she held
Her will alone responsible to rule
Her ways ; and if her ways were moody, sad,
Why, sad and moody they should be, if so
She chose.   She surely was the mistress and
Best judge of her own acts ? and to preserve
Volition independently of me ?
To live her life thus irrespectively
Of my approof ?   She seemed resolved to let
Me see how, notwithstanding fate had thrown
Her on my hands, she still reserved her right
Of born supremacy.   All this was not
Asserted ; nay, far from it.   But it was
To be inferred from every look and tone—
The eloquence of tacit, passive will
In ladies of high birth to one beneath
Themselves.
                One evening, when I brought
Her supper of wild honey, bread-fruit, and
Some pearly eggs, I was about to leave
Her that I might go eat my own apart

As usual. With a slight and languid lift
Of her bent head, she murmured: " Where do you
Contrive to lodge? You make this cave my house—
A very roomy, comfortable one it is,
With tapestry of moss, and curtained well
By long festoons of pendent climbing plants ;
A perfect bower of graceful green-clad warmth,
Yet shade ; a mingling of dry roof, dry walls,
With freshness of the open air, due heat
And cool combined; just what a house should be—
But where do you reside? " I told her I
Had shelter found within a crevice-nook
Of rock, not far from her house-cave. "And is
It tolerably habitable ? " she
Inquired, with half a smile ; " We're neighbours
     still,
It seems, as we were formerly, I heard.
Oh, by-the-bye, what is your name? I don't
Know even that ; and it is fit I know
My neighbour's name." I told her it was Helme.
" A name most suitable, indeed," she said,
A little scornfully ; " You've been the helm
To guide me into port, to steer me safe,
And to control my course e'er since you brought
Me to this haven ; but a helm's control,
You know, exists on sea and not on land ;
It ceases to have power when on shore."
" A helm exerts his agency when need
Demands, and when the helmsman's hand doth
     sway,"
I answered quietly : " The hand doth rule,
The helm doth but obey the hand. Your hand
Shall give the signal when the helm exceeds
Its proper office." I withdrew as I
Said this ; and afterwards I noticed that

Her manner changed to less of frigidness
And distance. But it varied much ; and she
Was sometimes querulous, perverse, just like
A petted saucy child ; at others, she
Was pensive, absent, wrapped in her own thoughts ;
But always ladylike and polished, and
Supreme in native beauty most refined.
  In one of her despondent moods, I tried
To waken in her a desire to see
And know more of the place in which we lived :
To visit some adjacent spots that in
Themselves were charming, and commanded views
Of exquisite enchantment ; for I knew
That exercise and freshened interest
In all that Nature had so plenteously
Bespread around us on this fertile land
Of rich production, beautiful, profuse,
And genial in extreme, would serve to bring
Her back to healthfuller condition. " Will
You not attempt a walk to yonder point,
Miss Merton ? " I once asked ; " You know not how
Transcendant is the prospect thence attained.
It grandly stretches far along the coast
Beyond this bay, and is a matchless scene.
The headland is within your easy reach,
And will not overtax your strength to climb."
" I am not easily fatigued," she said ;
" I thank you, but I care not for fine views,
New scenes. I told my uncle so, once on
A time," she sadly added ; " there's no place
To equal Merton Hall, in my regard."
" Alas, that you must wait ere you can hope
To see it ! " I replied. " Who knows if I
Shall ever see the dear old place again ! "
She said with falling tears, then checked herself,

And muttered : " Ah, this walk—suppose I were
To take it after all ?   I may as well,
Since *you* think it would do me good ; you are
My medical adviser, Doctor Helme,
As well as my adviser general,
You know, at present, when I must depend
On you for counsel, as for all." She spoke
With touch of bitterness in her sad tone ;
Then said abruptly : " Forgive me ; I
Am most ungracious, and ungrateful too,
I feel ; but you will pardon what must seem
Ingratitude for all that you have done
And been to me, when you remember my
Indulgent nurture, from my earliest years.
It little did to well prepare me for
The trials I have met with, and the strange
Sad fate that has been mine." "More strange than e'en
Your own sad fate appears to me the word
Of 'pardon' in your mouth, as asked by you
From me, Miss Merton," I returned ; "'forgive'
I cannot, since there's nothing to forgive."
" There is," she answered quickly ; " ah, there is ;
I know it but too well ; I'm angry with
Myself when I think over my remiss
Unthankfulness to you, kind Helme, who saved
My life at sea, and have preserved it since.
I do not think I should have been so base,
So wanting in due gratitude, while I
Was mistress of our old ancestral home,
How is it that I've altered thus, and grown
So other than my girlish self?" She turned
Away as she concluded, and set forth
To take the rambling walk I had proposed.
On her return she came to where I was
Engaged in fashioning a rude attempt

At garden near her cave, and stood beside
Me while I trained some climbing roses up :
She watched me silently for a brief space,
Then said abruptly, " What was it you meant—
Aboard the burning ship, when, firm and strong,
You lashed me to the saving spar—by those
Few words you said, ' Your uncle charged me to
Take care of you ; he trusted you to me.'
What did they mean ? "   " They meant what they
    expressed ;
For, once Sir Horace gave you to my charge,
Enjoined me to watch over you, to guard
You if he died while in a foreign land,
And see you safely back to Merton Hall."
" He did ? "   " He did ; he dreaded that his death
Might happen any unexpected time,
And leave you unprotected, far from home.
No less he dreaded that his fear might reach
Yourself, and keep you haunted with alarm
For him."   " Dear uncle, ever thoughtful, kind,
And provident for welfare of your child,
Your Clarice!" she exclaimed. " Then this was what
Your own words signified, when 'mid the flames
I heard you cry, ' Remember, Helme, the charge,
The trust I gave!'"   "It was," I said ; " you heard
Them, then, yourself ? "   " I heard them plainly," she
Replied ; " and wondered, even in that wild
And fearful moment, at his strange accost.
And surely 'twas most strange he should intrust
His niece to one well-nigh unknown and quite
Unproved."   " There are some natures thus at once
Confiding, ready to believe in what
They think they see plain written in a face
Of honest look," I answered.   " True," she said ;
" There are ; and my dear uncle had himself

This readiness to put his faith in those
He thought seemed worthy of his confidence.
And so, it now appears, he trusted you.
He gave me to your charge in solemn trust,
You say ; what were the special points enjoined
By this same trust ?   How far does it extend ? "
" I told you," I replied ; " it bade me guard,
Watch over you, and do my utmost to
Ensure your safety while away from home ;
And then to see you safely back again
To Merton Hall."   " My ' safety,' " partly to
Herself repeated she ; " and then to see
Me ' safely ' back to Merton Hall.   Ay, ' safe '
And well protected, ever was his care
That I should be ; my kind good uncle ! "   As
She murmured these last words she moved away,
And went into the cave to sit alone.
But, some time after, she returned again
To subject of the trust.   It happened thus.
I had been warning her against too late
Protracting her long walks—which often now
She took—at eventide.   " It is the hour
Of sunset that is most especially
To be avoided," I had said.   " In these
Hot climates, while the sun is going down,
There comes a sudden chill into the air,
Insidious, treacherous, and not to be
Encountered without really perilous
Effect : I hope, I beg, you will not thus
Run risk of being out at just that hour
Of danger."   " What ! grave Doctor Helme again
Prescribing ?   Is it his good pleasure that
I make my exercise, my air, my hours,
Accord with his opinion, his most sage
Decree ?   Is this included in the trust

He undertook?   Does it empower him
To guard my health, to watch my hours, dispose
My time, appoint my walks?" " The trust enjoined
Me to keep watch, to guard, and to ensure
Your safety with my utmost care ; I know
It is not safe to walk at sunset, and
I frankly tell you so, in consonance
With one injunction of the trust which I
Intend to steadily fulfil throughout,
If so I be permitted," I replied.
" Permitted?" echoed she ; "by me, you mean?"
" By Heaven's will and blest vouchsafement," I
Returned.   She paused an instant ; then resumed :
" Am I to understand that you engaged
In this same trust—and now intend to use
The full authority it gives for you
To carry out its dictates, and perform
The duties it enjoins—in deference
To my dear uncle's wish, or for the sake
Of benefiting me ?   Was it alone
Because you thought to satisfy his mind,
Or from the thought that I require your care ?—
In short, to please my uncle, or please me,
Did you accept, and now enforce this trust?"
" There could have been no thought of pleasing you,
Miss Merton, when I pledged myself to take
The trust your uncle gave.   He charged me to
Fulfil it faithfully : and so I mean to do,
Please God!" She said no more, but turned to look
At some white blossoms, growing close at hand.
    Another time, a captiousness, a half
Caprice and lady wilfulness displayed
Themselves in her demeanour.   " I have found
Some little purple blossoms that remind
Me of sweet English violets ; I thought

That you would like them planted near
Your cave, Miss Merton, so have brought you home
These clumps with roots." " I thank you, Helme,"
  she said,
But looked another way, with careless air.
The Merton lane, the roadside stile, the hedge
Near which I had so often lingered that
I might have chance of seeing Clarice pass,
And where I used to see the violets
In spring-time lurk beneath the hedge, came full
Upon my mind ; but memory I quenched,
And said sedately : " Will you tell me where
You best would like them placed, Miss Merton ?
  They
Require the shade, and, if you please, I'll plant
Them here." I pointed to the spot I meant.
She did not answer for a moment ; and
I looked at her for my directions. Then,
Still keeping her fair face half turned away :
" Pray call me Clarice," she exclaimed, in a
Disdainful pettish way ; " I cannot bear
The name ' Miss Merton ' ; it reminds me of
My old lost home and all its bygone joys."
I started ; I had used it to myself
A thousand times—her sweet, sweet Christian name ;
But use it to herself I dared not ; no,
I dared not ; for I knew how it would stir
My manhood, and betray the love I vowed
To keep concealed within my heart.
" I cannot call you so, excuse me," I
Replied ; " I cannot do it, e'en to please
Yourself ; forgive me." " Oh," she quickly said,
" I make no point of it, since you will not
Comply. Pray please yourself, not me ; I care
Not what I'm called, not I, now happiness

Is gone." She burst into a passion of
Sad tears ; and there was nothing left for me
To do but try and soothe her grief. At times
She was thus petulant and wayward ; but
At others gentle, smiling, docile to
My slightest wish. I could not make her out.
And yet sometimes I now began to have
A fancy I could guess but only too,
Too well what wrought these changes in her mood.
I was dismayed at my own thought, and put
It from me when it would recur and still
Recur.
      Next time we were together, she
Was in a sportively despotic vein.
" As you would not consent to call me by
My Christian name," she said, " now tell me yours :
I want to know it." " Mine is Edward," I
Replied. " A good old Saxon name," she said ;
" One borne by British kings. I like it well ;
And somewhere I have read its meaning is—
Stay—' Happy Guarder,' ' Keeper,' ' Warder ; ' Ay,
It is ; I recollect ; and suited to yourself
No less than is your surname. Let me see ;
I like not surnames in a woman's mouth
Addressed to men. I think henceforth I'll call
You Edward Helme ; it so exactly hits
Your character. Yes—Edward—Edward ; " she
Repeated in approving tone ; " it sounds
Appropriate and true." To hear her thus
Repeat my name, affected me with strange
Emotion ; but, according to my wont,
I held my feelings under strong control,
And naught appeared of agitation in
My speech or look. I more and more resolved
On this, the more I grew confirmed in my

Suspicion of the source from whence arose
These variable moods. What would have made
My proudest, fondest hope, had she been where
She could have still remained free mistress of
Herself to give or to withhold, now formed
My torture. Here, in this lone wilderness—
Dependent as she was upon myself
For sustenance, for all—and where no rite
Of holy union could be ours—how dared
I risk betrayal of my love, which might
Draw forth the sweet confession of her own
For me, if such indeed existed ? Should
I break my faith and violate the trust
So solemnly confided to my charge—
So solemnly accepted by myself ?
No ; never ; come what might, I would be true
And loyal to the death. None knew the cost,
The struggle, the incessant agony
Of this protracted strife between my love
And my resolve, but God ; and He gave strength
To vanquish self, and to preserve my trust.
" Your good sea-jacket looks the worse for wear,"
She once said, smiling with a half shy glance
At it ; " I wish you'd let me mend this rent."
Then, recollecting, she went on : " But, ah,
Forgetful that I am ! I have no thread,
No needle, nothing that a woman should
Possess who claims to be good huswife, as
I was at home." " A huswife ? You ! " I cried.
" Why not ? A Lady of the Manor should
Be notable, remedial, practical,
Well able to perform all useful things."
" Is mending Edward Helme's apparel one ?
Strange task, methinks, for any lady ; for
A Lady of the Manor, above all.'

" It may be strange, but strange has been the lot
Of this poor Lady of the Manor," said
Sweet Clarice, pensively ; " and strange tasks fall
To those who suffer strange reverse.   Why should
I not perform a simple office for
A friend who has performed such onerous
And endless ones for me ? "   " A friend ? " I said,
In lowest tone ; " Do you call Edward Helme
A friend ? "   "A more than friend," she answered with
A faltering voice ; " an earthly providence,
One sent by Providence itself to help
Me in my utmost need.   What would have been
My fate had you not saved and tended me ?—
Become my good protector and my friend ?
I well may call you ' friend,' " concluded she
With earnestness.   I made her no reply :
How could I, and preserve my secret still ?
We both remained in silence for a time :
And then I quietly arose, and went
To find some work : some good hard work might serve
To quell the torment I endured.   For I
Had found that manual labour, bodily
Exertion, best assuaged the tumults of
My mind.   And thus I made a hundred things
Were needed for the cave : odd, useful, quaint
Utensils of ornate device, and form
Antique : her moss-grown house of rock was filled
With plates and dishes, drinking-cups and jugs,
Or graceful pateras for holding flowers,
Deft moulded from the clay and baked in the
Hot furnace of a tropic sun ; with knacks
And trifles, curiously carved and wrought
In wood by my good clasp-knife, which, most true
To boyish habit, never left me, and
Was in my pocket when I 'scaped the wreck.

While working hard for Clarice I less felt
The trouble at my heart : and, as I toiled,
I whistled softly to myself some old
Remembered tune or village song.
                                        When next
We met, she had resumed her cold reserve ;
Which gave way once—but once again—before
It settled into steadily maintained
Return to freezing distance, as of old.
The conflicts I went through, the strict restraints
I put upon myself, the guard I kept
On every speech and word, on every look
And tone, began to tell severely on
My frame, as now I learned from what she said—
"You are not looking well; you're pale, you're thin.
You work too hard—you toil from morn to night ;
You ought to have some rest.   Let me prescribe—
I followed your prescriptions once, you know,
So now take mine.   I used to be a kind
Of Lady Bountiful, among the odds
And ends of things I did as Lady of
The Manor.   Let me order you some rest ;
You are not looking well—indeed you're not."
Her eyes dwelt gently on my face, her hand
Was raised as if about to lay itself
On mine ; her tone was womanly and low—
Nay, tender, in its soft persuasiveness.
I was so moved, so passionately moved,
By her appeal, that for a moment I
Had nigh forgotten all—my pledge, my vowed
Forbearance, and my trust ; but tore myself
Away in time and left her.   " Stony, hard,
Insensible, she must believe me ! " I
Exclaimed, as, writhing under my distress,
I plunged into the forest depths, that I

Might wrestle with my pangs alone. In her
Unconscious innocence, how should she know
Or understand the reason why I must
And ought to shun the growing tokens
Of her most generous affection, if
I still would keep my plighted word, my faith,
My honour, in allegiance to my trust?
" For her dear sake, for hers, I must and will ! "
Was ever now the secret sentence which
Sustained me through my fierce ordeal fire,
And kept my courage constant to the last.
The last was close at hand. Soon after our
Late interview, we clear descried a ship
That neared our coast, put in for water to
Our bay, and proved to be a merchantman,
Far driven from its course by adverse winds.
The captain took us both on board, and we
Set sail for England.
                        On the voyage home
Fair Clarice held the level calm of her
Indifference and lady quietude;
It served at once to re-establish the
Old space that set herself and me apart ;
It tended more than aught else could have done
To cast behind us the strange episode
Of desert life that we together spent,
As something done with, past, for ever gone.
She was all suavity and graciousness ;
Presented me to the sea-captain as
The saver and preserver of her life ;
She praised my courage and fidelity;
Dwelt largely on the energy and zeal,
The spirit and the self-possession I
Displayed amid the horrors of the wreck;
Still making *that*, and not our desert life,

The theme of her repeated narrative.
It wrung my heart to hear her thus polite,
Thus courteous, bland, conventional, and marked
In her acknowledgment of what I'd done.
But I accepted patiently her will,
Her tacitly expressed decree, that I
Should be again no more than Edward Helme,
That she should be again Miss Merton of
The Hall.   I sometimes felt inclined to smile
A little bitterly at this decree,
When I remembered the relations in
Which lately we had stood together ; she
The helpless, homeless waif, tossed to and fro
By unregardful waves, then cast ashore
Like some stray piece of sea-weed, broken from
Its fellows, till upgathered by the hand
Of one that sees its native beauty, and
Doth keep it, value it, nay, treasure it
For its inherent loveliness and grace ;
While I, the finder of the waif, did play
The part of keeper, guarder, treasurer,
In tender recognition of its worth.
She said the name of Edward meant as much,
And I was happy in the privilege
Of being to her these.   Well, if she chose
To re-exchange the characters we played,
And be to me protectress and benign
Approver, I would let her so esteem
Herself : but, once arrived on English land,
I, too, would back return to my old first
Condition—quiet watcher from afar.
On one occasion, while on board, it chanced
That she and I were left together, as
She leaned against the side and watched the stars,
That one by one came peering forth, while in

The east the sky was deepening into blue
Of darker tint, when crimson sunlight failed.
She held her head averted, fixed in gaze
Upon the firmament, the while she said :
" You soon will be relieved of your strange charge,
Your troublesome and duty-burdened trust,
Of which you have most faithfully discharged
So many of the points imposed by my
Lost uncle.   I, obedient to his will,
Have all along submitted to his terms
Without complaint, and so I still intend
To do, until you see me safely home again ;   .
As bidden by the trust.   When once we're there
The limits of this vaguely worded trust
Can be defined, adjusted ; for, you know,
We never could agree exactly what
It was that it enjoined.   But this can wait
Till we arrive."   She stayed for no reply,
But left me standing 'neath the starry sky.
To that mute comforter I inwardly appealed
Against the stabs her words had been to me.
    We reached beloved England; and when there
I thought we should have parted company
At once ; but on my showing this to be
My expectation, she declared the trust
Would not be validly performed until
I saw her " safely home."   That " home " did not
Mean English land alone, but, in her case,
Meant Merton, her belov'd ancestral home ;
" The words, you told me, of my uncle's charge
Were, ' See her safely back to Merton Hall.'
You know ; so there you still will have to go."
I acquiesced, and I escorted her
Unto the very gates, where she was met
By friends and tenantry with welcome loud

And joyfullest amaze, as one thought dead,
But now returned to be once more the prized
Young mistress of the mansion and domain.
I made escape from all of this as soon
As I discreetly could, and took my leave.
She gave a smile of gracious, affable
Farewell, while saying, " Pray remember, I
Expect that you will come some day, when we
Can settle any farther claims the trust
May justify." I merely bowed, and straight
Withdrew, reflecting on the words she used—
" She spoke of ' claims.' What claims? I have
    no claims
To make : no claim upon her gratitude,
If that were what she meant." And I resolved
That I would go no more to Merton Hall.
Rejoicings grand and festive took place there,
To grace her first arrival, and 'twas thought
A round of gay assemblages would then
Have followed these ; but Clarice Merton lived
A life retired, sequestered, when she had
Performed the hostess-duty that she owed
To greeters in her circle of kind friends.
Deep mourning worn for her lost uncle was
The cause assigned for this complete and close
Seclusion from society ; and she
Was left to follow her own chosen course.
    Meanwhile I also had returned to Merton ; sought
My old employer ; found him friendly as
He ever had been towards me, and he gave
Me cordial welcome ; told me how the news
Had reached him of the wreck ; how he believed
I perished in the burning ship ; and how
He felt assured that only accident
Akin to this would e'er have hindered me

11

From executing his commission : for
He knew my faithfulness of old, he said
With his approving smile of fatherly
Regard.   He made me take up quarters in
His house, as I had always done ; but now
He treated me more like a son than clerk.
" I'm growing an old man," he said, " and feel
The want of help and younger energy
In our good trade : from you, Ned, I can count
On both, I know ; so stay with me and give
Me what I need."   And thus it was arranged.

   I heard from time to time, through village talk,
Of Clarice.   It was said she lived alone,
Was seldom seen beyond the Merton grounds,
Except on some kind quiet errand of
Benevolence and gentle charity ;
Some visit to a cottage, where distress
Or illness called for aid and sympathy :
Unostentatiously and privately
She went about, engaged in doing good.

   A thirst, a yearning, irrepressible,
To see her once again, took feverish
Possession of me : I grew restless and
Unable to resist the strong desire
To wander forth in hope of one last chance
That I might look upon her face—myself
Unseen, unknown—ere I took leave of it
For ever.   In the throb, the rack of my
Fierce longing, I believed that if I could
Behold her but once more, I would persuade
My master to employ me where I might
Promote his interests away from our
Small country village ; then resolve to go
And never to return, till snow of age
Had settled on my head and on my heart.

Urged by my burning wish, I took my way
One evening to Merton Lane, and leaned
Upon the stile, deep musing on the strange
And varied scenes I had beheld since last
I lingered in this tranquil place.   My thoughts
Were soothed to something like serenity
By all its peaceful sweetness and repose :
The trees were coming into leaf, the birds
Were chirping their last hymn before the sun
Went down ; a green delicious twilight shed
Its softened shade upon the fading gold
Of western glow.   Ere quite 'twas passed, I spied
Beneath the hedge some modest violets
Just peeping 'mid the grass.   With eagerness
I stooped to gather the sweet blossoms, fraught
With thousand memories as fragrant as
Themselves : I fondled them, I pressed them to
My lips, inhaled their odorous breath, and
Unconsciously I murmured low-toned words
Of soft address to them ; when something near,
A shadow, a dark form, attracted my
Attention, and I saw a lady, tall,
And clothed in black, was standing but a pace
Or two from where I was.   So noiseless
Had been her approach, and now so motionless,
So silently, so phantom-like she stood,
That well I might have thought she was her own
Departed spirit, conjured to my side
By my intense remembrance of herself :
But, at a glance, I knew 'twas Clarice, and
With hasty impulse thrust the violets
Quick in my breast, and hid them there.   She
    smiled—
I thought disdainfully—and turned away
Without a word.   I walked as in a dream,

Returning home like one who had beheld
The spectre of his own dead happiness.
   That night there came a note from Merton Hall :
It ran : " May I ask you to come to me
To-morrow ? " Signed "C. M." No more. Its curt
Expression, cold politeness, all seemed meant
To show me distantly and freezingly
That I was naught to her; that I was but
The young man, Edward Helme ; she, well-born,
   rich,
The Lady of the Hall : and yet, to me,
As I stood gazing on those two well-formed
And clear-cut letters of her name, she rose
Before me as herself alone, the one
Sole woman I had worshipped when a boy ;
The woman I had faithfully preserved
From e'en myself and her own guilelessness
When chance intrusted her to me and my
Protecting care in manhood ; peerless, fair,
Devoid of any grace conferred by birth
Or wealth, her own sweet self presented still
To my adoring thought the image of pure,
Of womanly perfection.
              Sleep for me
Was none that night.
                  Next morning I went up
To Merton Hall ; and on the way I schooled
My beating heart to quietude might vie
With hers—that calm and frigid quietude
I knew too well in all its lady force
Of well-bred distance, and cold courtesy.
   I found her on the terrace, as before :
No peacock now was on the balustrade ;
But on her shoulder perched a little dove,
That from her palm took grain. She bowed her head

To me as I approached ; but still went on
Attending to her bird, that fed at ease.
Her colour varied ; but she strove to keep
Both look and voice composed, as she, with eyes
Still bent upon the dove, said :

                      " You would not
Oblige me by remembering my request
To come that we might settle any claims
Remaining unfulfilled of the old trust ;
I had to summon you by letter, and
Subdue whatever lady's pride forbade
My writing to remind you of my wish :
But I may well afford to sacrifice
A little of punctilio, sure, for you ;
Since in our desert life were levelled all
The usual forms of civilised regard
To set observances, distinctions, and
Conventional appointed rules."   " You speak
Of ' claims,' I answered ; I am not aware
That any claims exist.   I tried, with all
My best endeavour, to perform the points
The trust enjoined ; and I believed they all
Had been fulfilled, when I had brought you here,
And seen you safely home to Merton Hall."
" Ah, yes, we never could agree in what
Those points consist ; and therefore 'twas I asked
You to come hither, that we might decide
How far they reach, and how much they include.
You think them ended by your escort home :
You think protection, guard, and watchfulness
No longer needed for me, now I am
Returned to safety and to Merton Hall ?
You think your care for me may cease now I
Have once resumed my station and my rank
As Lady of the Manor—mistress of this place? "

There was a break in her sweet voice as she
Pronounced the words " your care for me," and that
Old playful title used between us in
Our desert life ; but with recovered tone
Of steadiness, she hurried on : " You think
Your task concluded, and my uncle's charge
Completed now?   Perchance it is, as you
Regard the trust and all the claims it gives
Me on your guardianship.   But may not I
Perceive some claims yet unfulfilled?   May I
Not feel I may advance my claim to show
The grateful sense I have, and ever shall
Retain, of your devoted, manly care :
Heroic bravery in saving me,
Unceasing labour, forethought, fortitude   .
For me, unfailing firmness, tolerance
Throughout, when whims of woman mood must oft
Have sorely tried your patience?   Do you think
That I possess no claims?   My uncle's charge
And trust, I know, must sure include the claim
His Clarice has to show her gratitude."
" Your gratitude is not what I would have ;
If any guerdon be my due, there is
One, higher far, I dare not, may not ask."
My heart gave a wild bound when I perceived
She shrank not at my words : I took her hand,
And held it in my own with firm close grasp :
" I never will ask this, if you forbid."
The dove had flown away ; but the soft eyes
Of Clarice still were downward bent, as she,
In gentle whispered tone, said :
                                        " Will you tell
Me what it was that made you treat those flowers
So strangely in the lane last night ? "   " You ask
The truth ? " " I ask the truth." " In one word lies

The truth ; but will you bear to hear it ?   Will
You not resent the truth ?"   " I ask it," she
Repeated, quietly.   "Then know 'twas love,
Love long ago conceived, love ever since
Concealed with careful painfullest attempt
To bury it within the depths of my
Own heart.   'Twas love that took me to the lane
In boyhood, that I might have chance to see
Fair Clarice riding by ; 'twas love that made
My rapture when I saved her from the sea ;
'Twas love that made my torture when I dared
Not let her see my passion in our home
Of desert life, lest she might grow to care
For me, and even learn (Oh, mingled bliss
And anguish !) to return my faithful love,
When no all-hallowed rite of sacred tie
Could there be ours : 'twas love and burning wish
To see her, if but once again, that brought
Me to the lane last night, and made me press
The violets with fervour passionate,
In thought of her and our sweet desert life."
" How could I guess 'twas love ? " she softly said ;
" Your manner was so strange, so grave, reserved,
Constrained, so almost—as it seemed to me—
Averse."   " For *your* sake it was so ; for yours.
All guardless, innocent, protectionless,
As you were then, how could I be but thus,
If I would not betray my charge, my trust ? "
"And now?" she asked, with frank, bewitching
    smile;
" Well, now, you are Miss Merton of the Hall,
While I am only "—   " Noblest, purest, best,
And truest-hearted man ! " she warmly said,
With eyes that sparkled through bright jewel
    tears ;

" The sea-bruised girl cast at your very feet
By tossing waves you took up tenderly,
You treated with all delicate respect
For womanhood, you cherished, treasured her—
What should she be but yours ? "   I clasped her to
My heart : she was my own by her free gift :
My TRUST was trusted to me evermore.

THE REMITTANCE.

―――

"A good woman is worth gold."

Young Bernard Thorpe and Richard Middleton
Were friends, fast friends, from time when they
    were chums
At school. A lively, sanguine, clever youth
Was Richard ; while his friend was earnest and
Industrious, content to win by slow
Degrees. Dick Middleton was rather for
An enterprise of dash and sudden gain ;
While Bernard Thorpe preferred a steady rise,
By diligence and perseverance earned.
Before they were of age they both were launched
In life, pursuing each the course was best
Adapted to his character ; and ere
Some years were past, they both were on the way
To make large fortunes. Richard Middleton
Went early out to India : Bernard had
His office-desk in London, where he worked
With assiduity and energy.
They both were merchants : but the ventures of
The one were made in the flush Orient ;
The traffic of the other chiefly lay
In the West Indies, where plantations large,
With luscious rums and sugars brought in cash.
Both were employed in making money ; one
Abroad, at times acquiring sudden sums
Of large amount ; the other, slow and sure,
Amassing solid wealth. Dick Middleton

Had married at eighteen, and taken his
Young wife to India with him when he went:
But Bernard Thorpe remained a bachelor.
His residence was good, substantial; one
Of those old roomy gloomy mansions in
The neighbourhood of Bedford Square, which once
Found favour with rich City men ; *warm*, like
Themselves, 'tis true, but wholly ugly and
Unstylish, unattractive, void of grace
Or cheerfulness.   In this dull dwelling he
Contented lived, his thoughts absorbed in gain—
Not sordid gain—but gain that should exalt
Him to the style of merchant-prince, the rank
Sir Thomas Gresham held with such renown.
Respectable in all, he had a most
Respectable old housekeeper, who once
Had been his mother's, and who knew him from
A boy.   She almost stood him in the place
Of mother now, so motherly and good
Was Mistress Wilson in her care of her
Young master.
            By the Indian mail one year
A letter came to Bernard Thorpe that gave
Him much delight.   It told him that he might
Expect his old school-friend, Dick Middleton,
In England shortly ; said the writer knew
That Bernard Thorpe would gladly hear of his
Return, and welcome him to English ground
Again ; " although " (so ran the letter) " I
Am only coming on a visit, and
Shall soon go back to India, where a man
May make a heap of guineas in a day.
There, there's the place for minting money, my
Dear friend : I almost wish the East and not
The West had been your chosen mart, old boy.

But I have something now in view that will,
Or I am very much mistaken, prove
A field between them—that's neither here
Nor there (I don't intend a pun)—which must
Bring in enormous profits, and turn out
A perfect El Dorado—truer far
Than that Sir Walter Raleigh went to find.
But more of this, friend, when we meet ; which will
Be soon I hope. Yours, ever faithfully,
DICK MIDDLETON."

When he arrived, his friend
Insisted he should come to him at once :
" You must, Dick ; " Bernard said ; " you must indulge
My wish, and make my house your home while you
Remain in England."   " But my stay will be
But short," said Richard ; " and it's scarce worth while
To put you out for such a little time."
" The less time you can give, the more I need
To make the most of it.   Come, Dick, you must
Consent."   " Oh, if I must, I must," said Dick ;
·' But Mistress What's-her-name, your housekeeper,
Will wish me farther, with my truant ways
Of darting in and out, at all odd hours ;
Of keeping dinner waiting ; being out
When I should be at home, and being in
When she'd be glad to have my room instead
Of company—as the old saying goes.
I know I am unpunctual, terribly
Irregular and unmethodical :
My wife has often told me so ; though she
Is gentlest of the gentle, and will bear
From me, ay, almost anything. But how
Can I expect your housekeeper to bear" —

" My housekeeper will bear whatever I
Think fit and pleasant," answered Bernard with
A smile ; " and your consenting to my wish
Is fit and pleasant both : so it's agreed."
The friends enjoyed their time together much.
While Richard Middleton was staying there
He entered headlong into the grand scheme
That he had mentioned in his letter to
His friend ; though Bernard Thorpe did all he could
To try dissuade the eager Richard from
A too rash entrance into this vast field
Of speculation, that presented such
Alluring prospect and large promise of
Returns.   " An interest of cent.-per-cent.
Dimensions always serves to startle me
From joining in a project," Bernard said ;
" Lest it should prove a bubble some fine day,
And burst, with empty nothingness for the
Investors, shareholders, and all concerned.
No, no ; I always rather trust to small
Sure gains, than to a dazzling possible
Result of magnitude immense ; for large
Percentage certainly implies large risk."
" Ay, Bernard," smiled his friend ; " you always
    were,
You know, a something of a plodder ; liked
To take the cautious, prudent course : while I
Loved rapid pace, excitement ; all the rush
The speed, the impetus, the triumph of
A swift arrival at my goal, to find
Myself the prize-crowned conqueror."   " Beware
Lest you the racer's fate experience,
Of check, impediment, or being thrown,"
Returned the other in a graver tone ;
" Consider, Dick, ere yet it be too late."

" It is too late already, if you call
' Too late ' my being early to secure
A thumping slice of this good thing, a lot,
A lion's share of shares, for next to naught,
For a mere song, in fact; they let me have
This first advantage, since 'twas I that first
Originated and promoted the
Affair.. It really is a splendid thing.
Moreover they have made me treasurer,
And one of the directors. I assure
You, Bernard, it is sure to do; it must,
It shall, it will ; I'm certain that it will.
I'll give you as a toast to-day—and drink
It you will not refuse, I know—' Success
To Richard Middleton's new scheme, and may
It bring him all the luck and cash that he
Expects ! ' And that is not a little, I
Can tell you, Master Bernard, dear old boy ! "
In highest spirits went on Dick, until
One day he came home late to dinner, and
Went up at once to his own room to dress.
A quarter of an hour elapsed—and then
Another—and again a third ; but still
No Dick appeared. Then Bernard rang the bell,
And asked if Mr. Middleton had yet
Come in. " Dear, yes, sir, to be sure,
A good half-hour ago," was the reply ;
" But p'rhaps he don't feel quite the thing," said Price,
The old grey-headed butler, in a tone
Of half mysterious, half fatherly
Concern ; for Dick's good-natured lively ways
And lavish pay for service done had gained
Him favour in the household. Price's tone
Drew notice from his master. " What is it

You mean?" said he; "Is Mr. Middleton
Not well?" "I don't exactly know, sir; but
He seemed to me to look quite queer—so white,
So drawn, so strange, somehow." "I'll go and see
To it myself," said Bernard; and he ran
Upstairs to see his friend. On opening
The door he saw Dick sitting with his face
Deep buried in his hands; complete despair
Marked sunken head, distracted attitude;
While on the table lay an open case
Of travelling pistols, close within his reach.
His friend advanced with noiseless step and laid
A gentle hand upon the shoulder of
The stricken man: "Dick, what is this?" he said
With voice as tender as a woman's; "tell
Me what has chanced." "A blow, a heavy blow:
It struck me on the head, I fancy; it
Affects my head, I think; but it will
Pass away; 'tis nothing, I dare say; leave
Me, Bernard; I will try to get some sleep;
I only feel a little stunned: the blow
Was hard." He tried to turn it off, and make
It seem he'd met with some street accident.
"Dick, tell me truly what has happened," said
His friend. Then Dick burst forth in torrent wild
Of words: "Impending ruin, utter loss,
Destruction! Worse than money loss, the loss
Of honour, credit, reputation; worse,
Far worse! I ne'er can raise my head again!
Best die at once, and end it all!" His eyes
An instant turned to where the pistols lay
Upon the table. Bernard closed the case,
And put it in his pocket. "Dick," he said,
"Be calm, be rational; come, be yourself,
Your bright and hopeful self; you always were

A hopeful chap, you know—too sanguine, p'rhaps—
But now 'tis best encourage hope. Come, let's
Consider how all this may be repaired,
Averted; think of ways and means; devise
Some mode of putting off the evil day.
This scheme, of course, has failed; I feared it
  would ;
It is so, is it not ? " "It is," said Dick ;
" Dolt, blockhead that I was, to be so rash,
So credulous!" "Is there no help ? No chance
Of staving off the crash ? " asked Bernard. "None,
None, none!" said Dick. "Unless I find the means
To raise before to-morrow noon a sum
Of fabulous amount, I'm beggared, and—
Still deeper misery—dishonoured, lost,
Undone ; for never after can I hope
To rise, recover ground, make one more strong
Attempt to try my fate with fortune, and
Retrieve the past by ardent, strenuous
Endeavour. Bankrupt, creditless, no chance
Remains for me in life ; and life I care
Not for, I will not have." "Dick, promise me
That you will be a man, commit no act
Of folly—worse than folly, wickedness—
Do nothing desperate, and I in turn
Will promise to think over this, and see
What can be done before to-morrow noon.
And now cheer up, my dear old boy, and come
With me downstairs ; we'll have a glass of good
Old Burgundy shall warm our hearts, and may—
Who knows ?—inspire me with the eftest way
To get you out of difficulty, and
To set you on your legs of mercantile
Stability again. Some food and wine
Will do you good. The dinner—no, I will

Not call it so—the supper has been kept
By us so long uneaten, that poor Price,
And mistress cook, and mistress housekeeper,
Are out of patience, sure, by this time." Thus
Did Bernard rattle on, that Dick might not
Relapse into his moody thought and black
Despair : the two men seemed, as they sat there
At table, to have changed respectively
Their characters : Dick, downcast, sad, and mute,
While Bernard was all brightness, passed the wine,
And strove to keep his friend in spirits, cheer, and
    hope.
When finished was the meal, and servants were
Withdrawn, the two fell into graver talk,
And Bernard made himself acquainted with
The full particulars of Richard's case,
The master of its every detailed fact,
Then bidding Dick good night, and charging him
To keep good heart, his friend retired to bed,
But not to sleep : he lay awake in thought
And earnest question with himself, how he
Might rescue Richard, yet escape without
The total wreck of his own fortunes ; for
The sum required was one that almost would
Demand his all, and leave him nearly stripped,
Comparatively penniless, reduced,
Restricted to the scantiest of means
For keeping still his honoured calling as
A merchant.   But at length he firm made up
His mind : " I cannot let old Dick be lost
For want of my assistance, come what may'!
He saved my life at school once, in his own
Impetuous and headlong way, without
Regard to consequence or danger to
Himself: just as he now is, he was then ;

A thoughtless, generous chap, resolved to win
Whate'er he sought at one bold dash, be it
The life of his school chum, or be it wealth
And eminence. Old Dick must not be lost,
If any sacrifice of mine can save
Him now. It is but going back to where
I was, beginning life anew. I'll start
Afresh with vigour and good will. I am
Not thirty yet : there's time enough to make
My fortune still." Next day he told his friend
Of what he had resolved upon. Dick made
Remonstrance; said he could not think of such
A noble sacrifice on Bernard's part ;
That he could not accept a loan so large,
So ruinously large ; but when he found
That Bernard still persisted and remained
Unmoved, Dick wavered, then began to yield,
And lent an ear to Bernard's arguments :
" Remember I, a bachelor," said Thorpe,
" Can better far afford to be a poor
And struggling man than you, a husband and
A father, can afford to be without
A shilling. Think a moment of your wife
And child, and then I know you'll see the force
Of what I say." " Besides," said Dick, " although
This heavy loan will leave you straitened for
A period, 'twill be but for a time ;
Since once I am again in India, my
Resources there will soon enable me
To send you a remittance ; such a sum
As amply will suffice to set you well
Afloat again, till I can forward more
And more, until the whole be gratefully
Repaid." And thus it was agreed. By noon
Next day the fate of Richard Middleton

I

Was saved; the fate of Bernard Thorpe was sealed:
The one was free, the other bound—bound hand
And foot to recommencement of his first
Dull drudgery in early days, when he
As office-clerk, began the mercantile
Career, day-dreaming of Dick Whittington,
His humble origin, and glorious end.
The time arrived for parting, and the two
Took leave. "God bless you, dear old boy! good-
  bye!
When once I'm over there I'll forward the
Remittance, never fear! Expect it soon,
Dear Bernard, generous friend!" And Dick set sail.
    Thus bare, thus cramped and maimed,
A crippled man in capital and funds,
Stout-hearted Bernard set to work to lay
Again the first stone of his edifice,
His building up a fortune regal in
Its vastness. He began by practising
The strictest prudence and economy,
Retrenched his personal expenses to
The merest need; wore plainest garments; took
No recreation save his books and walks;
Reduced his household; lived on simplest fare;
But dwelt in the same roomy gloomy house,
For three good reasons; one, because he there
Lived free of rent, since he had bought it for
His own when he was rich; the second was,
Because it looked substantial, solid, like
The dwelling of a well-established man;
The third, because to change it for a less
Expensive one would challenge notice and
Bespeak reverse and smaller means; for he
Endeavoured always to preserve the look
Of being still as able as before

To meet all exigencies and sustain
The business in previous magnitude.
Its old repute, its long-established name,
Its steady, firmly grounded credit, and
Repute for punctuality and prompt
Fulfilment of trade orders, constant in
Its industry, activity for years,
While Bernard's father was alive, and when
The son succeeded him to be its head,
Gave Bernard power to stem the tide
Of difficulty threatening to whelm
Him in its flood: and still he toiled and toiled,
And waited, waited, ever patiently,
In expectation of the promised large
Remittance coming from abroad, that might
Redeem Dick's solemn pledge, as well as shield
Himself from pressing calls, and urgent need
To be prepared against ensuing chance
Or imminent demand.
　　　　　　　　But time went on;
And still no news from India, none from Dick.
The lines increased on Bernard's knitted brow;
The crows of care began to set their feet
With deep indent about his wistful eyes;
His cheek grew haggard, wan, with that sad look
Is seen in faces early aged and worn
By carking, pondering anxiety;
By absent-minded longing for some one
Intensely wished occurrence; by a dull
Persistent dwelling on a single strong
Desire, to the exclusion of all else
That's healthful, cheerful, hopeful for a man
To think upon. Yet Bernard was still young,
And hardly yet had reached the prime of life;
The more, then, was it sorrowful to mark

The signs of that impending oldness in
His face and its expression, with the bend
Of his brown head ere it was grey, and stoop
Of limbs that had not shrunk, but still possessed
The firmness, suppleness, alertness of
Their youth.   He was a personable man,
Of figure fine and tall, with countenance
Refined, a forehead bland and thoughtful, eyes
That glowed with generous fire, or softened with
Benignity, and smile of sweetness most
Ineffable : but all these comely points
Were clouded by his growing care, and gnaw
Of ever-biting keen solicitude.
    At last an Indian mail came in that brought
The long-expected letter, which ran thus :
" Dear Friend,—Alas for the remittance that
I promised and I fully thought to send !
I've staked my last and lost : I thought to make
One final stroke of fortune would repay
You all, and more than all : but no, I'm ruined ;
Ruined past redemption, past recall.
I send you now, in lieu of the once-hoped
Remittance, all that now is left to me—
My beggared orphan child ; for orphan soon
I feel she'll be : her mother is no more :
Myself am struck to earth, am dying fast :
This blow has killed me with the bitter thought
Of my poor girl thus left, and you unpaid ;
I send her to you, Bernard, in my last
Extremity : a charge instead of payment :
And yet I know you will take care of her ;
For have you not been always good to me ?
Forbearing ?   Generous ?   A more than friend ?
Be kind to her, be kind to my poor Grace,
If only for the sake of bygone times,

When I was your old schoolfellow and chum,
DICK MIDDLETON."
            The girl arrived : a slim
Slight girl, scarce entered on her teens ; a shy
And timid creature, with large eyes that shrank
From gaze, yet seemed to fill her face, so out
They stood above her pale, wan, wasted cheeks :
A girl forlorn and unattractive she
Appeared to Bernard Thorpe, as he at once
Delivered her to Wilson's care, and gave
His housekeeper the order to attend
To all was needful for Miss Middleton.
" An unformed girl, an awkward unformed girl ; "
Was Bernard's muttered thought, as she withdrew ;
" ' A charge instead of payment,' were the words
Her father used, and true enough they are ;
A charge indeed ! an onerous charge ! a charge
The more for me to bear beyond what I
Have had to bear : a charge entailing more
Expense and outlay in the place of the
Remittance promised, my own sum returned,
Repaid : that sum so long expected, long
Relied on, long and ardently desired !
That sum which would have helped to make me all
I thought to be—a wealthy man, a man
Respected as a reigning potentate
Among his fellow-merchants, one who might
Have raised high merchanthood e'en higher yet.
What now is left me ? To remain for years
A struggling man, an ever-struggling man !
But, patience, Bernard Thorpe, be patient still !
With patience, courage, persevering work,
You yet may win the goal you've set your heart
Upon. Till now you have relied on one
Whose word you took : henceforth rely on none

But God and your own self; be brave, be calm,
Be firm and constant to your promised end ! "
That end he more than ever held in view,
Pursued, and still unflinchingly resolved
To gain : he laboured at his desk by night
As well as day; he spared nor toil, nor thought,
Nor hand, nor brain : all day he spent in the
Small pent-up city office, hard at work ;
The evening he gave himself for brief
Enjoyment of his dinner and his glass
Of wine ; but long into the night he wrote,
And looked into his ledgers, cash-accounts,
His long ruled pages bound in calf, and all
The rest of those important " books that are
No books," according to the author-clerk
Of London's venerable India House,
Dear Elia, ever-honoured writer-friend,
Sweet-hearted, witty, good and great Charles Lamb.
The time allowed by Bernard Thorpe for rest,
Repose of mind as well as hand, was when
Just once in the whole four-and-twenty hours
He saw the young girl, Grace, who had been sent
So solemnly to his own guardianship
And care.   Her diffidence, her shyness, her
Timidity, would fain have kept her from
What she imagined might be taken as
Intrusion ; but good Mistress Wilson would
Not hear of Grace's dining anywhere
But with the master of the house, and at
The proper dinner-hour of set and state
Repast for the chief meal of every day.
She had her ready dressed and ready to
Go down into the dining-room, against
The well-known knock was heard, that she might
   there

Be seated to receive the merchant, when,
Returning home, he ought to find and to
Be met with welcome, was the sage and kind
Assertion of the formal thoughtful dame :
" For you must know, my dear," she said, " that my
Young master has lived much too much alone,
In my opinion ; and he would be all
The better for a little company ;
Ay, even company of one so mere
A girl as you are, dear, is cheerfuller
Than dining by himself : so you must go."
Grace always went ; was punctual to the time ;
And sat beside the fire, its bright red blaze
Reflected dancingly, and lighting up
With starry sparkles the small locket and
The jet upon her mourning frock ; and so
Brought into fuller, stronger contrast the
Pale face and large dark eyes that spoke in dumb
But plainly written characters the tale
Of early saddened girlhood. There she sat
In deepest thought, her loosely folded hands
Across her lap, her eyes fixed dreamily
Upon the coals, in which she seemed to see
Strange pictures of the past old Indian life,
Until came Bernard's knock, to wake her with
A start from out her musing trance, and bring
Her back to present life with all its yet
More strange surroundings, as it seemed to her.
When he came in she used to quick look up
And see if in his face were aught amiss,
Of coming change or fresh anxiety ;
Then rose, and silently—as was her wont—
Drew forward his arm-chair a little, as
Presenting it, reminding him 'twas there
Beside the fire ; and pointed to the rug

Where lay his slippers, warming, ready to
Put on at once. ere he went up to dress
More leisurely before they dined.　All these
Attentions, paid with utmost quietness,
As quietly were taken by the man
To whom they were so mutely offered ; for
At most times Bernard was so absent, so
Immersed in calculations and accounts,
He rarely noticed what was passing.　His
Abstraction lessened somewhat as the meal
Went on ; and by the time dessert was placed
Upon the table, he became more free
Of speech, more genial, more inclined to chat
With Grace.　She had been in the house some
　　weeks,
When once he said, while eating walnuts peeled
By her, and put upon his plate with salt,
In silence : " I've remembered, child, that I
Ought long ere this to have bethought me of
A school ; for I suppose you should be sent
To school."　He gave a sort of little sigh,
As he said this, in thinking of the time
That he must give to choosing some good school ;
Some school well recommended, and well known
To be a good one.　" If you please," said Grace,
With her large eyes raised suddenly to his,
" I would much rather not be sent to school ;
My mother used to tell me that she did
Not like the thought of school for me.　But if
I'm troublesome or wrong in saying I
Object, or telling you my mother's strong
Objection, I will go to school."　" No need,
No need ;" said Bernard ; " we can think of some
Still better mode of education ; for
Of course you must be educated, child—

Now, mustn't you?" "My mother taught me
much,"
Said Grace; " from quite a little, little girl
She used to teach me all she knew, and take
Great pains with me; but I don't know; perhaps
I ought to learn some more. Do you think so?"
" I hardly know, indeed, myself," said he,
With puzzled look; " I know so little what
Is reckoned right for a young lady's due
And proper training; but, if not a school,
A governess might be engaged for you,
Or teachers, masters, could come here at hours
Appointed, certain days." " A governess
Would want a salary, and cost a great,
Great deal; while Mistress Wilson takes good care
Of me, and teaches me to sew and stitch,
And lets me watch her make preserves and jams,
With many other things it's well to learn;
And then there are the books upon the shelves
In your small study, that she said I might
Go into while you are away—you do
Not mind it, do you?—and from these I pick
Out several I like to look at and
To read." " You do?" asked Bernard, much
amused
At Grace's quaintly stated plan for her
Home schooling; " but I should have thought
those books
You speak of much too dry to please the taste
Of a young girl." " In one of them," said Grace,
" I found a number of most curious prints,
That entertain me always; queer monkeys,
Odd birds, strange places, heads of ancient men
And women, monstrous fish and insects, all
Of which I want to know about, and so

I read the pages near, and like that book
Beyond the rest."   " The Cyclopædia, eh ? "
Said Bernard, with a smile that lighted up
His face, and long had been a stranger there ;
" Well, well, your choice is rather different
From what the usual run of damsels of
Your age prefer ; but you are not among
' The usual run ' of girls ; and you know best,
Of course, what interests and pleases you."
" Not only pleases me, but teaches me,"
Said Grace, a little timidly, afraid
That Bernard's manner might imply he thought
She cared for nothing more than pastime in
Her looking through his books ; " I learn while I
Am turning over all those leaves, and if
I do not learn enough, you can engage—
But, later on—some masters for me, if
You please."   " Ay, very well," said Bernard, much
Relieved to find the matter settled for
The present, turning as he spoke to where
A writing-table always stood, that he
Might go at once to work when food and rest
Were taken.   Grace was also glad to have
Reprieve ; her haunting dread of adding to
The merchant's outlay, when she knew his means
Had been so straitened by that heavy loan,
Of being one more burden among those
Her father's act had laid on him to bear,
Inspired her with a constant wish to save
Him all expense, to spare in all she could,
To try and aid him by economy,
By active, helpful, frugal ways at home,
And by avoiding for herself whate'er
Cost money.   Grace was thoughtful much beyond
Her years : her mother delicate, she had

Been nurse, sick-cook, and comforter to her ;
Her father, thoughtless, lavish, careless, but
Most fond of wife and child, had been of both
The idol and the thought-for : thus it came
That, from her earliest childhood, Grace had been
Accustomed by her parents to be made
Their little confidant in all their joys
And griefs, their pleasures and their pains, their
 brief
Good fortune, and their frequent intervals
Of narrowed income ; causing her to have
Reflection, patience, prudence, foresight, quick
Perception, judgment, seldom seen in girls
Of age so tender.
 One among the few
Small luxuries that Bernard still allowed
Himself at table, after his resolve
To banish superfluities, was choice
Though spare dessert, and strong black coffee
 formed,
To him, its chief enjoyment. This he liked
Made carefully, prepared with duest eye
To preservation of its exquisite
Aroma. On a certain evening
He raised his coffee-cup, and sipped, and sipped,
With extra relish of its grateful scent
And flavour, till at length he asked : " Who made
This coffee ? Mistress Wilson, I suppose,
As usual ? Yet it seems to me she has
Surpassed herself. But was it she ? I ought
To be a judge of coffee, and I think
I could be sure that this was made by some
New hand. Who was it, Susan ? " " It was made
To-day, sir, by Miss Middleton," said the
Neat waiting-maid who served at table now

In place of Price, the butler, sent away
When Bernard had reduced his household. " I
Was sure I could not be mistaken ; it's
Delicious ; quite a different, and still
More delicate essential taste." He looked
At Grace. Her usual paleness now had changed
To scarlet. " Mistress Wilson let me try,"
She said, in answer to his look ; " I had
So often begged her leave to make it once,
Because I wished to see if you would like
The way I used to make it when I was
In India, for my mother, who was fond
Of coffee ; and she always liked it made
By me." " I do not wonder ; so should I,"
Said Bernard, smilingly. " Would you ? " answered
    Grace,
Delightedly. " Then might I make it for
You every day—at breakfast time as well
As dinner ? " " Certainly ; but breakfast time
Is early, and requires you to be up
At a still earlier time, if you would make
The coffee ready for my breakfasting,
Before I leave this house for office hours
And City business." " I'm always up
A good long while before your breakfast, and
I will be sure to have the coffee made
In time," she said. And so it was ; and Grace
Was there to pour it out for him. Till then
She had not liked to join him at that meal,
Lest he, in hurry to be off, should find
Her in the way ; but ever after, she
Took courage, and both breakfasted and dined
With him.
              Not only from the picture book,
That drew a smile from Bernard, did she strive

To gather knowledge, but with diligent
Attention she read through most carefully
The books he had thought "dry" for her, which in
The study she had found; they were a small
But well-chosen collection, mostly works
Of science, travel, and biography.
They aided her to form her mind and fill
It with a store of information, good,
Available, and solid; useful, fit
To make her practical and sensible.
She was already so, by nature and
By circumstance; her course of reading now
But tending to confirm her previous bent.
Another source of intellectual aid
She had.   There came sometimes at after-hours
To Bernard's dwelling-house, on messages
Of urgency, a young clerk from the house
Of business in the City, who was sent
Because he was a favourite of his,
A steady worker and intelligent.
This Henry Frankland worshipped Bernard; but
With certain awe and reverence inspired
By former patronage bestowed upon
Himself and family, and by the grave
Reserve, with aspect dignified, that were
The merchant's, even from his very youth.
When Henry Frankland brought these messages
It generally was when Bernard sat
Enjoying his dessert; but even that
Gave way at once to business; and he
Went straight to where his writing-table stood,
And wrote whatever letter, answer, or
Directions wanted sending back for next
Day's early morning post, first pointing to
The dining-table, saying, hurriedly,

But kindly : " Frankland, help yourself to wine
And fruit, or coffee, while I write this line."
The " line " would often take an hour or two
To write, as detail after detail would
Suggest itself to Bernard's mind for each
Minute and accurate instruction : thus
It came that Frankland stayed, while Grace
   performed
The hospitable duties, offering
The cates to him, instead of letting him
Attend upon himself; and often tea
Was served ere Bernard had completed all
He had to write.   The first time Grace poured out
A cup and offered it to Frankland, he,
In tone subdued that might not interrupt
The merchant as he wrote, said : " Shall I not
Take some to Mr. Thorpe ?   Will he not take
Some tea ? "   " No," was Grace's low reply ; " he
But seldom drinks it till it's cold, and does
Not like to be disturbed when writing ; he
Will come himself for some, if later on
He care to have any ; 'tis understood
Between us ; so I never offer tea
To him, but let it wait his pleasure."   And
Much low talk like this was held by Grace
And Frankland, then and afterwards while he
Awaited Bernard's written orders, and
She brought her needlework, to give her hands
Employment as she listened.   For 'twas he
That chiefly talked : habitually staid
And sparing of her speech, Grace much preferred
Remaining silent, when the clerk would tell
Her what he thought might serve to entertain
The lonely quiet girl thus living set
Apart from all society, from all

Communion and companionship with those
Of her own age. Till, by degrees, Grace learned
To look for evenings when most probably
Young Frankland might arrive with City-sent
Despatches for the merchant; since she then
Heard something of the outer world, and, what
More interested her, some touches of
That inner world wherein she dwelt and close
Concentred all her thoughts. She heard from him
Of Bernard's goodness to himself and all
He dearly loved, when they in penury
Were steeped, and, but for what the merchant did
On their behalf, would probably have sunk
O'erwhelmed: she heard from Frankland of the
    large
Benevolence, the charity, the bland
Mild kindliness that marked the merchant's mode
Of giving ear to sufferers; e'en when
He could not give them aid in money, from
His own less ample means, he furnished them
With letters to his wealthier friends, and took
Best pains to help them on their way to earn
An independence for themselves. Besides
These narratives, Grace gleaned from the young
    clerk
Some knowledge that she wanted, for the clear
And better comprehension of a branch
Of information she had made her more
Especial care to cull from those " dry " books
She studied ; it was commerce, traffic, trade
In mercantile and international
Regard, she strove to understand ; and to
Become acquainted with their various
Requirements—skill in book-keeping, and in
Arithmetic, in calculations of

Percentage, annual and compound rates
Of interest, in home and foreign goods,
In exports, imports, markets, prices, and
The rest of those essential points for one
Who wished to be proficient, and might be
Efficient, as a merchant's helping-hand.
She once heard Bernard say that his young clerk
Was versed in business particulars,
And first-rate as accountant ; so she asked
Of Frankland help in certain points that still
Perplexed her, and of which she could not quite
Yet solve the mystery from what she read.
Sometimes, when Grace's difficulties of
Commercial study were adjusted, the
Young clerk would turn to other subjects ; and,
As gradually more and more at ease
Became this murmured talk, he would confide
To Grace some items of his personal
Affairs ; as where his parents lived, and how
He had an only sister, who with them
Made home a paradise of peace and joy
And comfort to him ; ne'ertheless, how he
Looked forward, some fine day, to make his home
A still more happy one, by bringing there
As wife a certain Lucy Mildmay, whom
He loved and hoped to wed, when he should earn
Sufficient income to support them all.
Grace took great interest in this the first
Love-story that her girlish life had known ;
She felt a pride in being told so young
Its secret, and she wished it all success
With earnestness and warmth.   It made a theme
Of kindly social thought for her amid
The solitary course her youth maintained.
And yet, though solitary, it was far

From dull to her. She took delight in all
She did ; and worked with zest at each pursuit
With which she filled her time, in hope to make
Her education what it should be, while
Still keeping Bernard free from the expense
Of schooling, governess, or masters. One
Expense there was she could not spare him from ;
For he himself insisted that she should
Have an allowance quarterly, to spend
As best she chose, for clothes, for trifles, such
As all young ladies need, he had affirmed,
And would not hear of any other plan.
He told his housekeeper that Grace had showed
Such great discretion, for so young a girl,
In all she said about her learning from
The books already in the house, he felt
Assured she might be trusted to control
Her own expenditure, and thought it best
Young people should be early used to lay
Out money for themselves, and learn betimes
To regulate their income with a true
And just economy. " I think so too,"
The dame had answered ; " and of all
Young ladies that I ever saw, Miss Grace
Is, sure, the cleverest at making and
Arranging dresses, keeping them so neat and nice,
So spick and span, they look bran new,
Though now they're getting rather worn, it must
Be owned ; but then they're still those same black
    frocks
She brought with her from India—poor dear thing ! "
" Then let her get some others," answered he,
And so the subject of allowance ceased ;
For Grace deferred to Bernard's wish in this
As in all else. Her stipend once begun,

K

Among the first large purchases she made
Was no less than a cottage piano, that
She might keep up her music, taught her by
Her mother, which she thought she could make
   means
Of earning, if need were, some day ; and so
She practised hard in her own room ;
She also worked at drawing, sketching, as
She had much aptitude for these,
And fancied they, too, might be useful, if
She had to earn ; for Grace was constant to
Her character—prudent, provident, and wise.

   Two years slipped by with almost unperceived
Transition, since she had been dwelling in
The merchant's house ; when, after dinner, once,
As Bernard sat engrossed with papers at
His writing-table, Grace heard drop some words
Of muttered worry from his lips : " How's this ?
How's this ?   To-night it seems as if I could
Not reckon.   Pshaw ! a simple sum like this !
Let's see, let's see ; the interest upon
Eleven hundred pounds, at six per cent.,
For twenty-seven years, would bring—how much ? "
He looked up for an instant, as in doubt,
When Grace said softly, scarce above her breath :
" One thousand seven hundred eighty-two,
I think, sir, is it not ? "   A cannon-shot
Could hardly more have startled Bernard than
This answer from a girl of Grace's age.
He looked at her and laughed outright, a good
Loud hearty laugh, a laugh that had not come
From him for years.   " Why, child ! " he said,
" How long have you been mistress of accounts ?
How long is it that you can tell about
A capital with interest, and such

Hard-sounding mercantile up-reckonings?"
Grace blushed bright crimson—partly shame to be
Found out in what she secretly had learned,
And partly with delight at Bernard's laugh;
For never had she heard him laugh—not once,
Since she had known him: and the consciousness
Of how his gravity was caused had oft
Depressed her heart, which now leapt up at sound
So new, so welcome. Through her blushes bright
Her eyes were dancing; and as Bernard looked
At that young face, so usually pale,
But now one glow of colour, vividness,
And animation, wondered how he could
Have ever thought her "unattractive."
"You do not answer me," still laughing, he
Continued: "Tell me how it is that you
Have come to be a good accountant? Why
I might engage you as a clerk, if your
Accomplishment be what it seems." "I ask
No better," Grace replied; "I'll be your clerk
At home, if you will have me. You can try
My services; and if they please, they're at
Your service, sir." She spoke with playfulness,
Inspired by pleasure at his laugh. "But yet
You have not told me how it is you gained
Your clerkly knowledge?" Bernard said. "I
   learned   .
Much from your books; and what I could not quite
Make out from them, I asked your clerk to tell
Me—to explain more clearly, fully. He
Had patience, and his explanations I
Could always understand." "My clerk? What do
You mean? What clerk?" "The clerk that
   sometimes comes
With messages to you. I heard you call

Him Frankland, did I not ? "   " Oh, ay, of course,
Young Frankland ; yes, he is an excellent
Accountant ; one well able to instruct
You in the rudiments and science of
Our noble mercantile pursuit : but still "—
Here Bernard stopped, and said no more ; he turned
To look again into his papers, while
Grace plied her needle, happy in the thought
Of Bernard's pleasant look and hearty laugh.
And, after that, he often gladly used
The clerkly knowledge and the clerkly hand
Of Grace, in helping him to calculate
And write ; he found her thoroughly well versed,
Most competent, and ever happiest
When she was busy helping him.
     Thus, two years more passed by unmarked, until
One day an illness came to Grace : 'twas slight
At first ; but soon became much worse, and then
Proved fever ; fever that for long kept her
A prisoner upstairs, nursed carefully
And tenderly by good kind motherly
Old Mistress Wilson, who from earliest
Had taken Grace to her affection, loved
Her like a daughter ; calling her " My dear "
When speaking to herself, though always spoke
Of her to Bernard, as " Miss Grace," and to
All others as " Miss Middleton," with true
Old-fashioned properness of due and right
Distinction.   Grace's illness was a time
Of grief to all, for all had learned to love
The gentle girl, so quaintly self-possessed,
Yet modest, quiet, mild, in all her ways :
But most of all the merchant felt the time
While Grace was ill a period of grief
And misery ; a want, a vacancy,

A blank, a loss, seemed fallen on his life;
At breakfast how he missed the light quick step,
So noiseless yet alert, that came to bring
The coffee freshly made ; the sweet young face,
So cheerful, placid, bright, that bade him a
" Good morning," e'en before she spoke, and gave
Him blithe " Good-bye " when he departed for
The City ; but when most he missed her was
Returning home for dinner ; missed the rest,
The peacefulness, the soft repose yet cheer
Of Grace's presence ; all the sympathy,
The welcome, that her look, her tone, expressed
Without the need of words to say how much
His home-return delighted her.   Instead,
The news of " Not much better, sir, to-day,"
From Susan, with her former briskness now
Subdued to stillness ; then the silence of
The solitary meal, the sighs that oft
Broke from him as he ate, in lieu of that
Gay interchange of chat, which, since he had
Become less absent-minded, she less shy
And timid, passed between them while they dined.
    At length, however, came an evening
When Susan met him with a brisker face
And voice : "Oh, please, sir, Mistress Wilson bade
Me give her duty and to say that if
You'd like to come upstairs, sir, after you've
Had dinner, she believes it wouldn't hurt
Miss Middleton to see you, and to have
A little chat for half an hour, as she's
A good deal better, sir, to-day."   He made
An end of dinner very quickly, and
He ran upstairs with lighter step than had
Been his for days and days.   He found Grace in
A large arm-chair, propped up by pillows ; but

With beaming eyes, that shone like stars above
Her hectic-flushed thin cheek, as he approached.
The wavy chesnut hair hung loosely down
Upon the muslin wrapper that took place
Of those plain sober greys she wore when well ;
Her arms fell languidly on either side,
And wasted hand—when once it had been held
Out greetingly to him—dropped feebly too.
The shock of seing her so changed, so weak,
Held Bernard silent, motionless ; while she
Said little, in the joy of seeing him.
" We're getting nicely on, sir, now," remarked
Dame Wilson, cheerfully ; " we have been ill,
Ay, very ill ; but we are coming round,
I'm glad to say, and hope soon to be well,
Quite well, and looking bonnily again."
" We're looking ' bonnily ' already, as
It seems to me," said Bernard, trying to
Speak cheerily in tone.   " These rosy cheeks
Tell hopefully of coming health, I trust ;
And, Grace, you've grown quite tall in this short
   time."
" Ay, always during fever we grow fast,"
Said Wilson, with sententious primness ; " tall
And slender—just a shade too slender, sir,
Mayhap, at present ; but with feeding up
And care we shall grow plump, and strong, and
   stout,
All in good time."   " Nay, ' stout ' we'll leave
   to you,
Good Wilson," Bernard smiling said.   " I meant,
When I said ' stout,' " said Wilson, laughing at
Her own full cheeks and double chin, " I meant,
Of course, robust and hearty ; and I hope
It won't be long before Miss Grace is that ;

For though she always was a slip, a mite,
Yet wonderfully healthy, active in
The house, she always was, that must be said.
See what a pretty place she's made of her
Own sitting-room; it's all her doing, all
Her planning and contriving; and it cost
So little too—ay, there's the beauty—cost
A merest nothing; for she worked at it
Herself, and made the curtains, carpet, with
Her clever little fingers, bless her; sewed
Away as if she got her living by
Her needle; stitched the seams, the hems, as though
She liked tough work; and then, by way of rest,
Embroidered all these cushions, soft low chairs
And footstools; drew these pictures that are hung
Around the walls, and "— " Stay, you must not thus
Tell tales, nurse, out of school," said, laughing,
  Grace;
" How you are running on." " My dear, I do
So just o' purpose, making talk for you
And master, that my patient mayn't be made
To talk too much herself, the first time she
Receives a visit." " ' Patient,' nursey? It
Is he that is the ' patient ' now, I think,
If.you run on at such a rate." " No one
Can say that I am given much to talk,"
Said Wilson; " goodness knows, I only talk
To keep you lively, and amused, my dear,
When you seem willing to enjoy a chat
Sometimes while you are sewing at your work."
" Suppose I say ' Good-night,' " said Bernard; " if
Allowed to come, I must not make my stay
Too long, lest nurse should scold, and tell me that
Our invalid exerts herself too much.
If I behave with due discretion now,

I may, I hope, be promised I shall come
To-morrow. Good night, Grace ! God bless you,
  Grace ! "
As Bernard went downstairs he thought of his
Last word. He had repeated " Grace " instead
Of saying to her " child," as formerly :
But now he felt he could not call her " child,"
He felt, while he was with her, that she had
Become no longer like a child, a girl,
A little creature sent to him for home,
Protection, care, and guidance ; but a young
And beautiful and sentient being, with
A nature righteous, spirit wise and good,
Well able to conduct itself by pure
Instinctive innocence of impulse and
Perception : no—no child ; but a young girl
Irradiated, hallowed, by the bloom
Of early womanhood that touched her with
A saint-like glory, as she lay back there,
So smiling, and so gentle, and so faint—
More helpless than before, and yet more clad
In spiritual strength, exalted, strong
To help herself and others throughout life,
If life were granted her. As Bernard's thought
Arrived at this last clause, he inwardly
Ejaculated : " God of mercy ! had
She died, had she been taken from me, what
Would life have now become to me ? A void,
A weary, worthless void." He shuddered, turned
From e'en the shadow of that possible,
And drew his chair beside the fire that he
Might dwell with thankfulness upon the blest
Relief of knowing she was spared to him ;
And then in mental fond review he passed
Successively through all that Grace had been

To him ; her quiet unobtrusive help,
Her pretty thoughtful, active, silent ways,
Her never-failing punctuality,
Her constant care, devotion, watchfulness
For all his likings, comforts, and pursuits :
No mother that he lost, no sister that
He might have had, no chosen woman whom
He might have made his wife, could better have
Divined his every wish, or studied to
Fulfil them pleasantly and welcomely.
A something in this " might have been " there was
That made the merchant start, as stung by what
Had crept about his heart while musing thus.
He rose abruptly, crushed the creeping thing,
And turned to write till long past midnight, when
All else but he had gone to rest.
                                        Next day,
No sooner dinner done, than Bernard sent
Upstairs to know if he might come and pay
The invalid another visit, with
Much sportive ceremony and parade
Of deference to nurse's orders.   She
Sent down to say that " Master may, as soon
As he thinks fit, and welcome, for we've made
A great improvement since last evening."
And Bernard found 'twas true; Grace looked much
    more
Her former self, in quiet strength beneath
A slender frame.   The nurse permitted her
To chat herself, and let her answer when
The merchant spoke ; so he availed himself
Of Wilson's gracious sanction, and addressed
His questions freely to the invalid.
He went about the room, examined its
Adornments, praised their grace, simplicity,

And taste; then paused significantly, just
Before the cottage-piano, looking straight
At Grace. "Ah, yes," she said, "that was my one
Extravagance; but thought it well to make,
Lest I should lose the little music that
My mother taught me; and I might have need
Some day, I fancied, for accomplishments,
In case I had to teach." "To teach?" "Yes,
　teach;
Give lessons; go as governess myself,
If·you became unable still to keep
Me here. Such things have been, I know; and if
You had grown poorer, and could not have kept
Me here, I should have liked to earn myself
A living independently, and—who
Can tell?—helped you, besides, if you would let
Me help." She spoke so gravely, with her own
Old quaint and simple self-possession, blent
With modest gentleness, that Bernard heard
Her gravely in return. "You paid a large
Amount for it, now, I suppose?" he asked.
"A large amount for me to spend," she said;
"But not too much, considering what I
Should surely lose had I not had the means
Of practising." "Quite true," he answered, with
A smile he could not now repress; "you made
A prudent calculation: how much gained
By a judicious outlay, set against
The price you pay—the best economy.
And pray, now, may I ask what is it that
You practise? Playing, singing, what?" "I play
Four hours a day; and sing, at intervals,
A couple more." "And might I farther ask,
If I'm not indiscreet, to hear you play
And sing?" said Bernard, laughingly. "I'm not

Accustomed to do either, as you well
Can understand, to any ears but mine
And nurse's ; but if you will promise to
Be audience lenient as ourselves, I'll try
My best." She had her chair wheeled over to
The piano ; and played unaffectedly
Some favourite pieces of her own, then sang
A simple air or two she liked herself.
Her voice was sweet, pathetic, capable
Of giving full expression to a strain
That needed feeling chiefly ; and her songs
Were mostly these—soft Indian tunes, and scraps
Of melody—regretful, wild ; replete
With mournful, dirge-like, sad lament and wail.
The merchant rendered duest homage by
His silence and his moistened eyes, as Grace
Concluded : she, a music-lover, well
Could understand this best of praise. He then
Resumed his walking round the room, and stopped
At each successive sketch and picture ; found
Them principally old remembered bits
Of Indian scenery—rock, mountain, and ravine,
Small fisher-hut, or ancient temple, with
A single lofty tree of cocoa-nut,
Thick jungle, tangled underwood, or else
A river-side with boat fantastic-shaped.
Amid them all there hung a portrait-sketch
That Bernard knew at once—his old friend Dick ;
The face was capitally hit—that look
Of bright expectant eagerness and hope,
So well remembered by the merchant, as
He gazed upon the likeness. " Grace, did you
Draw this ? " he said, at length. " I did," was her
Low-toned reply ; " I took it once when he
Was reading to my mother, full of glee

At news he had received : she thought it like."
" 'Tis very like," the merchant answered with
A deep-drawn breath—" poor Dick ! poor Dick ! "
Grace had
Been nervously observing Bernard, as
He looked upon the crayon-sketch ; but when
She heard his sighing word there came a light
Into her face—a sweet glad light—a light
That seemed a softened reflex of the bright
Expression in her father's : " Then you love
Him still ?   I thought—I feared "—she stopped.
" I loved
Him from a boy, he saved my life ; I love
His memory still, in thinking of his bright
And kindly nature.   Could you fear I ceased
To love your father ?   Dear old eager Dick ! "
" I fancied—dreaded—the remittance that
He failed to send, might cause you to"—   " He
sent
A treasure, priceless household treasure, that
Outvalues all the sums of India ! " said
The merchant in an earnest under-breath ;
And, for a moment, not a word beyond
Was uttered by himself or Grace.   He then
Began to talk of other things, and fell
To asking her about the simple white
Soft draperies that curtained shadingly
The windows in harmonious contrast with
The grasslike green of carpet, and of walls
That papered were with trellis, bowered in
By woodbine, jasmine, climbing rose ; while round
The base there ran a garland-bordering
Of clustered ferns and wild anemones,
Recalling rustic gardens, woodland glades,
And pleasant, country, open-air retreats.

" How did you manage, Grace, to ornament
Your room with all these elegancies for
So small a sum as Wilson vouches that
You spent?   You must not henceforth limit your
Ingenious thrift to furnishing your own
Apartments only ; through the house your care
And taste must now extend ; and let me, too,
Enjoy the pleasure and the benefit."
" Most gladly," she returned.   " I never dared
Attempt a change downstairs ; I fancied you
Preferred to have all left exactly as
It ever had been.   Now beware the wave
Of Grace's fairy wand ; its potency
Shall be most fully tried, thus summoned by
Your invocation ; you have called it forth
To exercise its spell ; take care it does
Not ruin you in articles undreamed
Of by the former furnishers employed—
Conventional upholsterers, with all
Their heavy durable moreens and stuffs."
" I'm reckless, Grace !   Perform your fairy will !
Be boundless in your magical behests !
And play the powerful enchantress in
Your vast commands !   I can afford to meet
Prosaic bills, and write out cheques, with aught
Else may assist to summon up the aid
Of ministering spirits you may need
To bring you silks from Samarcand, or rich
Brocades and damasks from the looms of far
Cathay or Persia—where you will."   " You talk
Of bills and cheques, and such ' prosaic ' charms
Of incantation ; but methinks your thoughts
Have wandered to the realms of poesy :
I fancy I have somewhere seen the words
Of ' silken Samarcand ' and ' far Cathay.' "

" I know but little of the poets, Grace,"
Said Bernard, " saving one, who wrote a play
Beginning with a spirited account
Of what a merchant's haunting fears must be
Lest 'rocks' should split his 'gentle vessel's side,
Should 'scatter all her spices on the stream,
Enrobe the roaring waters with her silks.'
But let's return to prose—and understand
That I am now no longer poor, but rich :
You look surprised, Grace ; well you may ; for I
Have gone on quietly at work to gain
The ground I lost, through these few years, and
    made
No outward change, although at present I
Possess abundant wealth ; so, in plain prose,
Be sure you use it freely, Grace, and turn
The house to Palace of Aladdin in
A trice." " Free use of cash, with liberty
To use my taste, I have Aladdin's lamp,"
She answered, " therefore you may soon expect
To see the magic change you authorise."
    But modern genii, although they're swayed
To speed by money, still take time to bring
About their transformations ; workmen once
Within a house, the marvels of their slow
Advance vie with the marvels they effect :
So, while her gnomes wrought out her mandates
    with
Precision equal to her own in all
She ordered, Grace was taken down to the
Seaside by careful Mistress Wilson, that
She might recover perfectly before
The mansion was arranged according to
Her wish.   The time of Grace's absence was
A weary one to Bernard ; but he plunged

Into his merchant work, and slipped away
At intervals from town, with pretext that
He must tell Grace how gnomes and genii
Got on while she played truant by the sea.
    At length the whole was finished, and return
Was gladly made to the old London home ;
Old home, but newly, tastefully adorned :
The "roomy," now no longer "gloomy" house,
Had brightness, cheerfulness, and elegance,
The dining-room where Bernard so enjoyed
His genial hour of rest, good fare, and chat,
Was made chief scene of Grace's care and taste.
The lumbering old sideboard, horsehair chairs
Ranged side by side along in formal row,
The window curtains, with their rigid folds
Of stiff, unyielding, thick moreen, in hue
A dingy brown half faded into drab,
The clumsy girandoles, the ugly grate,
The high old-fashioned chimney-piece, beyond
One's reach, its marble yellowed through by stain
Of smoke and age, the walls left pictureless
And blank, with ponderous flock-papering
That dull absorbed the light into its own
Grim red—were all replaced by paintings choice,
By sculpture exquisite, by colours of
A delicate harmonious tint ; while the old
Monotony of "willow-pattern" plates
And dishes now gave way to porcelain
Of dainty flowered device, set off by glass
And silver, sparkling in a million rays
Of shifting jewelled light—now amethyst,
Now topaz, sapphire, ruby, emerald.
As crowning loveliness to all the rest,
Grace decked the table daily with rich groups
Of ruddy fruits, placed on the frosted glass

And frosted silver of a branched epergne :
While freshest flowers she placed with artist eye
And fingers ; some in feathery sprays down drooped
From crystal brim of a tall vase, some massed
In flatter tazzas of Etruscan ware
And form.   Contrasted colour, shape, and scent
Delicious, all were there to yield delight.
Now Bernard's home was what a home should be,
A shrine of beauty, comfort, and repose.
   Thus time moved on apace, and two years more
Had nearly passed, when in the City was
Announced a ball for some large charity
That interested all the world, and roused
The mingled sympathies of love for deeds
Benevolent, and dancing.   Bernard was
Entreated by the Lady-Patroness
To give his aid and to promote the thing.
He sent a handsome contribution and
Took tickets home to Grace, with smiling look,
Demanding if she cared to go.   " Of course
You will.   The question hardly need be asked.
What girl would think of saying ' No ' to ball
Proposed ?   What sensible young lady would
Refuse a dance ?   " Not I," said Grace, " the
   thought
Of my first ball already flutters at
My heart ; in part because it is my first,
In part because I fear I may not know
Enough of dancing to acquit myself
With credit.   But I mean to try, and if
I fail, I can amuse my eyes, if not
My feet, by looking on at others."   " Ah,
That shows how little of a dancer you
Have ever been.   I've heard that to a good
Enthusiastic dancer few things are

More hard than playing the looker-on.   Be that,
However, as it may, I've asked the wife
Of an old business friend of mine to act
The chaperone, and take you, Grace."   " But you
Will go yourself, will you not ? " she asked
With quick look up ; " you do not mean to stay
In peace at home, and shabbily leave me
To go with this strange lady, do you ? "   " No,"
Said he ; " for once I'll play the youngster, and
Again enjoy a ball.   For this one will
To me be an enjoyment, since I mean
To see how Grace 'acquits' herself."   " Don't go
With sly intent to entertain yourself
At my expense, and laugh at my defects
Of inexperience ; for if you do
I'll make you dance one dance with me, and show
How your unpractised steps exceed my own
In awkwardness."   " I ask no better than
You should accept me for a partner, Grace ;
I fear the stoop my shoulders have acquired
By years of bending o'er my merchant work
At office-desk would make you hesitate,
Ere figuring with one would cut so bad
A figure in a ball-room.   You would blush
To have a partner like myself."   He spoke
In playful tone, but glanced with earnestness
At Grace's face, which at the moment wore
Just such a blush as he alluded to,
While answering with smile should match his
   tone :
" You want a compliment ; you know how good
The figure is, you thus—conceited that
You are !—draw notice to, affecting to
Dispraise.   But fear not I shall e'er invite
You ; lest I might become the envy of

L

All ladies in the room." He could not quite
Determine how much irony might lurk
In Grace's laughing speech ; but hid whate'er
Of trouble and disturbing doubt he felt
Beneath responsive rallying.
                              The night
Arrived, and Lady Bullion came, arrayed
In matron lappets, diamonds, and gown
Of velvet, to conduct the novice, Grace :
Who, robed in simple white, looked lovelier,
The merchant thought, than any maiden he
Had ever seen. He asked himself if this
Could be the " unformed awkward girl " he called
Her to himself when she had first arrived ;
This graceful, modest, perfect creature, fair
And beautiful in nature as in form.
And others found her fair no less than he :
Fat Lady Bullion vowed she was quite proud
To have the charge of one who'd prove to be
Without a doubt the beauty of the ball ;
And the event confirmed her ladyship's
Prediction. Partners pressed in numbers to
Be introduced and granted leave to ask
If she would hold herself engaged for next
One after fourth ensuing dance ; and thus
Did Bernard find he should have little chance
Of *the* dance she had said she meant to make
Him dance with her. But just as he began
To give up hope, Grace beckoned him beside
Her chair, and said with archness in her tone,
But with a rosy flush upon her cheek :
" You've seen how Grace ' acquits herself '; should
    you
Refuse to try how ' bad a figure ' you
Would make with her as partner, if she told

You she has kept one dance—the promised dance—
For you ? " For answer, Bernard took her hand,
His eyes expressing speechless joy, and led
Her to her place, with more of triumph in
His heart than had been there to gladden it
Since he had been a happy boy, elate,
With life before him, full of conscious power
To reach his highest aim of glorious
Achievement.   But when once the dance was done,
And Grace was claimed by younger partners, more
Accomplished dancers, a reaction came :
" Fool, self-deluder that I am !   Why do
I let my thoughts take that most fruitless bent ?
Why will they wander in that hopeless track
I have so often told myself is closed
Against me, past all chance of leading to
The paradise of happiness that might
Have been, were I a younger man ?   She likes
Me as her father's friend, no more.   Be mute,
Be patient, Bernard !   Be not you your own
Misleader, and destroyer of what joy
Is still within your reach.   Her innocent
Devotion and affection are now yours ;
Why risk their loss by rash betrayal of
Your deeper feeling for herself?   Be mute,
Be prudent ; rest contented with the share
You have in her most gentle, loving heart,
And lose it not by seeking love itself."
    But on the following day his self-communed
Resolves were put severely to the proof.
A certain Mayfair Baronet had seen
The City Belle and danced with her.   He asked
Her name, her parentage, and found she was
The ward of Bernard Thorpe, with whom Sir John
Had had some money·dealings recently.

He called at once upon the merchant at
His office ; and in easy way began
To speak his mind : " Look here, you see, I'll tell
You frankly what has brought me here to-day ;
At your great City Ball last night I saw—
Was introduced to your Miss Middleton—
I danced with her ; I hear she is your ward ? "
" She is my ward," was Bernard's answer, with
A cold incline of head. " Well, then, she is,
Without exception, the most beautiful—
The finest girl I've seen for many a day.
I was so struck with her, that—'pon my soul—
I came to you at once to-day to ask—
A beauty such as hers excuses what
May seem abrupt, unusual, my dear sir ;
But she herself is so unusual in
Her handsomeness that really, now, a man
Can't help himself, you know. Of course, you staid,
Calm, middle-agers hardly understand
This sort of thing : you money-worshippers
Can scarcely be expected to allow
For hare-brained fellows like myself, who can't,
By Jove, be prudent where a lovely girl's
Concerned ; but still, dear sir, you'll pardon me
For coming straight to ask you "—   " What, Sir
      John ? "
Was Bernard's curt inquiry. " Well, to ask
If you'll permit me—beauty, my dear sir,
Is irresistible, and so "—   " And so,
Sir John ? "   " And so, my dearest sir, you see,
I come at once to ask your leave to court
Miss Middleton—to offer her—to pay
Her my addresses."   " You're aware, Sir John,
Her father left her portionless ? "   " I've heard
Some story of a loan not paid—of a

Remittance never sent—I'm not quite sure
About the facts ; but think that I have heard
Her father was a careless scamp, who "— "Stay,"
The merchant cried, "her father was my friend,
My dearest, oldest friend, Sir John ; I will
Not hear him spoken ill of." "Well, at least
I've heard he was a thoughtless chap, who left
His daughter without fortune ; you, dear sir,
Just said as much, that she was portionless,
Worth nothing, did you not ? " "Worth nothing !
 —I ?
Grace Middleton worth nothing ? " "*Has* nothing,
Dear sir, is what I should have said, of course ;
I meant Miss Middleton is dowerless ;
You understand ? " "Oh, yes, I understand,"
Said Bernard quietly. "But you may give
Her something, though, yourself, you know, dear sir;
She's almost like a daughter to you ; or
Perhaps do something for her at your death."
"My death ? " "Of course it's to be hoped that may
Be long deferred, dear sir ; but when it comes,
You know, you might leave something handsome in
Your will." "My will ? " "Ay, in your will : of
 course
A man like you, a wealthy man, a man
So prudent as you are, has made his will.
It needn't make one's death more near, you know.
You must be getting on, though, now I come
To think of it ; yet not by any means
Advanced in years : to fellows like myself
Of twenty-three, a man like you seems old.
If fair the question, now, what is your age ?
It can't be fifty yet." "Just thirty-six."
"Indeed ! I should have given you more, I own.
But then, hard work, you know, and laying up

The lucre, makes us all look older, eh?
You'll think of my proposal, my dear sir,
And give it the advantage of your own
Good word, when you submit it to the fair
Miss Middleton?"   " I promise you I will lay
Before her your proposal for her due
Consideration," answered Bernard Thorpe;
" And now I'll wish you a good morning, if
You please, Sir John; my time is not my own;
I have appointment with the directors of
North Western at eleven o'clock.   I know
You will excuse me."   " Certainly, dear sir;
You wealthy City men are never at
Your own disposal.   We West-enders have
Advantage of you there; but as for more
Substantial cash advantage, why—ha, ha!
It must be owned you have decidedly
Advantage over us."   Sir John took leave;
And that same evening, when Bernard sat
With Grace beside the fire, he said: " You danced
Last night with young Sir John Bodapperton."
" I did?" said Grace; " I daresay that I did,
And knew but little of the honour I
Enjoyed, there were so many candidates
For my poor hand to dance, I hardly could
Distinguish them apart, still less by name.
I think, though, now, I do remember that
One name among the several that were
Pronounced by Lady Bullion, when they came
To bow and beg to be presented.   He
Is fair and lanky, is he not? with just
A morsel of light sandy whisker, that
He pulled and pulled, while he was dancing, with
The bright intention—as it seemed to me—
Of making it grow longer ere he'd done."

" You thought it ' honour ' to be asked to dance
By him : what will you think when I inform
You that he offers you the honour of
Becoming, if you please, the partner of
His life ? " " Of his ? " she answered, in a tone
So unmistakably contemptuous,
That Bernard laughed outright, and she in turn,
To witness his amusement. " Poor Sir John ;
I see that I shall have to break his heart
By telling him of your refusal, your
Point-blank refusal." " Well, please say that I
Decline the honour he proposes ; that
Will be the proper style, I fancy." " Ay,
Exactly," Bernard said. " Among the rest
Of those who danced with me last night, at least
A dozen were worth fifty of Sir John ;
And one there was, an old acquaintance, that
I was quite glad to see again—your clerk,
Young Mr. Frankland, who so frequently
At one time used to come with messages
To you. I've often meant to ask you why
He never comes of late ; I hope he still
Is with you as a clerk ? " " Yes," Bernard said,
" He still is in our house of business."
" Then how is it he never comes now to
Your dwelling-house ? I feel quite sure he has
Done nothing that should forfeit your esteem.
I know he prized it highly, and from what
I know of him, I'm confident he can
Have done no ill." " You speak with warmth,
   Grace, you
Avouch your confidence in one of whom
You've seen but little ; what can you have known
Of Henry Frankland that should warrant such
Full confidence in his desert ? " " I speak

With warmth because I warmly feel," she said.
" I feel quite certain Mr. Frankland has
Committed nothing base, unworthy ; no
Dishonourable action that should cause
You to forbid his coming here ; now tell
Me, has he ? "   " None," said Bernard, drily.   " I
Was sure of it ; I told you so ; I knew
He could have done no ill.   From what I've seen
Of him, I feel that he's incapable
Of meanness or disgraceful conduct ; and
In justice, nothing less should make you change
The former friendliness you showed him,
And damage his good name by letting him
No longer enter your own private house.
Consider, how his feelings will be hurt,
And how his prospects injured by so marked
An alteration.   Knowing well the high
And honouring regard he has for you,
The gratitude he feels for all you've done
For him and his, I can imagine his
Unhappiness, to find himself no more
Entrusted with your messages, nor sent,
As previously, to your own home.   Forgive
My warmly speaking—if too warm it be—
But I feel earnestly in this ; and I
Must always speak to you exactly as
I feel."   " Nay, God forbid you ever should
Do otherwise," said Bernard, warmly as
Herself ; " but how, Grace, comes it that you know
So much of Henry Frankland's character,
Of what I have done for him and his,
Of his regard, his gratitude, to me ? "
" I saw a great deal of him when he used
To come and wait while you wrote out replies
To papers that he brought," said Grace ; " you know

I told you how I asked him to explain
Whatever I could not make out from books
On calculation and accounts : well, when
All that was done, he sometimes talked of you,
And sometimes of himself; and all he said
Convinced me of his grateful nature, of
His honourable character ; so I
Was sure he could have done no act that ought
To forfeit him your trust." " He used his time
With good effect, and made the most of it,"
Said Bernard bitterly ; " it seems he talked
So eloquently of himself, that you
Imbibed impression of his worth enough
To render you his advocate and make
You plead his cause with warmth and fervour that
Might fill with envy any other man
Less favoured. What would poor Sir John have said
Could he have made a like impression ? " " He ! "
Said Grace, with scornful emphasis again.
" Sir John's not worthy to be named with such
A man as Henry Frankland ; though the one
May be a baronet, the other but
A merchant's clerk." " The merchant's clerk
Is to be envied, Grace, if he have gained
The favour that the baronet has sought
In vain." " The ' favour ' ? " echoed Grace, at length
Observing Bernard's strangely bitter tone
Of sadness. " Yes, your favour, favouring
Opinion, preference." " I have a high,
A very high opinion of the one,
While of Sir John, I fear, 'tis very low ;
But if by ' preference ' you mean the sort
Of liking asked by the lank Baronet,
For neither of them have I that," said Grace,
With laughing frankness. " All the better for

Myself it should be so," continued she ;
Since Henry Frankland told me once his hope
To marry Lucy Mildmay, his betrothed,
When better salary shall justify
The match." " To marry ! " Bernard cried, in tone
Now clear as clouded 'twas before ; " I've heard
No word of this : how comes it that you know
A secret so important, while to me
'Twas never breathed ? " " He thought me likely, I
Suppose, to sympathise with what he said ;
Of you he has too great an awe ; and feared,
Perhaps, you might not quite approve ; or, still
More likely, dreaded mentioning his wish,
Lest it might seem like begging you to raise
A salary that you yourself had been
The means of his obtaining." " ' Awe ' of me ?
He thinks most probably that I'm too old
To have much sympathy with lovers, and
Their hopes of marriage." " You ! too old ? " said
    Grace,
With genuine surprise. " Too old to think
Of love, to care for love ; and if he should,
What wonder ? An old bachelor like me
Is sure to be regarded as stone deaf
To lovers' hopes, and dead to love itself."
A sudden pang of vital agony,
That gave sharp negative to Bernard's words,
Shot through him as he spoke, and made him start
From forth his chair to pace the room in wild
Disorder irrepressible. Then by
An effort, mastering himself, he came
To Grace's side, and strove to steady down
His voice to more of calmness as he said :
" I can no longer bear this torture of
Perpetual struggle to suppress the truth.

Grace, what would *you* think were you told by me
A love-story? Would *you* think me too old
To care for love? Would *you* believe me deaf
And dead to love?" "Too old?" again said Grace;
But now with agitation in her tone,
Besides surprise; "confide to me your love
You'll have my sympathy, believe me; your
Commencement tells me that your story is
Of hopeless love; how strange it should be so!
How stranger still I never guessed you loved;
Yet saw you all that is most loving and
Most loveable. But tell me who she is:
I know so little of your outer life, you know;
I only know you in your home." Grace spoke
With firmness, spite of agitation and
A secret pain she ne'er had felt before;
But very low and gentle was her voice.
" It is my inner life I tell you of,"
Said Bernard. " True," Grace answered; " what I
    meant
Was life outside this house—your friendships, your
Attachments, which are all beyond the sphere
Wherein I've seen you, known you, learned to make
You centre of my interest and thought."
A little tremble came in Grace's voice
As she said this, but she went on: " You need
Not fear indifference because I do
Not know the lady; I shall feel for you."
" You have not heard my story, Grace," he said.
" No; tell it me." " You do not know how mad,
How rash I've been; how I have let my thoughts
Entwine themselves around perfection in
A gentle woman's shape: a creature so
Endowed with every quality of good,
Of tender, and of true; of sensible,

Of gifted, and of prudent; of modest,
Of diffident, devoted, kind; withal
So beautiful, and—more than all—so young,
That my own difference of years makes such
Enamoured sense of her fair excellence
No less than madness, and consignment of
Myself to hopeless, endless misery—
Unless, indeed, this young, this beautiful
Perfection could perceive the youth of heart,
The freshness of affection that survive
To render years of small account, and serve
As sacred light to cast into eclipse
Defects that else would be but only too
Apparent.   Grace, 'tis you, 'tis you alone
That can decide this doubt which long has made
My secret torment of suspense, and now
Impels me to speak out, that I may learn
At once the worst—or best." As Bernard spoke,
There spread a gradual beam of happy, glad
Delight o'er Grace's face, a radiance of
Content, that made her look as beautiful
As even his adoring words proclaimed.
He was not slow to read the speaking look;
And murmured : "Grace, you do not bid me fear
The 'worst'?" "I bid you know the 'best'—if 'best'
You call the certainty that you have long
Been loved by Grace; unconsciously, but yet
Most deeply, truly : without knowing it
Herself, she must have loved you from the first,
I think," she said, with sweet ingenuous eyes
Soft raised to his.   "When first she came to you,
A helpless, timid girl, afraid to find
Herself a burden and a worthless charge,
A graceless, profitless young thing, you let
Her try her best to expiate the wrong

Her father did you ; suffered her to help
You and endeavour what she could to make
Your home a home to you ; well might she learn
To love you with a love that was at once
Revering, grateful, worshipping, and fond ;
Spontaneously it sprang, and unawares
It grew to be the love you wish ; ay, love
Itself." He folded her within his arms,
And drew her to his heart of hearts. " My Grace,
My own, my wife! From first to last you've been
A wife to me, a priceless home delight
And treasure ; wifely in your childish care
And ministry, most wifely in your youth
Of sympathy and aid in my pursuits ;
Now wifeliest in your acknowledged love.
A thousandfold you have redeemed the pledge
My old friend gave, and made me nobly rich :
My Grace has proved the best REMITTANCE that
Her father could have sent to Bernard Thorpe."

AN IDYL OF LONDON STREETS.

With fog and mud and drizzling rain the town
Was murk: the very gaslights blurr'd with damp,
Thick, heavy air: the sky hung like a pall
Above the houses dimly seen in rows
Of shadowy height. A carriage stood before
The portal of a stately mansion there,
As ready for its mistresses: to take
Them forth to some bright scene of dance
Or festive music, ball, or opera;
Where lights and luxury were things of course,
As much a portion of the scene as were_
The mud and darkness of the streets that night.
  Upon the pavement, like a half-seen ghost,
There loiter'd near the figure of a girl,
A woman; something feminine of form,
But most unfeminine withal; a creature
With lost abandon'd look, a dogged look
Of bold defiance, yet a scared and dread
Expression, as of a hunted-down wild beast.
She stood with savage glance, half furtive, half
Disdainful, reckless, impudent; a glance
Not good in any human face, still less
A woman's; there she stood—and shrank and
  shiver'd
Thin wrapp'd in her old threadbare shawl and
  gown,
With gaunt wan cheeks, and restless sunken eyes.
All youth and freshness seemed gone out of her,
Although but twenty autumns she had seen.
And yet a touch of childlike fancy lurk'd

In what she did—to stand there gazing at
The grand luxurious carriage, and to wait
Until its mistresses came forth, that she
Might see their dresses—that was all—their dresses !
To stand there, shivering in the wet and cold,
That she might catch a glimpse of finery
And rich attire ! so potent is the taste
For elegance and grace in girlish mind,
It rather sees a handsome dress adorn
Another, than see no good dress at all.
And yet this girl half mocked herself for so
Remaining there : " Why should I stay ?   What
     for ?
I know what I shall see ; some haughty minx
Step out, and trip across the pavement damp
In satin shoes ; like a sleek cat, that can't
Abide to wet its squeamish velvet paw.
Proud cat ! what right has she to be so fair
And fortunate, and I so foul and poor ?
Forsooth, because she's born a lady, I
A nobody ; one doomed to be a drab,
An outcast, refuse of the pavement edge,
The gutter ; filth that's only fit for drains
And sewers, made to drift away the orts
From cities.   Ay, what better am I than
The dirt and offal swept along yon kennel ?
While she "— By this, the mansion door was flung
Wide open, and a burst of light appear'd
Within the spacious hall, that showed where down
The stairs came stepping with a stately pace
A lady elderly and portly ; cloaked
In furs and ample folds of costly silk.
Two powder'd footmen waited her descent ;
Two more attended to the carriage-door,
And gave their aid, while she placed foot upon

The step and made the light-hung carriage swerve
And swing with her important weight, as in
She stepp'd.   Then down the stairs came gliding
   soft
A graceful figure; lithe and easy, quick
In movement, yet composed, and full of that
Possessed demeanour that belongs to those
Brought up from childhood never to commit
A single act of awkwardness or aught
Ungain.   The figure had a face that match'd
In beauty and attraction : bright, and young,
And very frank; beaming with kindliness ;
Sweet violet eyes, and mouth like rosebud fresh.
A little hood of blue and swan's-down clos'd
Around the winning face, and seemed to pet
And fold it in with loving warmth, as if
'Twere glad to nestle near and minister
To so much loveliness : and on she came,
This young bright lady beauty, and stepp'd out
Into the night, where stood the outcast girl.
From moment that she first caught sight of that
Sweet lady face, the girl had fix'd a rapt
And fascinated gaze upon its beauty :
She seemed unable to withdraw her eyes,
And made involuntary movement forward
To look the more intently at the face
That so enthrall'd her.   "Now, young woman," said
The footman, " where are you a-coming to ?
Stand back, and don't block up the way; stand
   back ! "
" Take care, Nathaniel ; " said the lady voice
In gentle tone ; " take care, or you will throw
The poor girl down ; don't push her off so roughly.
How pale and scared she looks ; she totters—is
She ill ? "   " No, no, my lady ; no, not she :

She's drunk, I think." "Poor thing! Poor girl!"
and with
A look compassionate, the lady young
Moved slowly on and stepped into her coach.
 It rolled away; and with it passed the fair
Bright vision that had bless'd the eyes of her
Who gazed, and left her haunted. Like as one
That, after many dreary weeks of fast
From seeing the green fields, has spent a day
Amid their glories, still beholds a host
Of leaves and boughs beneath his lids whene'er
He shuts his eyes, so this girl's sight was fraught
With images of the fresh beauty she
Had seen; it seemed to fill her senses to
Th' exclusion of aught else; to take the place
Of darkness, wet and mud; to let her see
No other than its radiant self, and flood
Her eyes, her thoughts, with brightness, purity
And beatific grace. She drew a deep
Long sigh, and turned to go, as if she walked
In sleep, possess'd by some entrancing dream.
"She look'd at me—she pitied me—she would
Not let the fellow drive me off! Good heart!
It looks from out her face! That bright young
 face!"
Thus coursed her still-recurring thought, as back
She took her way through crowded thoroughfares
And jostling passers-by.
                    Night after night
The girl returned to linger in the square,
Where she had seen the face that spell-bound her.
It drew her there; it kept before her eyes
All day, and fill'd her with the need to go
At night and see its veritable self
Again and yet again. It came to be

M

The object of her idolising fancy,
The one bright starlike point in all her grim
And dingy life's horizon : something that
Supplied the famine of her heart for goodness,
For purity, for kindliness, and beauty—
All things that are instinctively a want
To even natures most depraved by vice
And vicious teaching ; yearn'd for, p'rhaps, un'wares :
But still they're yearn'd for, bent to, ay, and held
In secret worship. So by her. She learn'd
The name of her young lady cynosure,
The rank, the whereabout, the daily wont ;
She follow'd all her doings, knew her hours
For driving out, for riding in the park,
For visiting, for being at home ; and when
She went to Court—and what the dress she wore ;
Spell'd out the newspaper that gave th' account
Of Lady Blanche de Lyle's costume at last
Court ball or drawing-room : and when the time
Arrived for all the London world to flock
Away from town, she read of how the Earl
And Countess Chute, with Lady Blanche de Lyle,
Their daughter, had departed for their seat
In Oxfordshire ; and then a blank seemed
Fall'n on the city which no longer held
The bright young lady star of her adoring ;
But still she search'd the columns of each old
Stray paper that e'er chanced into her hands
For news of where and what her charmer was
And did ; would hang enchanted o'er the lines
That told of how the Lady Blanche rode to
The Meet ; of how her Ladyship was seen
To follow with great spirit through the run ;
And how her party came up with the hounds,
And she was chosen County Beauty to

Receive the fox's brush ; or how, at some
Great archery affair, the prize was won
By Lady Blanche de Lyle ; or how the Earl
And Countess Chute and family were soon
Expected back to town : then leaped the heart
Of her who read ; and felt she then as if
A light were shed around, and all things seemed
The brighter.
             Spring was come : and e'en into
The town came some reflection of the hues
That flushed the vernal meads and skies away
From smoke and grime ; soft slants of sunshine touched
The tops of houses, fell upon the sides
And angles of the tall white mansions, or
Upon the long brick ranges of the streets,
And glorified them with effects of light ;
Above the roofs, a line of tender blue
Took place of that grey streak that mostly marks
The ridge where housetops meet the firmament
In London ; wafted scents of balmy air
Come playing through the thoroughfares at dawn,
And carry sense of open downs afar
Where grass and thyme are swept by breezy gusts
Of morning wind, that crisply dry the drops
Left by some passing shower of the night ;
The baskets of the primrose-sellers bring
Sweet thoughts of turfy banks rich-cover'd with
The dainty yellow blossoms pale ; the cry
Of " Violets, sweet violets ! Come buy
My violets ! " recalls the shady lane
Where 'neath the hedge lurk coyly the blue gems
Of modest loveliness, like true and gentle eyes ·
That lie in wait to bless the look which seeks
To win them earnestly : the parks have lost

Their brownest driest tint, and something like
Green sward carpets their centre space ; their drives
Are neat and smooth, and sprinkled duly by
The dust-bedewing water-cart, that sends
Its gush of wide-shed silvery jets adown
In plenteous stream, and mimics well the fall
Of mighty cataracts, cascades, that pour
Their sheeted weight o'er rock, and fell, and steep.
The grand old elms of Hyde put forth their leaves;
St. James's and the Green Park wear a look
Of urban-rural verdure ; while the trees
Of gardens Kensington rise massively
Against the western sky, their emerald tufts
Of tender shoots and budding leaflet-sheaths
Soft woven into one broad velvet surface
Bespreading all those swelling curves that look
At distance like the domes of sylvan fanes,
Green cupolas.   Tall beeches with their large
Expansive branches, fanlike stretching out ;
The grace of drooping birches, silver-stemm'd,
The stately growth of regal oak ; the boughs
Of Spanish chestnut, horrent with their spiked
And taper leaves, the vividest of foliage ;
The straight horse-chestnut, almost clumsy-shaped,
So round and heavy is its outline, with
Those formal rows of blossoms white and red
Uprising one by one, a pyramid
Of girandoles ; and yet formality
That has its handsomeness among the more
Irregular design of neighbour growths.
The spring had brought out early token of
The summer promise by and by ; and town
Was smiling with the sunny sheen of May,
When May is May indeed in dear old England.
    The girl had sauntered to the rails that skirt

The level line of Rotten Row ; to watch
For that gay cavalcade of riders, men
And women, mounted on the finest beasts,
Equipped in trimmest trim ; among them there
She looked for one, the fairest in her eyes ;
The slenderest of waist, the winsomest
Of form ; the one whose habit fell in folds
Of sweep most graceful, with the hat that had
The feather most bewitching in its droop
Against the rich dark hair and rosy cheek
And throat of purest white.   And, hark ! yes, hark !
Now ! clatter-tramp, clatter-tramp, clatter-tramp !
On, on they come, pelting along, a throng
Of gallopers, a crowd on horseback, at
Full speed ! a sound of rippling laughter light,
A merry buzz, ran pattering among
The thump and clatter of the horses' hoofs,
As on they raced.   When suddenly a stop,
A reining-up, a check confused of all
The riders, as a wretched urchin boy
Quick darted, close beneath the very feet
Of the advancing throng, to cross the road.
An oath of angry sympathy escaped
The lips of sundry gentlemen ; a cry
Of horror from the lady horsewomen :
      Bent down with pitying looks and eager voice
The young sweet face, to ask how fared the lad ;
If he were hurt—if badly—if 'twere much.
They took him up and lifted him away ;
And bore him to St. George's Hospital
Close by ; the girl still watching how her own
Bright lady star (as now she always called her)
Went sorrowing after him to hear
What said the surgeons to the case, and if
They thought the boy would die, or whether they

Deemed hopefully ; and rode away with sad
Soft mournful eyes, when she was told there was
But little chance for him.   " Poor ragged Bill ! "
The girl low mutter'd to herself—(she knew
The boy—a crossing-sweeper orphan lad—
A reckless daring chap, in fifty scrapes
A day)—" Poor ragged Bill !   I wish it had
Been me had been run over, 'stead of you !
I'd give my life to have her look like that
For *me !* her eyes were wet, ay, really wet ;
She has a feeling heart, a true kind heart,
My own bright lady star ! "   And after that,
She noted not a day pass'd by without
The Lady Blanche's going to inquire
How fared the boy : and when she heard he would
Recover, went to see him, took him help,
And sat beside his bed with kindly words ;
And when he left the hospital, she put
Him to a school, where he might learn to gain
His bread, and be a steady honest lad.
And now the girl's fond worship knew no bounds ;
It interblent itself with all she thought
And did : she breathed it with her very breath ;
It was her vital air of moral good,
The one sole element of purity
She lived in.   From it came to her a sense
Of better things ; of beauty in good deeds,
Of trust, of truth, of virtue, in their own
Divinest essence ; abnegation and
Disinterestedness ; benevolence,
And pleasure in the gentle exercise
Of charity and kindliness ; the joy
And solace of indulging generous thoughts
Of others ; and the comfort in mere trying
To rise above the slough of selfishness ;

Th' ineffable delight of impulse to
Be good for goodness' sake : all these became
Unconsciously apparent to the soul
Of her who consciously beheld the bright
Young beauty of her lady star, and saw
Its fair effulgence—visible reflection
Of spiritual life within.   The girl,
With softened nature, fell into the way
Of thinking over things that ne'er before
Had struck her, while she leaned against
The back of some park-bench, and watch'd the sun
Sink slowly down behind the distant trees
Of bosky Kensington.   " How glad I am
I've seen her, known her ! "   Thus her musings ran :
" I'm better for my love of her ; it makes
Me feel the better, do the better—try,
At least.   I can't be pure, like her, of course ;
I can't be good, like her ; but I can give
Up things I like to do, as she does ; I
Can do things that I do not like to do,
As she does.   How she'd give up, day by day,
Her rides and drives to go and see poor Bill !
And how she'd sit and listen to his talk,
Poor chap, and make him tell her how he felt
And what he did, and how he lived, and where !
She couldn't much ha' liked all that o' course ;
But she did it, ay, day after day.
She did it, 'cause she know'd it did him good ;
She did it, 'cause she know'd 'twas right and kind.
And how she used to look when out she come
From sitting with him ! how her bright young face
Was just as if the sun was on it, like !
Her eyes all sparkle, and her cheeks flush'd up
As if she'd heard some joyful news, or had
Some present given her—my beauty bright !

How God must love her! how He must be pleased
With her!—God help me! I've heard tell of God :
I wonder what he thinks of such as me.
I didn't make myself the thing I am ;
Perhaps he knows all that, and won't be hard
With me because of it.   Perhaps he sent
Me her to make me better ; who can tell ?
Perhaps he sent me her to love and think
About, that I might be more happy, and
Have something I can call my own that's good.
Who knows ?   At any rate, I've got her, and
I'm glad and thankful that she's mine, mine, mine :
I've made her mine myself, by loving her
And watching her, and calling her my own,
And feeling somehow that God gave me her."
   And time went on : and still the outcast girl
Kept loving watch and worship, secretly,
At lowly distance ; most content, nay, glad
To know and be unknown, and make of that
Pure lady bright her own life's guiding star.
   One day—a burning day, when the hot sun
Came flaming out, and shone with tropic force—
A day when London pavements struck a glare
Like Afric sands against the eyes, and walls
Reflected oven heat, scorching the hands
Unwary laid upon them, casting o'er
The shoulders an oppressive copper cloak,
As walkers dared to skirt along their length—
A day when shade became necessity,
And people cross'd the way to gain a strip
Of darkly cool relief—a day when dogs
Were eyed askance and shrunk from with distrust—
A day when beggars crawled away from spots
Where usually they bask'd, and sought instead
Some friendly refuge from the glow and warmth
Of afternoon—a day when idlers most

Complain of languor, weariness, and bore
Of having nothing upon earth to do ;
While workers half incline to envy them
Their power to sit at ease and lounge away
The lazy hours, attempting to get rest—
A day when eating is a task, and naught
But ices seem a possible approach
To food—a day when broil and brazen dazzle
Seem wholly to pervade the air, and make
A furnace of the town—on such a day
As this the girl beheld, with beating heart,
A carriage she well knew draw up before
The entrance to a fashionable shop,
Its glittering front o'ershaded by a blind
Of ponderous slope ; out stepp'd a youthful form
Of graceful buoyancy, and took its way across
The flagstones at the very moment that
The iron uprights of the blind gave way,
Made sudden slip from some unwonted cause,
And let the weight descend with crushing force.
The girl, who saw the peril at a glance,
Dashed forward, thrust the lady back, herself
Receiving the whole brunt of the descent ;
And dropp'd to earth, felled by the deadly blow.
     In that precedent particle of time
Who knows what compensating flash of thought
Was then vouchsafed? The brain perchance conceiv'd
The consolating image: " Death endured
For *her !* For *her*, my own bright lady star !
Thank God for letting my life purchase hers ! "
And then there stood beside the fallen girl
The lady pure, with hallowing tears of ruth
Shed o'er the bruis'd and bleeding form of one
Who died to save, of one whose instinct taught
'Twas blessedness to nobly sacrifice
The erring self for innocent belov'd.

LINES

FOUNDED ON AN INCIDENT AT THE BATTLE OF
MELAZZO, RECOUNTED BY AN ITALIAN VOLUN-
TEER IN THE SICILIAN BAND OF PATRIOTS
UNDER GARIBALDI.

Our night bivouac on that lone ground,
  The ruined castle on the hill,
Our sleeping soldiers scattered round,
  The summer air so calm, so still,
The watchfires casting fitful light—
  Now deepest shadows here and there,
Now patches lurid red or bright—
  All soft subsiding into where
The distant eastern sky began
  To pale and streak with coming dawn;
That dawn the herald to each man
  Of struggle 'gainst the yoke had gnawn
Into his soul: I see it now—
  The whole of that impressive scene—
My fellow-soldiers lying low,
  Steeped in their death-like sleep serene—
(Alas, how soon it might be death
  Itself, I thought!)—the night—the morn—
The starting up with earnest breath—
  The snatching up those arms we'd borne
Already in the sacred cause—
  The eagerness of forming ranks,
Without a moment's stint or pause—
  To join the glorious brave phalanx

Of him who led us on to gain
　Our heart's desire, our country's trust,
Full freedom from the galling chain
　So long had crushed us in the dust.

We found him, Garibaldi, there,
　Alert and ready for the strife ;
His mouth firm-set, composed his air ;
　Yet in his eye a fire and life
That spoke his purpose glowing, strong,
　Unquenchable, as from the first
It ever hath been : there among
　Us all he stood, his look athirst
For action ; quiet all the rest,
　And calm, and simple ; one brave hand
On sword, and one on hip ; his breast
　With no more corslet than the band
That carelessly about him girt
The red, the well-known martial shirt.

　He sent our small battalion forth
To make a passage good across
　A bridge of most important worth :
With some advantage, and some loss,
　We faced a battery defended
By certain Naples *cacciatori :*
　On this, we knew full well, depended
The great, the enviable glory—
　Achievement of the bridge.　A roar
Of guns now summoned us away
　And farther on : the thunderous pour
Of cannon, and the lightning play
　Of bayonets, marked well the spot :
There stood our General, face to foe,

Unmoved amid the hail of shot,
As if he fated were, or no
Perception had of fatal risk ;
Right cheerfully he looked, and brisk.

At sight of him, so gallant-brave,
So gay, in peril of his life,
My fellows burst into a rave
Of " *Viva Garibaldis !* " rife ;
And " *Viva Italias !* " rent the sky :
I led the charge, and on we rushed :
When, seeing us, he raised on high
Both arms ; and, running towards me, crushed
Them down with heavy blow of fist
Upon my chest, outshouting clear :—
" Go back, you madmen ! Back ! Desist !
You'll all be cut to pieces here ! "*
But nothing could have thrust me back :
I saw, to gain that post was all
In all ; a second rush, attack,
And charge, in front of cannon-ball
Not forty paces off ; around
I glanced : but four or five were near—
My faithful " *valorosi*," bound
By brotherhood of buying dear
Our fondly hoped success at last :
The path was strewn with dying, dead ;
Some breathless struck, and prostrate cast,
With gaping wounds that oozed and bled ;
Some staring wide with stiffening eye ;
Some placid-smiling as a child ;
Some with a last despairing cry,
A tortured prayer, or farewell wild.

---

* Garibaldi's actual words are even more roughly strenuous in
his own vernacular : "*In dietro, canaglia, che andate a far vi
massacrare !*"

Beside me kept my valiant friend,
  The brave Lombardi, who had dashed
Among the foremost ; a cruel rend
  Of musket-shot his right hand smashed :
And I was struck upon the breast
  So stunningly I almost thought
I must be killed ; but then a test
  I still survived was swiftly brought
In shape of pain—another ball
  Came piercing through my leg, and told
Me feelingly I lived : my fall
  Was only groundward : whence I rolled
And crawled to shelter of a house :
  Behind its corner there I found
A group of comrades refuged close,
  With Garibaldi safe and sound ;
Though near and round them flying still
The balls came whistling loud and shrill.

  Brave Migliavacca sudden dropped,
A ball had struck him on the head ;
  Our eager talk it scarce had stopped,
Ere we beheld him lifeless, dead !
  And while with pitying shuddering gaze
We looked upon him, Cosenz next
  Received a shot that open lays
His throat ; but he with laugh unvext
  Declares " 'Tis nothing, not a wound
To signify." Ay, one and all,
  We'd reason to exult and sound
A victory ; since that day's fall
  Beheld us masters of the field—
Th' important bridge was ta'en and passed,
  Melazzo's self was forced to yield—
A conquest surely not our last.

TIME'S HEALING.

Time worketh wonders in his onward course :
To those who bear their burdens with meek heart
He lendeth courage, energy, and force.
    Then, "bring forth fruit with patience," O my
    soul !

Time creepeth with a feeble ling'ring pace,
He bendeth down his aged back and stoops ;
Yet aids the suff'ring in their toilsome race.
    Then, "bring forth fruit with patience," O my
    soul !

Beneath the shelter of his soft dusk wing
He leadeth on in welcome shade to peace,
And gently smoothens every rugged thing.
    Then, "bring forth fruit with patience," O my
    soul !

His scythe, with noiseless surely sweeping swath,
Mows down abuses, prejudices, wrongs ;
Induces amity, assuages wrath.
    Then, "bring forth fruit with patience," O my
    soul !

His kind old hand, for all its trembling eld,
Hath oft the skill to disentangle knots
That we have hopelessly intricate held.
    Then, "bring forth fruit with patience," O my
    soul !

The silent dropping of his hour-glass sand
Is like the unheard stealing on of "joy"
That "cometh in the morning" from God's hand.
    Then, "bring forth fruit with patience," O my
    soul !

MEANWHILE.

A REVERIE OF "SWEET SIXTEEN."

Repeating sophisms worn and tame
  In self-complacent even tone,
They tell me 'twill be all the same
  When fifty years are past and gone:
         But what, meanwhile?

They bid me think, when I am old
  How trivial, slight all this will seem;
How little I shall care, I'm told,
  For what so vital now I deem:
         But, ah, meanwhile!

If half a hundred winters hence
  I find my heart grown still and cold,
If time have blunted keenest sense,
  And buried feeling 'neath the mould,
         Yet, ah, meanwhile,

The fifty springs and summers warm,
  The autumns with their fading hue,
The gradually coming calm,
  Will have to be endured, gone through,
         That sad meanwhile.

The crushing down of hopes and fears,
  The quenching out of youthful glow,
The keeping in of countless tears,
  The teaching oneself not to show
         The pain meanwhile;

The seeming to have conquer'd grief,
  The trying to appear at ease,
The resolute withstood relief
  Of weeping, sobbing, when we please,
      Those hours meanwhile.

Those "hours"? Those days! those dismal nights!
  Those long, long nights that drear'ly glide;
When even by ourselves our rights
  To cry aloud are stout denied,
      That dark meanwhile!

Whereas, instead of preaching now
  Renouncement and reflection dull,
If they would give me leave, I trow,
  I well could prove to them in full
      How my meanwhile

Should pass in gloriously bright
  Anticipations, bringing fruit
And harvest ripe; my heart, still light,
  Would plant and set with firmest root,
      The glad meanwhile,

A range of blossom-yielding flowers
  Of fertile growth and produce good;
They'd bring me happy shining hours,
  They'd bring me wholesome joyous food,
      The sweet meanwhile;

And when the fifty years were past,
  I should be mistress of a store
Of garner'd golden grains at last
  Would make me rich for evermore.
      Ah, my meanwhile

Is surely better worth than theirs !
　Why should remonstrance interfere ?
Why seek to load me with their cares ?
　Why mayn't I be allow'd to rear
　　　　　My own meanwhile ?

Sixteen, sometimes, when all is said,
　May best discern the true and wise ;
Its-younger sight may come in aid,
　When sixty fails from dimmer eyes :
　　　　　And so, meanwhile,

I'll cherish hope and trust and faith ;
　I'll try to win them to my creed,
Persuading sixty, till it saith
　My sixteen years are right indeed
　　　　　About meanwhile.

DO !

There is a little English word,
Soft as the twitter of a bird ;
And though its letters are but twain,
Its power mighty is, and main :
    Do is the word ; do—do.

If properly it be express'd,
As though your voice the ear caress'd,
'Tis simply irresistible,
A magic spell ineffable :
    Just utter'd so : " Do—do ! "

Just think of it, when murmur'd low,
'Tween lovers walking, ling'ring slow ;
A tender, fond, inducing tone,
Meant for one listener alone :
    " Do, my dearest ; do—do !"

A note invites you to a visit :
Perhaps you'd rather like to miss it—
But after all the usual form
A sentence comes, so brief, so warm :
    " Do come, dear friend ; do—do !"

Suppose you're asked to play or sing—
You can't endure to do the thing—
You've got upon your thumb a tumour,
You're hoarse, you're ill, you're out of humour ;
    But when they say : " Do—do !

" You'll give us so much pleasure, dear ;
Some choice Gounod we long to hear,
You can't refuse us just one air ;
Come, take your seat, love—here's the chair ;
    Now, there's a darling ; do ! "

Imagine being call'd away
When you would give the world to stay
At writing, in some quiet nook
Or reading, p'rhaps, a pleasant book ;
    Yet if the call be : " Do

" Come here ! just look at this ! " Or, may be,
" Just listen to this news ; Maude's baby
Has caught the whooping-cough ; pray send
The maid to say our help we'll lend ;
    Be quick, my dear ; do—do ! "

You can't refuse if thus besought ;
For my part, I have often thought
There's not a thing can be refus'd
If only this small word be us'd,
    This witching word, do—do !

When next you wish to gain a point
Take my advice and try the joint
'Effect of voice, and look, and word ;
Just breathe it out, with tone half heard :
    " Do, my beloved ; do—do."

Should you desire to win consent,
Essay this sure experiment ;
Accept this precept that I preach,
Adopt the lesson that I teach—
    Do, my good friends ; do—do !

If you, young men, would court a wife
And gain a partner for your life,
Now, take my word, you can't do better
Than follow this out to the letter :
                Think of it, youths ; do—do !

Her hands you clasp in both of yours ;
Her eye your gaze implores, adjures ;
In accents that both please and press,
Your lips say this, with fervent stress :
                " Do, my own sweet ; do—do ! "

If this don't win her straight to wed,
I'll forfeit, willingly, my head ;
I've faith in my instruction ; you
Should have as firm conviction too.
                So try my word ; do—do !

This pretty little English word,
I know no second, nor no third,
That can compare with it in force,
Considering its size, of course.
                Love it with me ; do—do !

When spoken, most persuasive 'tis,
Scarce less so than a coaxing kiss ;
When written, it has winning sway
If used in a peculiar way ;
                Quite simply put ; do—do !

Its very sound is like the coo
Of ringdoves who in woods do woo ;
It fits the mouth of—I know who
(A certain sparkling Cousin Prue,
To match her there are very few !

With lips of budding roses' hue
And balmy as the morning dew.
If she but call me " Cousin Hugh "
And say : " You must, dear Hugh, do, do ! "
With that sweet glance of hers, so true,
A glance of goodness shining through
Her merry eyes of heaven's blue,
I yield at once—and so would you.
Most charming !—if you only knew—
But I must mind, or I shall rue ;
I'm parenthetic more than due),
When she entreatingly doth sue :

     " Do, my dear one ; do—do ! "

SISTERLY CONFIDENCE.

Yes, I met him again,
  But I wasn't to blame:
I was ask'd to the dance;
  And I went—and he came.
      Stay—I think that I said,
      I'd be sure not to tell.

And he brought me some flowers
  Of the loveliest hues,
And would dance with me, Nell,
  And I could not refuse.
      Stay, I fancy I said,
      I'd be sure not to tell.

And he spoke to me low,
  When no others were near,
And I felt, darling Nell,
  He was more and more dear.
      But, stay—what have I said?
      I had meant not to tell.

And he look'd at me long,
  Held my hand close in his!
And then, somehow, oh, Nell!
  He press'd on it a kiss.
      Stay—I'm certain I meant
      To be sure not to tell.

And he pour'd forth some words
  That express'd how his life
Would be worthless to him
  Without me as his wife.
        'Twas so sweet, what he said!
        Yet said *how*, I can't tell.

I intended, you see,
  Not a word, dear, to tell;
But I could not refrain
  From confiding in Nell.
        After what I have said,
        She'll be sure not to tell.

You will promise me, dear,
  Say you will, sister Nell,
To keep secret all this—
  Not repeat—never tell.
        Come, now—all I have said
        I am sure you won't tell.

INFANT SUPREMACY.

Baby, with thy starry eyes
Full of innocent surprise
At the wonders that thou see'st
Round thee in perpetual feast.

Tugging at thy sister's curls,
Diving in her mouth for pearls,
Clutching at her eyes of blue,
Seizing everything that's new.

Staring at the candle white,
Tipp'd with flame of dazzling light;
Screaming out in sudden glee,
Crowing in thine ecstasy.

Stretching chest, and legs, and arms,
Doubling up thy tiny palms,
Fighting, foining lustily,
Sprawling on the nurse's knee.

Half awake and half asleep,
Burying thy nose full deep
In thy mother's downy breast,
Blinking, drinking, quite at rest.

Smiling when thou look'st in space,
Dost thou see an angel's face ?
So 'tis said : we'll think it true,
For the sake of us and you.

Toss'd on high by dear papa,
Watch'd by happy-proud mamma,
Flying up with all thy might,
Kicking out for sheer delight.

Doting aunts around thee throng,
Thinking something must be wrong,
If thou hast not all thou cravest
While thou, red-faced, roar'st and ravest.

Uncles meekly stand about,
Waiting till it's well found out
What the darling Baby wants
That so puzzles all its aunts.

Grandmamma is Baby's slave,
Infinitely pleased to have
Spectacles it fain would wear,
Anything it likes to share.

Grandpapa is Baby's fag,
Glad to pick up ball or flag
Dropp'd by Baby's heedless hand,
Ready at its beck to stand.

Diligently are construed
Each of thy small accents crude;
Sagest meanings oft are heard
In thy murmurs, pretty bird.

Chirping in thy cosy cot,
Crooning to thyself what not,
Playing with thine own ten toes—
Wisest wisdom, we suppose.

Though thou utter'st ne'er a word,
Confidently 'tis averr'd
This thou say'st and that thou say'st
Aptly, patly, fitly, best.

Only need'st thou look a wish
Noted is it with a " Hish !
Baby wishes for the moon.
Yes, sweet, it shall have it soon :
Take, meantime, this silver spoon."

Mighty art thou, little mite !
Reignest thou by Baby-right :
All thou wilt thou hast, because
All thy whims are held as laws.

Cooing like a woodland dove,
Fed on kisses, milk, and love ;
First in every thought and heart,
Ruler of the house thou art !

Universal is thy sway,
From Land's End to far Cathay ;
Sovereign, the world around,
Every home where Baby's found.

Shakespeare's words—with difference—
Suit me for a reference ;
Measure of the lines the same,
Varying the theme and name.

" Come, thou monarch dear, divine,
Plumpy Baby with bright eyne !
In thy fat our lips be drown'd ;
With thy grace our joys be crown'd !
    Hug us, till the room go round ;
    Hug us, till the room go round ! "

TWO LIFE-PICTURES.

I once was seated in the upper tier
Of boxes at the theatre: by me sat
My husband; both of us were deep absorbed
In watching Edmund Kean Othello play.
Between the acts, a thing of painted cheeks,
And powdered throat, and hardened eye and smile
Put on, flounced rustling in and placed herself
Beside us; lightly looked around the house;
Then fell into a dull abstracted mood
And gazed out straight before her into space,
As if she nothing saw of playhouse, stage,
Or audience, but as if her sight beheld
Some inward mournful thought of haunting force
That drew her spell-bound to confront it still.
A listless recklessness was in her air;
But in her hand she held with rigid grasp
A bunch of freshest flowers, sweet and pure,
That made strange contrast with her tainted self:
White lily-bells of spotless innocence;
Pink rosebuds, all one blush unto the core;
And—mockery of name!—heartsease were there,
With gold and purple opulence of bloom.
She desperately seemed to clutch at them
As at one last remaining source of clean
Immaculacy left to her in life.
The odour of the roses and the scent
Of delicatest valley-lilies shed
A balmy fragrance that surrounded her
With atmosphere of freshest purity,
Wherein she seemed to draw a freer breath,

Away from that foul stench of sin in which
She dwelt.   Methought it was redeeming gift
Vouchsafed by Heaven to keep alive in her
The faith in virtue, the belief in good,
The yearning after purity, e'en though
Herself had forfeited its holiness.

I once was seated in a railway train :
My husband by my side : just opposite
To us there sat a quakeress, young, fair,
But dressed in primmest suit of dust-like drab ;
Demurely silent ; folded hands across
Each other ; eyes cast down ; her mouth set close,
Expressionless ; her thoughts apparently engaged
With vacancy and nothingness, as though
She'd strictly bid them ne'er admit one glimpse
Of aught unseemly, worldly, or profane ;
She looked as if to her unseemliness
And worldliness and vile profanity
Included were in naturalest things ;
As if 'twere worldly to admire God's world,
Unseemly to behold his fairest works,
Profane to witness all their glorious
Perfection : so, complacently she sat,
Unsympathising, cold, unsensitive,
Concentred in herself, and ne'er cast glance
At scenes of rural beauty which we passed,
Or saw the setting sun that threw his rays
Athwart the landscape in a stream of gold.
She kept the red silk blind drawn closely down
On her side of the carriage, and her eyes
Ne'er once she raised.   But Nature, outraged at
The pretty quakeress's steady slight,
By its own magic willed her to obey
Its laws, and steeped her in the ruddy light

Cast by the fulgent sun right through the blind,
Until she sat amid a halo of
Soft roseate bloom, her cheeks, her forehead fair,
Her folded hands, aglow with colour rich ;
Her very dress, for all its stony drab,
Was made to flame in gorgeous ruby hues,
While flush carnation tinged her kerchief white.
Unconsciously she sat, bathed in the flood
Of crimson glory; forced, against herself,
To wear the livery that best beseems
Fair youth, and let her face express the tide
Of warm and vivid feelings proper to
Life's bounteous springtime.

DONALD'S COURTING.

Young Donald leaned with folded arms,
  And chatted at the window-sill :
I listened, but I spoke no word ;
  My spinning-wheel kept going still :
      Old Grannie sat in her arm-chair.

Young Donald told her all the news,
  Repeated them all o'er again :
I listened, but I spoke no word ;
  My spinning-wheel I plied amain :
      Old Grannie nodded in her chair.

Young Donald crept round to the door,
  And lifted quietly the latch :
I heard him, but I spoke no word ;
  My spinning gave a sudden catch :
      Old Grannie dozed in her arm-chair.

Young Donald sat him by my side,
  He looked at me, but held his peace :
I hardly breathed, I spoke no word,
  And somehow let my spinning cease :
      Old Grannie slumbered in her chair.

Young Donald asked me in my ear,
  If love for him I e'er could feel :
I gave him answer with my eyes ;
  Unheeded stood my spinning-wheel :
      Old Grannie slept in her arm-chair.

My Donald caught me in his arms,
  And clasp'd me close as ne'er before;
We neither of us spoke a word:
  My spinning-wheel fell on the floor:
      Old Grannie woke up in her chair.

My Donald went to her and said:
  " Dear Grannie, will you let us wed?"
I knelt before her, spoke no word:
  She laid her hand upon my head;
      Old Grannie smiled in her arm-chair.

My Donald smiled to see her smile:
  " My bairns," she said, " I give consent;
I see now why the spinning-wheel
  Was overturned, and what it meant!"
      Old Grannie laughed in her arm-chair.

STANZAS ON CORREGGIO'S PICTURE
OF "THE FLIGHT INTO EGYPT."

(FOR SETTING TO MUSIC.)

Saint Joseph holds the sacred Child,
While gently sleeps the Mother mild ;
Who, weary, and with travel spent,
Enjoys the slumber Heaven has sent.
  Rest, Mother, rest ! Take soft repose,
  While smoothly on the vessel goes.

Small guardian angels guide the boat,
That on the shining stream doth float ;
One dips the oar with graceful ease,
His curls blown lightly by the breeze.
  Rest, Mother, rest ! Take soft repose,
  While smoothly on the vessel goes.

Three others lift an awning spread
To screen the sun from Mary's head,
And, shading her from noontide heat,
They make it canopy her seat.
  Rest, Mother, rest ! Take soft repose,
  While smoothly on the vessel goes.

Two little angel faces more
With smiles the Babe divine adore,
In rapture note the Infant charms
Close nestled in Saint Joseph's arms.
  Rest, Mother, rest ! Take soft repose,
  While smoothly on the vessel goes.

Amid the sedges calmly glides
The shallop with its angel guides;
Their wings uplifted seem to waft
An aiding motion to the craft.
 Rest, Mother, rest! Take soft repose,
 While smoothly on the vessel goes.

Benignest Peace doth brooding wait
Above the happy hallowed freight,
And sheds reflected soothing rays
Upon our spirit as we gaze.
 Rest, Mother, rest! Take soft repose,
 While smoothly on the vessel goes.

Oh, choice Correggio! Painter rare!
To whom was given this vision fair;
Thine art enables us to see
The tender picture granted thee.
 Rest, Mother, rest! Take soft repose,
 While smoothly on the vessel goes.

O

LINES TO HENRIETTA MORITZ.

That damsel in the story-book, whose lips
  Dropped diamonds and pearls whene'er she spoke,
Prefigures thee, whose gifted finger-tips
  A stream of brilliant pearly notes evoke
Whene'er thou wilt—bright, rounded, liquid gems,
  Like those that leap and sparkle, trembling
    swim,
Then mingle with the sheeted glass that hems
  A fountain's edge, broad-spreading to its brim ;
Light rippling water-drops that race amain
  Adown the brook, now lingering to bedeck
The grass that skirts the bank, now caught again
  Amid the swirl of onward rush and wreck
Resistless of the torrent sweep.   Anon
  The mighty wash of waves, that surging dash
With aye-recurrent ponderous swing upon
  The rocks ; or sudden elemental crash
Of thunderous wind, uprooting mountain pines,
  Loud storming thro' ravines with giant groan,
Till sobbing, gasping, spent, it shrilly whines
  Discordant, sinks into a long-drawn moan,
And lulls to silence.   Wealth of jewel-sounds
  In grandest magnitude, in deepest thrill,
In softest, sweetest touch, with thee abounds,
  Dear lady-friend, to richly give at will :
And we, thy grateful listeners, ever long
  For more, still more, from that small bounteous
    hand—
So small in size, so large in gift—so strong,
  Yet downy soft—so like a fairy wand

Its potency of magic sway and might
  To conjure visions 'fore th' enchanted eye
By simple wafture, forcible yet light.
  Of all thy spells, methinks, there's one that I
Feel most subduing, most enthralling, though
  I fancy thou dost rate it but of small
Account—a trifle—slight, demanding no
  Great execution ; but, to me, its fall
And rise, its tender depth of sweet appeal,
  Unspeakably excite me, e'en to tears ;
And when thou play'st it, in my heart I feel
  How music can arouse yet calm our fears—
How a musician's dainty little hand
  Can summon spirits of divinest kind
To give us glimpses of a Heavenly Land
  And soothe to peace the aching mind.

OCCASIONAL ADDRESS
FOR A DRAMATIC EVENING.

APRIL 13, 1864.

This April month, this pleasant month of spring,
With Shakespeare's ever-honour'd name doth ring!
And through all corners of the peopled earth
Men vie in celebration of his birth!
Three hundred years ago he first drew breath—
A life of fame began that knew no death;
An actor-author, writer for the stage,
Who made the plays he wrote a mirror-page
Wherein mankind might see themselves display'd
In living colours that will never fade.
Some pay him homage with a sculptured stone,
Some found a scholarship, and some are prone
To think a grammar-school "the eftest way";
Some plan museums, book-rooms, and defray
The cost of spreading knowledge as the mode
Of best revering him who truly show'd
That "Knowledge is the wing wherewith we fly
To Heav'n;" and some, again, there are who try
To fitly honour him who play'd and wrote,
By playing too, and therefore aptly quote
In his own words "The play, the play's the thing,
Whereby we Shakespeare greatest honour bring!"
For this, my gentle audience, now you see
Us here to-night—my actor-friends and me.
  The Philadelphion Society,
With super-excellent propriety,

Have thought it suitable to act a play,
As practical and eligible way
Of manifesting reverential love
For one whose poet-genius ranks above
All other playwrights ; one who wisely knew
The value of the drama as the true
Refiner of the thoughts and aims of man—
At once a potent and delightful plan.
If, then, you think we've pleaded well our cause,
Give us your hands in token of applause ;
For Shakespeare's Birthday Tercentenary
Bestow your plaudits loud and plenary :
For him, for us, his humble fellow-actors in a play,
Now kindly raise a hearty, English, univoiced
   Hooray!

OCCASIONAL ADDRESS
FOR AN AMATEUR PERFORMANCE

OF

SHAKESPEARE'S

"MERCHANT OF VENICE."

WEDNESDAY, DECEMBER 14, 1864.

The knights of old, to prove their ladies' charms
Oft broke a lance, and did their feats of arms :
To-night we *Shake* our *Spear*—or act Shakespeàre—
In honour of a truth he shows most clear :
The rights of man to man, and what is due
From Jew to Christian, Christian to a Jew ;
That harshness shown to one of alien creed
Is sure to sow the pestilential seed
Of hate, revenge, and all unholy fruit
That in oppressed races take deep root.
   Antonio's most unchristianlike disdain
Of Hebrew Shylock and his sordid gain,
His "Jewish gaberdine" and "patient shrug,"
Inevitably stirr'd and surely dug
The depth of deadly malice and despite
Which only waits its turn to sharply smite
Its former foe, when once beneath its heel,
And teach th' oppressor stingingly to feel
That those who 're treated with unjust contempt
Will "better the instruction," and attempt
To crush the one who crushed them when he could,
Repaying ill with ill—not good by good.

Ne'er shown forbearance, justice, kindness, trust,
What wonder if they naturally must
Imbibe the lesson taught them all along
Of enmity, of rancour, and of bitter wrong?
If Shylock's cruel, who was cruel first?
If he demand, with fierce, insatiate thirst
For blood, fulfilment of the forfeit bond,
He scarcely goes but one short step beyond
Th' example they themselves before have set;
And they but sheer retaliation get.
Who call'd him "dog," and on his garment "spat"?
Was Shylock likely e'er to pardon that?
If "as a stranger cur" they oft him spurn'd,
Was it not likely that his bosom burn'd
With thought of vengeance at some future day,
If e'er the chance should come within his way?
'Mong Christians he had seen revers'd the law
That bids us love our enemies, and saw
How so-called Christian men could scoff and rail
On those without their own exclusive pale;
Instead of practising what they profess'd,
In their own persons their own laws transgress'd.
　　But not alone the moral of the Jew,
In this immortal play, the Poet drew:
The story of the caskets serves to show
How judgment and discrimination go
To make a chance a certainty, and gain
For wife a peerless lady, who doth reign
In all our hearts as most supremely *fair*
Among a class who have the name—not rare—
Of being *un*-fair; I mean the lawyer race;
They all, you will allow, maintain a case
Through thick and thin, and try to gain the
　　day;
Whatever right or wrong beneath there may

Be compromis'd, or inward conscience hurt,
To win, they'll spatter lots of legal dirt.
    But Portia, as a woman-lawyer should,
Still preaches " mercy," gentleness, and good ;
She strives to lure the Jew into relenting,
To touch his wolfish heart into repenting ;
She first attempts to make him " tear his bond,"
And not pursue his vengeance thus beyond
The bounds of human brotherhood with such
Remorseless, eager, murd'rous, bloodhound clutch ;
She leaves no point unurg'd, no word unsaid,
That might him from his fell intent have led ;
And only when she finds it all in vain,
Defeats him by conviction clear and plain.
    The *fairest* lawyer yet upon record,
The noblest amongst judges—not a lord—
Sweet Portia lives acknowledg'd and receiv'd :
A verdict that at once will be perceiv'd.
    And now dispose yourselves to kindly hear
Our play, ourselves, and, more than all, Shake-
    speàre :
Be pleas'd to think 'tis him you chiefly take ;
And judge us leniently, for his good sake.

OCCASIONAL PROLOGUE
FOR AN AMATEUR PERFORMANCE.
FRIDAY, DECEMBER 22, 1865.

To-night we've taken for our chosen play
A comedy that's matchless in its way—
" The School for Scandal," fam'd among revivals,
In fact, that's rivall'd only by " The Rivals ";
For wit like Sheridan's, so choice, so rare,
With naught but with itself can fit compare.
Less artfully built-up than Congreve's style,
Where sentence follows sentence in a pile
Of studiously constructed repartee,
And each retort we almost can foresee :
Less gross than Wycherley's or Farquhar's vein,
Where humour is so broad that it doth stain
The hearer's cheek with blushes, and arrests
The cordial laugh that follows purer jests.
But Brinsley scorns the double-meaning word,
The ribald hint, suggested more than heard;
His finer wit relies on its own force,
And seeks not aid from equivoque or coarse
Allusion : free, and unconstrained and gay ;
Full of airy and spontaneous play ;
Of pungent satire that is void of gall ;
Of pointed lessons that come home to all ;
So gracefully, so easily it flows,
So full of verse-like harmony his prose,
So neatly are his phrases turn'd and tim'd,
That every line's an epigram unrhym'd.
His characters are portraits, every one ;
His plots are most ingenious, full of fun ;

His scenes are " situations," still maintain'd ;
His " action " ever lively, well sustain'd ;
His dialogue a diamond, whose ray
Is all one sparkle in perpetual play.
  The present drama is indeed a " School "
Where every one may learn—not born a fool—
That scandal is a fashionable vice ;
That malice is genteel, and slander nice ;
That calumny can stab in accents bland ;
And, by th' insidious wave of a white hand,
Or nod, or whisper, reputations fall,
When subtle inuendo poisons all.
Joe Surface, with his sentimental cant,
His moral axioms, and his virtuous rant,
Enacting the immaculate, defames
By scores the characters of men and dames ;
And while pretending to a blameless life,
Seeks to pervert his friend Sir Peter's wife.
Fair names and fames by dozens are at stake,
Attack'd by such a gentleman as Snake ;
And Lady Sneerwell's arrows hit the mark,
Though aim'd at reputations in the dark ;
Her secret machinations shun the light,
But visibly and surely cast their blight :
The tongues of Crabtree, Backbite, are accurst,
While Mrs. Candour's is of all the worst ;
For open slander one may meet and dare,
But treach'rous partisanship who can bear ?
All this our author makes us feel and see,
All this he teaches us most wittily.
  And now, for us, the actor-scholars in his " School,"
We hope you'll kindly bear in mind the golden rule,
" Take will for deed " ; and, if you can, award the
  prize :
'Tis your approval : then—applaud us to the skies.

OCCASIONAL PROLOGUE
FOR AN AMATEUR PERFORMANCE
OF
SHAKESPEARE'S
·"MUCH ADO ABOUT NOTHING."

FRIDAY, DECEMBER 21, 1866.

The modest title that our Shakespeare gave
His play, accords with many other things
Besides the drama that we're met to enact:
For instance, with the fuss and fume for place,
Position, empty name and sinecure,
Whose very soul is pay for "nothing" done;
With all the trouble ta'en by thieves to rob
Some "lute-case," which, like Bardolph's, borne
    "twelve leagues,"
Brings but "three-halfpence"; or with swindler's
    pains,
Bestow'd upon some trick not worth a straw,
A world of care and skill that's thrown away
On fruitless fraud, which, if devoted to
An honest industry, would lead to wealth;
With all the struggle, bloodshed, cost of life,
Of cash, the wounds and mutilations, grief
Of friends surviving, nation's gen'ral loss,
That go to make up all that is involv'd
In that three-letter'd little word of WAR;
With backbiting, ill-natur'd calumny
And spite, that drudge unceasingly to strip
A neighbour of his name and fame, which when
They're lost, what gain results to the detractor?

Just "nothing," after all his "Much ado!"
And thus with myriad other things beyond,
The title of our this night's play conforms
E'en better than with Shakespeare's plot itself:
Was Hero's slander "nothing"?   Or her shame,
Her misery, her agony to find
Herself a bride rejected in the face
Of all her friends by him she hop'd
Would be her husband, her protector, yet
By him to be revil'd, thrown off, cast back,
Beside the very nuptial altar-rail?
Was all this "nothing"?   Surely, no.   But then
Shall we complain that Shakespeare nam'd his play
Amiss?   Not so: the title that he gave,
Has this in common with his every line
And word—it comprehends inclusively
A wide extent of application, serves
Not only playfully to mark the fact
That all th' aspersion in the play is false
And naught, but serves to satirise the large
Amount of "Much Ado" that's going on
In this good world of ours "about" sheer "Nothing."
Our chief concern regarding it to-night
Is your acceptance of the name in such
A spirit, that you will not think it hits
Our acting: since we pledge ourselves to take
The utmost pains in our performance: then,
We trust you will not say 'tis "Much Ado
About" a "Nothing"; but that you will say
Our "Much Ado" is "Nothing" to the gain
You make in pleasure, seeing Shakespeare's play
So lovingly enacted by the troop
Of Philadelphions,* your faithful friends.

* Written by M. C. C. at the request of the members of the
Philadelphion Society.

PROLOGUE TO A SHAKESPEARIAN
ACROSTIC CHARADE.

'Tis often said, if you're at loss to find
A motto for whatever comes to mind,
You've only to look into Shakespeare's page;
And there you'll see all sorts of maxims sage
That suit all subjects, and that illustrate
(Without concerning your own empty pate)
Their subtlest meanings with much fuller force
Than you can hope to do by any course
But this : he always furnishes a word,
A passage, or a line that ne'er occurr'd
To any brain so perfectly as his :
And therefore, for this reason clearly 'tis
That he's consulted when apt words are wanted :
Thus much, we think, will readily be granted.
   Well, granting this, we thought we couldn't do
     better
Than search his book for every needed letter
In our to-night's proposed Charade acrostic;
And, if we do not fail in our prognostic,
We fancy we'll succeed in pleasing you
By this device Shakespearian and new.
   Attend, then, while its plan we thus explain :
A scene from "As You Like It" first makes
   plain
Th' initial letter of our chosen word
(To miss it would be certainly absurd);
The second by a scene from "Much Ado"
Is shown; the third by sample touch or two

From charming " Winter's Tale ; " while fourth
and last
A scene from " Midsummer Night's Dream " is
pass'd
Before your eyes ; concluding with the whole
Completed word, denoted by a sole
And simple leaf-crown'd portrait of the man
We all delight to honour.   Then you can
Have no more doubt what is th' acrostic word ;
Its guessing then need no more be deferr'd.
　　And now there's nothing farther to be said,
Than to entreat attention may be paid
To one small fact.   Our actors hope you'll be
Indulgent to whate'er defects you see ;
And bear in mind they're nervous at the thought
Of playing Shakespeare as he should and ought
To be enacted : but they'll do their best ;
And put your lenient judgment to the test,
By making up in love to Shakespeare's verse
For want of skill in speaking, or aught worse.
　　Our scenery, moreover, is as plain
As that which Shakespeare's stage did e'er attain
When he did write and act : or, older still,
When classic Grecians summon'd at their will
The fancies of spectators to believe
In whatsoever place they should receive
As represented, by the simple means
Of writing up above the several scenes
The phrase, " a grove," " a temple," or " a
room " ;
" A royal palace," " garden," or " a tomb."
And so we only follow in the track
Of antique Art, when we inscribe at back
Of stage the name of each successive scene,
And trust to your imagination keen

For filling up the vision of the spot
That's requisite, according to the plot.
   In winding up this p'rhaps too long oration,
Accept a little note of preparation :
Permit us just to give you this one hint :
Of loud applause be sure you do not stint ;
You've naught to do, to make all things seem right,
But kindly clap your hands with all your might.

OCCASIONAL EPILOGUE

TO

SHAKESPEARE'S

"LOVE'S LABOUR'S LOST."

(WRITTEN FOR AN AMATEUR PERFORMANCE AT THE
REQUEST OF MR. ALFRED LITTLETON.)

"*King.*   Come, sir, it wants a twelvemonth and
   a day,
And then 'twill end.
   Biron.   That's too long for a play."
Princess.   Nay, good my Lord Biron, you do
   mistake ;
A play, if ably writ and played, may make
The onward lapse of years seem simply true
And natural : the task appointed you
Of playing out your play in forcing smiles
From sick-bed wretches, you will see, beguiles
The term of waiting for your lady's love,
If well you play your part.   Be, then, above
Despondency ; since that will never serve
To win your cause : be hopeful, lords ; *deserve*
To conquer, and the victory is yours.
Triumphant is the courage that endures.
Farewell !   Success attend you all !   But now
I drop my royal princessship to bow
Before our friends, and humbly crave for leave
To speak the Epilogue, which may receive
Acceptance as the substituted close
To this our acted play, instead of those

More antique forms of songs in praise of Spring
And Winter, that demand good voice to sing.

[Advancing, and addressing the audience.]

Thus far, then, gentles all, Love's Labour's lost :
But yet, not wholly so ; for in the end—
The year's probation honestly gone through—
The word is then to be, Love's Labour's won.
No labour underta'en for love can e'er
Be lost entirely : it repays itself.
The love of springtime sends us forth in hope
To gather violets : not one we find :
But none the less the search has been enjoy'd,
The walk, the open air, the clear blue sky,
The wide green sweep of lawn or meadow's sward,
The sun-bejewelled rivulet, the hedge
Of hawthorn, with its tangled mass of briar
And bramble, intervolved with briony—
The well-named " Traveller's Joy "—that straggles
        o'er
In rich confusion and profusion : there
We stoop and peer amid the wayside turf,
Amid the emerald blades of vernal grass,
The giant sturdiness of dock-leaves broad,
The delicater fronds of palmy fern,
The hemlock umbels, and the grey-green stalks
Of ragged-robins red, that lift their heads
With saucy carelessness of picturesque
Effect, like hedgeside ruddy gipsy boys
Unconscious of their native beauty wild,
But gladsome in their right to grow and thrive
By Nature's law alone. We hardly miss
The violets we came to seek, repaid
By so much unsought loveliness instead.
No poorest little deed that's done for Love's

Sweet sake but brings its own sure recompense.
We hold a twig to save a drowning midge,
The insect crawls upon the proffer'd stem,
And drags its saturated weight along,
Until the deadly burden wet is left ;
Then fluttering emancipated wings,
Flies off to airy freedom, leaving us
To gaze forsaken : ne'ertheless we've had
The joy of rescuing the fragile thing,
With all its mysteries of hair-slight limbs,
Its gauzy pinions, and its crest of down.
    No toil or enterprise is ever lost,
That hath the consecrating motive, Love :
The gravest work, the gayest avocation,
If but pursued from purely loving cause,
Unfailingly reaps harvest and bears fruit.
The getting up a play for love of Art
Implies a labour manifold, 'tis true :
The casting characters, the studying parts,
The reconciling claims of self-esteem,
The due regard to fit ability ;
The long rehearsals, and the patient wait
For zest of actual performance-night :
But still, our pains are balanced by our gains ;
The care bestowed in conning Shakespeare's line
Has earned us truer knowledge of its worth,
Its grace, its inner core of meaning deep ;
And now we hope to win a crowning test
That we have not in vain essay'd to please,—
If you your kindly plaudits will accord,
Our Loving Labour has its best reward.

HALF CONFESSIONS.

Who it is I met yestreen,
With winsome face and simple dress,
Who it is has gentlest e'en,
I will not tell, but you may guess.

Who it is that whispers low,
With glances shy that *look* a yes,
Who it is that says not no,
I will not tell, but you may guess.

Who it is with blushing cheek
And tell-tale eyes that still confess
Love for me she will not speak,
I will not tell, but you may guess.

Who it is that lets me kiss
Her snowdrop hand, her golden tress,
Who it is makes all my bliss
I will not tell, but you may guess.

Who it is will be my wife
When once I win her word to bless,
Who'll be mine, my own for life,
I will not tell, but you may guess.

HERSELF.

Her bonny mou', her bonny mou',
How weel it says the words " I lo'e ! "
Her ruddy lip, her ruddy lip,
How soft it yields the sweets I sip.

Her gleefu' e'e, how bright its glance !
It gars my very pulses dance,
When near my cheek I feel her curl,
As through the reel we swiftly whirl.

Her winsome form, her waist sae slim,
Her little feet, her ankles trim,
Her shapely shoulders smooth and white,
How gracefu' are they in my sight !

But 'tis na lip or sparkling e'e—
Though very, very dear they be,
Nor yet her little twinkling feet,
Though they are very, very sweet.

'Tis na her shape or slender waist,
Though they're exactly to my taste,
Nor yet her wavy shining hair,
That mak's her sae surpassing fair.

It is her *thochts* sae honest, clear,
That in her artless e'en appear,
It is her *look* sae pure, sae true,
That penetrates me through and through.

It is her *heart* that winneth mine,
Her heart of innocence divine ;
Her heart, from its own goodness light,
That makes her lo'ely in my sight.

It is her *spirit*, chaste, yet warm,
That gi'es to her her greatest charm ;
It is *herself* that I adore,
That mak's me hers—ay, to the core.

NEAR AND DEAR.

In all her moods she's dear to me,
She's ever welcome near to me ;
      Dear, most dear,
      Near, most near,
    Is wifey mine to me !'

Her voice is gentle, sweet, and low ;
She hath an ear for others' woe ;
She hath a smile for others' joy ;
She's neither over-free nor coy.

She hath a grave attentive look,
When hearing read a thoughtful book ;
She hath a laugh that ringeth out
With gladsome little tuneful shout,

When listening to a merry tale ;
She hath a cheek that turneth pale,
When crime or cruelty she hears ;
An eye that brimmeth o'er with tears

At word of sorrows nobly borne,
Or fortitude of soul forlorn ;
A quivering lip, a trembling start
Betray th' emotions of her heart

At sound of treachery or wrong ;
But murmurs she an inward song,
In happy sympathy of pure delight
With all that's high and just and right.

She has a woman's instinct true,
A genuine native spirit-clue,
That draws her towards the nobly pure,
As with a strong resistless lure ;

That her repels with equal force
From aught that's evil, foul, or coarse ;
That makes her cheerful look, or sad,
In consonance with good or bad.

She's kindly kind to every one,
She's kindest kind to me alone ;
She's loving to all folk that be,
Her love of loves she gives to me.

In all her moods she's dear to me,
I'd have her ever near to me ;

Near and dear,
Dear and near,
Is wifey mine to me !

HER EYES.

Those charming, merry, dancing eyes,
　That seem to say a thousand things ;
Those darling, roguish, glancing eyes
　From which a world of gladness springs.

Those curly upturn'd lashes bright,
　That twinkle archly golden shade
Amid the dazzling beams of light
　From forth her eyelids white are ray'd.

That frank yet modest open gaze,
　That fearless yet most gentle look—
I watch them all, in every phase,
　And read their meaning like a book.

I follow them with mine, until
　I dread lest she may think me bold ;
And then my very·heart turns chill
　Lest she, reproving, should be cold.

And change that candid, winning glance
　For looks of distance and restraint ;
The very thought of such a chance
　Doth make my breath come short and faint.

Yet still my rebel eyes will keep
　Pursuit of hers, in spite of me ;
Do what I can, they furtive creep
　Away, and after, constantly.

And whether grave or whether gay
　Th' expression of those eyes of hers,
They've always something fresh to say
　That still allures me, ne'er deters.

They eloquently shine thro' tears,
　When aught pathetic is the theme ;
But soon as mirthfulness appears,
　·With animated smiles they beam.

On me those eyes too rarely turn ;
　But when they do, I feel my own
With eager joy dilate and burn—
　Ah ! joy too swiftly past and gone !

For fleetingly as rarely look
　Of hers meets mine : a lightning flash,
And then 'tis o'er ; as if it took
　A pleasure in the sudden dash

Of answering brightness it illumes
　In mine ; yet chooses not to stay
To see the fire it kindling dooms
　As soon as born to fade away.

I ask myself if this be sign
　Of little liking or disdain ;
Or p'rhaps indifference so fine
　It cares not if her look remain

To scathe, or quickly be withdrawn
　To disappoint : but then, if not ?
My life I sometimes think I'd pawn
　To know the truth ; if not, then what ?

What, what doth mean that look of hers?
  That little tantalising look
Which, oh, so sparingly occurs,
  No sooner darted than forsook.

If not dislike, disdain—or worse,
  Indifference—then, can it be,
She feels for me the sweet reverse
  Of these, and has for me—for *me*—

A preference, a liking, *love?*
  I tremble as I *think* the word,
I dare not utter it above
  My breath; I murmur it unheard.

If love indeed it should be—LOVE!
  And love for me, that makes those eyes
Still shrink from mine! My gentle dove,
  It thrills me through, the bare surmise.

It gives me courage to implore
  To know the truth: this very day
I will compel those eyes, before
  They turn so flittingly away,

To rest on mine, to speak the truth,
  To tell me what their look doth mean;
To say, without or reck or ruth,
  If it bespeak aversion keen,

Or if, indeed, it augurs bliss,
  And leaves me free, in mine own fashion,
To thank those eyes, by sacred kiss
  Imprinted on their lids with passion.

Dear, charming, merry, dancing eyes,
   O say to mine those thousand things
You're wont to say to others' eyes;
   Let my chief gladness be't that springs
From forth those darling cherish'd eyes:
Their looks of love alone be mine;
For others let their brightness shine!
Be mine those dearest eyes for life,
When she who owns them is my wife!

HER TWINKLE.

What is the magic lurking in her eyes ?—
'Tis not their shape, their colour, or their size ;
'Tis none of these I worshipfully prize :
It is that little, radiant, roguish twinkle.

The dimple in a maiden's blushing cheek,
The look that in a picture seems to speak,
The lustre in a silver planet meek—
Is to her eye its loving little twinkle.

The ruby sparkle in a priceless gem,
The point in epigram or apothegm,
The zest intent that lives in each of them—
Is to her eye its sprightly little twinkle.

A thousand pleasant things it seems to say,
More jocund sweet than children at their play
Or tumbling in the meadows 'mong the hay—
That lovely little, dancing, glancing twinkle.

When on myself its merry light doth beam,
A blissful flood throughout my frame doth stream,
And all my being saturate doth seem
With rays of happy sunshine from her twinkle.

It fills my heart with rapture at her charms,
It makes me long to catch her in my arms,
To shield her throughout life from all its harms,
And thank her in my own way for her twinkle.

NO AND YES.

Her modest words they say " No, no ; "
 Her gentle looks still " Ay " express :
Which I obey, you well may guess,
 Between these signs of No and Yes.

For though her lip, in word, says " No,"
 When I its ruby red would press ;
It says, I blissfully confess,
 In its own way, " Yes, yes ; yes, yes."

ASKING.

(SET TO MUSIC BY THE REV. W. BORROW.)

He stole from my bodice a rose,
 My cheek was its colour the while ;
But ah, the sly rogue ! he well knows,
 Had he ask'd it, I must have said no.

He snatch'd from my lips a soft kiss ;
 I tried at a frown—'twas a smile ;
For ah, the sly rogue ! he knows this,
 Had he ask'd it, I must have said no.

That " asking " in love's a mistake,
 It puts one in mind to refuse ;
'Tis best not to ask, but to take,
 For it saves one the need to say no.

Yet, stay—this is folly I've said ;
 Some things should be ask'd if desir'd :
My rogue hopes my promise to wed ;
 When he asks me, I will not say no.

BELIEVE ME !

I will not vow by yonder moon,
Or by the balmy breath of June :
   I'll only tell thee that I love :
      Believe me, dear, believe me !

I'll love thee with a faith sincere,
With meaning honest, simple, clear,
   I'll love thee with my truth of heart :
      Believe me, dear, believe me !

Thine own sweet graces all attest
Thou'rt form'd to be belov'd the best ;
   Believe, then, in my fervent love :
      Believe me, dear, believe me !

SERENADE.

Music, with thy downy wing,
Fan her senses while we sing ;
O'er her fancy subtly creep,
Lulling it to dreamless sleep.

Music, softly sung and play'd,
Shed thy balm upon this maid ;
Through and through her fancy steep,
Soothing it to dreamless sleep.

Music, with thy magic wand,
Touch her by supreme command ;
Spell-bound yet her fancy keep,
Charm it into dreamless sleep.

SERENADE.

O, come to thy window! Sweet one, appear!
Thy lover, his friends, are waiting thee here :
Our music receive, 'tis homage to thee ;
He sues for thy love, his pleaders are we.

O, come to thy window! Sweet one, appear!
And lend to our strain thy favouring ear ;
Approve of our music, happy are we ;
Accept of his suit, and happy is he.

O, come to thy window! Sweet one, appear!
If music and moonlight be to thee dear,
Enjoy them this night, in pure air and free ;
Our serenade hear, thy lover's fond plea.

VALENTINE.

(SENT TO JOHN LISTON, BY SABILLA NOVELLO, FEBRUARY 14, 1845.)

With scrupulous modesty, suiting a prude,
I'll venture to "hope that I do not intrude"; ([1])
But really, so many fair graces combine,
I cannot but choose thee for my Valentine.
My heart dwells with rapture on many a thought
By Adam Brock's ([2]) laughter to memory brought;
Billy Lackaday's ([3]) humour so cockney and smart,
And Lubin Log's ([4]) family, dear to his heart;
Tony Lumpkin, ([5]) the lout, so rude to his Ma,
And Acres ([6]) with new-fangled oaths and French
pas;
The pathos of Russet ([7]) so manly and touching,
That left to be wished for an absolute nothing.
But why, then, this *list* should I farther insist *on*,
When all is combined in th' unmatchable LISTON?

([1]) His constant and famous speech in "Paul Pry."
([2]) In "Charles XIIth of Sweden."
([3]) In "Sweethearts and Wives."
([4]) In "Love, Law, and Physic."
([5]) In "She Stoops to Conquer."
([6]) In "The Rivals."
([7]) In "The Jealous Wife."

UNLESS.* (No. 1.)

(SET TO MUSIC BY JOSEPH ROECKEL.)

When yesterday I left you, darling Nell,
I felt as tho' it were for ever, dear ;
You look'd so cold, so *how* I cannot tell,
You seem'd to banish me for evermore :
              Unless, indeed—
You'd make it up, and let's be friends again !

Our lovers' quarrel grew from nothing, Nell,
How it arose, I can't imagine, dear ;
If you or I began, I cannot tell ;
I only know 'twill part us evermore :
              Unless, indeed—
You'd make it up, and let's be friends again !

I'm very, very wretched, darling Nell ;
I fancy you are fretting too, my dear ;
Nay, sure of it, tho' *how* I cannot tell ;
In short, we're both unhappy evermore ;
              Unless, indeed—
We make it up, and be good friends again !

---

* Imitated from the Italian "Stornello," a kind of national
ballad, the chief characteristic of which is playful familiarity.

(Suggestion to Composer and Performer.) No. 1. In setting
these words to music, the first four lines should be made a slow
and mournful strain of regret; then, the "Unless, indeed"—
should be lingering and very hesitating, and, finally, the concluding line should be in extremely quick time, with rapid and joyous
tune. The singer should put much sadness of expression into
the commencement; changing to archness and vivacity at the
close of each stanza.

MAKING UP MY MIND.* (No. 2.)

He often teases me to frankly say
If I like best Sir William or Sir John ;
He presses me to tell him whether they
Or others take my fancy most of all :
And I reply,
I can't make up my mind.

He plagues me to be partner in the dance ;
To promise him my hand for next quadrille ;
T' engage myself three waltzes in advance ;
To let him lead me to the supper-room :
But I reply,
I've not made up my mind.

If he would ask me whom I love the best ;
If he besought my hand for life ;
If he but spoke in earnest, not in jest,
And told me he loved me as I love him—
I might reply,
I've quite made up my mind.

---

* Imitated from the Italian " Stornello."

AFTER ALL.* (*No.* 3.)

I'm sometimes puzzled which I most admire,
　Belinda's wealth of lovely golden hair,
Letitia's jet-black eyes of sparkling fire,
　Or bright Matilda's skin so dazzling fair :
　　　　　But—after all,
　My little Flo' loves me, and I love her.

My fancy now and then is led astray
　By Lucy's graceful shape and slender waist ;
By Milly's dainty feet I'm drawn away,
　Or half beguiled by Dora's tact and taste :
　　　　　But—after all,
　My little Flo' loves me, and I love her.

When steadily I think of her, I'm safe ;
　My heart its loyal constancy avers ;
I'm not a fickle wandering stray or waif ;
　I'm proof against all other charms but hers :
　　　　　For—after all,
　I love my little Flo', and she loves me.

---

* Imitated from the Italian " Stornello."

AND YET.* (No. 4.)

I see him look at Linda's wavy hair,
I see him watch Cecilia's winning smile,
I see him notice Maud's complexion fair ;
   My heart with dread is beating all the while :
           And yet—
I'm almost sure he loves me best of all.

I see him glance at Milly's fairy feet,
And follow all their movements with a smile,
I see him charmed by many maidens sweet ;
   My heart with dread fast beating all the while,
           And yet—
I'm almost sure he loves me best of all.

For when he takes my hand in both of his,
And looks at me with his confiding smile,
My every doubt and fear are set at ease,
   Although my heart is beating all the while :
           And—*yes !*
I'm sure, quite sure, he loves me best of all.

---

* Imitated from the Italian " Stornello."

THE TWENTY-SECOND OF NOVEMBER.

This day to Saint Cecilia's name
Devoted in perpetual fame,
Was chosen well to be the date
Of sealing Clara's wedded fate.
The Patron Saint of Music's Art
And she, whose voice goes to the heart,
In songs of sacred faith and trust,
Their celebration surely must
Deserve to have on self-same day;
And though November 'tis—not May,
Yet points of harmony there are
To make the distance far from far
Between the Songstress and the Saint,
On floral grounds—as I shall paint.
Cecilia's wreath of blended rose
And lily, that with odour flows;
Unseen, but fragrantly perceiv'd;
From angel hands divine receiv'd,
Was typified when Clara crown'd
With English rose the man who found
Th' Italian lilies of his name
Lack'd rosy bloom—that very same—
To make them flowers of perfect hue
For endless beauty, fresh and true,
In love and purity to live,
United by young buds that give
Immortal bliss to married pair,
Still newly springing, ever fair.

A LOVE SONG.

(SET TO MUSIC BY MISS MACIRONE.)

So dearly do I love thee, dear, in sooth,
  I cannot hope thy love can equal mine :
But love me with thy heart and with thy truth ;
  They needs must satisfy me, being thine.
      Then love me well, my love, and love me true ;
      Oh, love me half as well as I love you !

So boundless is my love, my sweet, for you,
  That half would fill my measure of content ;
A double portion is of right your due :
  To this agreement let us both consent.
      Then love me well, my love, and love me true ;
      Oh, love me half as well as I love you !

Our mutual share of love thus order'd fair,
  Shall ne'er become the source of fond dispute :
I'll love thee with a love beyond compare ;
  Thou'lt love me to the utmost of my suit.
      Then love me well, my love, and love me true ;
      Oh, love me half as well as I love you !

BE TRUE TO ME, MY LOVE!

(SET TO MUSIC BY THE REV. W. BORROW.)

With thee my thoughts are calm and sweet,
  Without thee they are wild and sad ;
With thee my life is all complete,
  Without thee it is stormy, mad :
      Be true to me, my love, be true !
      I'm nothing, if I have not you.

With thee my heart is aye at rest,
  Without thee it is tempest-tost ;
With thee my life is fully blest,
  Without thee I am wreck'd and lost :
      Be true to me, my love, be true !
      I'm nothing, if I have not you.

SHAKESPEARE'S BIRTHDAY.

The twenty-third of April, O !
St. George's day, and Shakespeare's day,
The pride of merry England ho !
Sing all a hearty hip, hurrah !
     Hurrah ! hurrah !

The twenty-third of April, boys,
Is for us all a glorious day ;
Then sing it with a merry noise,
A musical hip, hip, hurrah !
     Hurrah ! hurrah !

The twenty-third of April, lads,
Should be a celebrated day ;
Then celebrate it, sons and dads,
With our united hip, hurrah !
     Hurrah ! hurrah !

WRITTEN AT DAWN,

ON THE 23RD OF APRIL, 1869.

Five decades have elapsed since I, a child,
Was taught to know and love thy poet name,
O Shakespeare mine! I may say " mine "; for art
Thou not possessed by all who have the boon
To see thy wondrous merits, and perceive
The boundless good thou art to men? As for
Mine own poor part, I owe to thee a debt
Of gratitude through life : thou'st been to me
A comfort and a stay in many a pinch
Of sore distress ; a soother of sad thought :
A help in time of trouble ; a good friend
And counsellor at need, whose sage advice
Came ever unobtrusive, yet sufficing ;
A gentle monitor, that took to task
Unseen, unheard, by witnessers, and spared
The shame of aught save self-avowal, led
To quiet self-reform ; enhancer of
Delight when joys arrived ; bestowing sight
More keen in things of Art ; an aid to view
The wealth of Nature with an eye of love
And heart of thankfulness, to raise the mind
In rapture, exaltation, and devout
Emotion to the Giver of all good :
Yea, this and countless more I owe to thee,
Thou nobly, truly great! Accept my lines
Of faithful fervent homage on this day
That saw thee born.
     Now breaks the coming morn :

Now peereth out the first pale streak of East :
Now faint grey lines with ambient hints appear :
And presently a more pervading haze
Of silvery-yellow hue : lastly, the sun
Himself upriseth, like the lord of all,
And floods the sky with universal light ;
So, Shakespeare, thou ; thy beams are cast abroad
To pour upon the world effulgence wide,
Impartial : on the lowliest cottage thatch,
As on the lofty palace roof, they shine :
On solitary headlands, and on peaks
Where snow eternally doth lie, the sun
Bespreads his roseate lustre at approach
Of dawn ; or turns to gold the mountain tops
At eve : so thou, the lornest, most remote
Of nooks dost visit with thy bright and large
Beneficence ; dost bring the warmth and glow
And cheer of geniality, the sense
Of growth and progress, culture and refinement,
With fruitfulness and ripe prosperity,
Where'er thine influence rests : Thou, like the sun,
Prevailest to illumine and to bless !

SONG.

No sound doth break the silence of the night,
Save yonder fountain's ever gentle play
In measur'd fall of softest show'rs alwày,
    That time the beating of our hearts, my love.

And, hark ! the nightingale, embower'd near,
Breathes forth its happy plenitude of song
In notes of fluty sweetness, ling'ring, long,
    That chant the music of our hearts, my love.

MUSIC'S BLESSING.

Music man's great blessing is :
Changes dolour into bliss,
Gives his cares a gentle kiss,
Setting them at rest, I wis.

Trouble it doth softly ease,
Bidding it be still and cease ;
Joyfulness it doth increase,
Bringing happiness and peace.

MUSIC'S DELIGHT.

Sing we now a grateful measure,
Praising Music as our treasure :
What so good for spending leisure ?
What so sweet in giving pleasure ?

Music hath no jot of badness,
Music filleth all with gladness,
Music comforteth in sadness ;
It hath power to soothe e'en madness.

{ *When distracted we are driven,
{ All our mind at six and seven,
Music as a boon is given,
Turning earth into a heaven.

---

* Occasional couplet, to be substituted when appropriate :—
{ Music brings us here at seven,
{ Keeps us here until eleven.

INVOCATION TO MUSIC.

When o'er the keys my fingers stray
In search of tones to lull my care,
I feel my sadness melt away,
As clouds dissolve in summer air.
    O Music, sent to soothe and bless,
    Vouchsafe me thy divine caress!

Come, fold me in thy soft embrace,
And waft my spirit into bliss!
With tenderness my cares efface,
As by the touch of mother's kiss.
    O Music, sent to soothe and bless,
    Vouchsafe me thy divine caress!

INVOCATION TO SLEEP.

Sleep, thou balmy comfort, Sleep,
Near my lady's bower keep!
Smoothly from her grieving sweep;
Sorrow in oblivion steep:
On those eyes late made to weep,
Lay thy fingers, gentle Sleep!
Sweetly o'er her senses creep;
Fold her 'neath thy wings, O Sleep!

THE DESPAIRING LOVER.

She let me take her hand in mine,
　She let me keep it folded there ;
She let me look her in the eyes,
　And yet she left me to despair !

She let me think I'd won her heart,
　That I was fondly shrinèd there ;
That she had given me her faith,
　And yet she left me to despair.

And she is gone, my cruel love !
　As heartless as supremely fair !
She went without a word or look,
　And left me to my dark despair !

That she is lost, is bitter grief ;
　But that I'd try to bravely bear :
That she is false is keenest pang,
　'Tis that that darkens my despair.

SONG.

There is a stile beneath a tree,
Is very—very dear to me :
The stile gives rest, the tree gives shade,
And there for many an hour I've stay'd.

But neither rest nor shade, you see,
Quite gives the spot its charms to me ;
    Another reason, I must say,
    It is, that makes me like to stay.

An arm that holds me on the stile,
Frank eyes that look in mine the while,
    A voice that murmurs in my ear,
    All make the place so very dear.

Oh, pleasant stile ! oh, shady tree !
A cherished thought you are to me :
Oh, faithful arm, frank eyes, fond voice !
You make my inward heart rejoice.

THE DECLARATION.

(SET TO MUSIC BY CHAS. R. TENNANT, ESQ.)

What makes my heart so wildly throb?
I'm glad, not sorry—yet I sob:
    What ails me that I cannot rest?
    He told me what I partly guessed.

Why will the tears o'erflow my eyes?
It must have been the glad surprise:
    Surprise to find I rightly guessed,
    Delight to hear he loved me best.

The words he said I hardly knew;
But—eager, ardent, rapid, few—
    Their meaning flashed upon my sight
    In flood of almost blinding light.

My quivering lip, my varying cheek,
Revealed the truth I could not speak:
    Contented with my tell-tale look,
    He silently my answer took.

A sudden joy affects like grief:
But with joy's tumult comes relief
    To feel all fears are set at rest,
    As when he drew me to his breast.

I COME TO THEE, MY LOVE, I COME!

SONG.

In tedious bondage long held fast
The weary hours of absence past,
I come to thee, my love, at last!
   I come to thee, my love, I come!

Fulfilled the part allotted me,
Hard duty done now sets me free,
On wings of joy I fly to thee!
   I come to thee, my love, I come!

Endured with many a stifled moan,
An age of waiting sad and lone:
But now—oh, happiness!—'tis gone!
   I come to thee, my love, I come!

GOOD-MORROW.

(SET TO MUSIC BY MISS MACIRONE.)

Good-morrow to my lady bright,
  I'll early sing beneath her bower;
Let others serenade by night,
  I choose the brilliant morning hour:
      Good-morrow, love, good-morrow!

The morn is fair, and like my love;
  Benignant, gracious, so is she;
It sheds a radiance from above;
  It smiles on all, as she on me:
      Good-morrow, love, good-morrow!

Appear, my love, and beam with light;
  Thy lattice is mine orient;
Arise, and bless my longing sight;
  My heart awaits thee, jubilant:
      Good-morrow, love, good-morrow!

TOO LATE.

Two mournful words, minute in length,
   Fall on the ear with dire import ;
Though seeming small, of greatest strength,
   They shut out hope, of earthly sort :
            Too late !   Too late !

When erring man would fain atone
   For injuries that bring remorse,
He finds his purpose futile grown
   By those two words that check his course :
            Too late !   Too late !

They strike, as with a dooming chime,
   The soul that vainly would retrieve
The past, the lost, lamented time ;
   And leaves it nothing but to grieve :
            Too late !   Too late !

One sole resource to man remains,
   When his sick heart hath made this moan
Divinest mercy still contains
   A cure for all : with that alone
            'Tis ne'er too late.

MR. RIGHT.

They press me to make haste and choose;
　They pester and they worry;
They tell me I've no time to lose:
　But surely there's no hurry—
　　　　　　　I'll wait for Mr. Right.

They say that I'm too hard to please,
　Too dainty, too fastidious:
I only ask to choose at ease;
　And—not to be invidious—
　　　　　　　To wait for Mr. Right.

They recommend me Colonel Blank,
　Because he's rich as Crœsus;
They introduce me men of rank:
　That's not the way to please us—
　　　　　　　I'll wait for Mr. Right.

I will not wed till I can love,
　Of that I am determin'd;
Mere interest I am above:
　So, once for all—I'm firm in't—
　　　　　　　I'll wait for Mr. Right.

"HE."

He won me with that look of his,
  So manly and so clear ;
He won me with that glance of his,
  So gentle and so dear.

He won me with that laugh of his,
  So pleasant and so frank ;
He won me with that voice of his ;
  Into my heart it sank.

He won me with that eye of his,
  So eloquent and pure ;
He won me with that tongue of his,
  Which did my love allure.

You shall not know that name of his,
  Nor hear it breathed by me :
You cannot guess that name of his ;
  I said no more than "*he*."

MY BONNIE BIRDIE !

(SET TO MUSIC BY CHARLES DESANGES.)

The lark may sing with mountain glee ;
The blackbird warble mellowly ;
The throstle pipe full clear and free ;
But let me hear my own sweet bird—
        My bonnie Birdie !

My bird has eyes of azure bright ;
Her song alone is my delight ;
But wings she has not yet for flight :
An *earthly* angel is my bird—
        My bonnie Birdie !

Then come, my bird, and with me rest ;
And stray no farther than my breast ;
But make this heart thy home, thy nest,
My mate, my wife, my own sweet bird !
        My bonnie Birdie !

THE LITTLE BIRD.

A little bird whispereth me
As softly as softly can be ;
And, perch'd on invisible tree,
Deliciously low singeth he.

He twittereth close in mine ear,
That none but myself may him hear :
To *me* he is perfectly clear ;
And tells me of one the most dear.

He says to me many a thing
That no other bird did e'er sing ;
Delightfullest news does he bring,
And never's in haste to take wing.

He's a strange little wonderful bird,
As ever was seen or was heard ;
He lets me know many a word
Of a person who makes up our third.

My little bird's secret and sweet,
Through him we in spirit oft meet ;
My love and I kindly him treat,
And give him our bosom for seat.

THE MARINER'S WIFE.

My sailor husband's on the main,
            Far, far away !
Oh, send him swiftly home again ;
            Let him not stay !

He thinks upon his faithful Sue,
            Far, far away !
He will return, as fond and true ;
            Let him not stay !

Ye winds and waves in foreign seas,
            Far, far away !
Ah, set this anxious heart at ease ;
            Let him not stay !

Be gracious to him, Powers above ;
            Far, far away !
Oh, waft him to his waiting love ;
            Let him not stay !

THE FISHERMAN'S WIFE.

A BALLAD.

Come home to me, Willie,
  Come home from the sea,
Come home to thy baby,
  Come home, lad, to me.

The wild winds are raging,
  There's storm in the sky ;
I tremble while singing
  Our babe's lullaby.

I try to be brave, Will ;
  I try, lad, I do ;
But hard is it, Willie,
  When watching for you.

The sound of the waves, lad,
  The sound of the sea,
It fills me with terror,
  While waiting for thee !

I fancy the tumult,
  The turmoil, the toss,
The darkness, the struggle,
  Oh, Heaven, the loss !

What ails thee, my babie ?
  Did mother give start ?
Oh, hush thee, my darling,
  Lie close to my heart.

I'll hope for thy father,
 I will not think thus;
I'll trust him to One
 Will send him to us.

What ail'st thou, my baby?
 What see'st thou, out there?
'Tis only the storm-clouds
 At which thou dost stare.

'Tis naught but their shadow,
 That flits by so fast;
But heed it not, baby,
 'Tis past, dear, 'tis past.

Turn this way thy face, babe,
 Turn close to my breast;
'Tis nothing thou look'st at,
 Oh, rest thee, babe, rest!

'Tis I have disturbed thee
 With fanciful fears,
'Tis mother has wak'd thee
 With fast-falling tears.

Now still thee, babe, still thee,
 'Tis *not* father's wraith;
Oh, gaze not about thee.
 He's not come to scath.

I will not believe it,
 I will not e'en think
The horrible fancies
 That make my heart shrink,

I'll pray for thy father,
I'll fervently pray ;
Now, close thine eyes, baby,
'Tis nothing, I say.

But, hark! There *is* something!
A footstep—hark, hark!
A swift-coming footstep,
I hear through the dark.

Joy, joy! It is Willie!
'Tis no one but he!
I know it is Willie
That thus claspeth me.

Thou'rt come to me, Willie,
Thou'rt come from the sea ;
Thou'rt come to thy baby,
Thou'rt come, love, to me!

Oh, welcome, my Willie,
Oh, welcome from sea ;
Oh, welcome to baby,
Oh, welcome to me!

ENGLAND.

(SET TO MUSIC BY J. L. HATTON.)

England, O England! dear land of our birth,
　Land of the fair, and the brave, and the free.
England, dear England, the first of the earth!
　Some pride is forgiven us, singing of thee.

Near thee, away from thee, still 'tis the same;
　Still we must cherish thee, thrill at thy name;
Joy in thy nobleness, honour thy fame;
　Even to vaunt of thee, are we to blame?

England, O England, belov'd native land!
　Land of the generously helpful and strong,
Sing we thy praises in brotherly band;
　Lift we our voices in heartiest song.

SPRING.

(SET AS FOUR PART-SONGS BY WALTER MACFARREN.)

A glee for jovial, happy Spring,
The season when the nightingale
In rapture doth her heart outfling,
Rejoicing every hill and dale.

With song we'll laud the jovial Spring,
As doth the voiceful nightingale;
We'll let our voices cheerful ring,
And tuneful make the woodland vale.

All glory to the jovial Spring,
The season of the nightingale;
Like her, its praises will we sing,
And greet it with a loud "All hail!"

SUMMER.

Summer, with your genial noons,
Summer, with your golden moons,
Summer, with your skies of blue,
Warmly will we welcome you!

Summer, gladd'ner of the young,
Ever be your praises sung!
Summer, banisher of cold,
Truly welcome to the old!

Summer, with your leafy bowers,
Softest showers, heaps of flowers,
Open, airy, happy hours,
We rejoice to have you ours.

AUTUMN.

Thy praises, Autumn, will we sing!
    Thou, ruddy as thy ruby wine;
Compar'd with thee, how pale the Spring!
    Thy colouring how richly fine!

Ripe golden corn and purple grape,
    With peach and apple's rosy cheek,
Combining hue with grace of shape,
    Who shall their beauties fitly speak?

The eye, the taste, thou dost rejoice;
    To love thee, Autumn, who can fail?
Then let us pledge thee, heart and voice,
    In loving cup, thine own bright ale.

WINTER.

Winter hath its merits too;
Never think that they are few;
Winter hath its blazing fires;
Right good cheer at hearths of sires.

Winter hath its frosty stars;
While, within, its household Lars
Shine with tenfold sparkling light
Near the holly, glossy bright.

Sing we then the Winter cold,
Sturdy, vigorous, and bold;
Winter sing, with all our might;
Have we not his Christmas night?

THE FAIRY GHOST.

(WRITTEN FOR A YOUNG GIRL'S ALBUM.)

The sky had been aflame with burning gold ;
Down sank the sun, with crimson splendours
crown'd ;
As deepen'd the cerulean into blue
Of darker, fuller depth, out shone the stars,
Revealing their glad eyes ; then rose the moon,
In radiance pure, filling the vast serene
With universal glow of mellowness,
Benignity, and soft pervading light :
What time Aurelia—tempted forth alone
T' enjoy the middle summer's lovely night
In quiet musings, open-air'd and free,
Betook her to a wood, which legends said
Of yore was haunted by the fays and elves ;
And where they held their wonted revelry
Of song and roundel in quaint circling maze ;
Frisking and darting thro' the bladed grass ;
Now wafted floating, o'er the rushy pool ;
Now pendent, flaunting from some bloomy spray ;
Just swinging lazily, by zephyr's breath
Mov'd to and fro in idle lightsome play ;
Anon all eagerness and busy work,
Rifling the sweets from musk-buds or the cups
Of bean-flowers, lime-blossoms, the stor'd wealth
Of jasmine, eglantine, and thymy banks
Where fragrant sweeps of scent in clouds arise,
Lulling and swelling, lingering in their fall,
Expanding in their soar, like music-strains

Charming the sense with alternated flush
Of upborne richness, or subsiding down
To dwell in latent still-returning flow
Of perfum'd freshness, or melodious sound.
Aurelia mus'd of those small fairy folk,
Their sportive graces, deeds, and airy ways,
Their frolics, gambols, mirthful antics, wiles,
Their freaks of mischief, innocent in fun,
Too playful to be fraught with any harm,
And griev'd to think their reign should be no more;
She felt regret that reason and belief
Taught her no longer to expect the sight
Of elfin troops, of Oberon the king,
Of bright Titania, and the tricksome Puck;
For " gone were all that merry band "; so wrote,
At least, a poet sage who doubtless knew
The truth ; and sinking down upon a bank,
With half-heav'd sigh, Aurelia paus'd to rest,
And ponder, and deplore the bygone race
Who peopled bravely the green forests old,
Adorning them with shapes of beauty rare,
Of fancy strange and fair, of fashion quaint,
Of hue most brilliant, dainty in device,
Of form the gracefullest—nimble, merry sprites,
Emphatically nam'd " the good "; and good
In fact they were, if not of purpose good ;
For they gave rise to good, in happy thoughts,
Ideas of mirth and sprightliness, and all
The train of cheerful imagery born
Of such believ'd existences :   And so
Aurelia deemed; and so regretful sat,
With eyes bedimm'd by dewy trembling tears
That seem'd prepar'd to fall and weep the loss
Of Fairies and their kind : until a sound,
Scarce loud enough to start a little mouse,

A lizard, or quick-neckèd watchful bird,
Light fell upon the ear of her who lay
Reclining on the bank in museful mood,
With brush or rustle such as falling leaf
Might cause upon a heap of leaves below.
  Aurelia turn'd her head, and was aware
Of something pois'd upon a pliant branch
Of briony that flung its garland length
Beside Aurelia's seat: the something seem'd
A figure small; of undefinèd shape;
Of shadowy indistinctness; yet as if
Compos'd of sheeny substance, silv'ry grey;
As though a filmy gossamer, that spreads
Its bright-weav'd threads across the summer fields,
Had wrought a garment to enwrap the form
That rested on the wreath of briony.
Aurelia gaz'd: and studied to discern
Aright the tiny being perch'd so near:
Yes, there it stood; dim, faint, but surely there;
A slender, misty, insubstantial thing,
But still an atom visible—a point
Whereon to concentrate the sight, and make
It feel assur'd it sees; and still, the more
She look'd, the more she knew she saw a thing
Slight, silver-hu'd, minute—a flitting shade—
Like greyish flue, or down of cygnet stirr'd
By sudden puff of air. Wistful its glance:
And then the maid bethought, how she had heard
That beings unearthly wait till first accost
From mortals come; and thus she strove to break
The spell of silence brooding o'er the wood,
Which held her beating heart in mute surmise.
With aw'd and breathless lips Aurelia said:
" What art thou, shadowy slender thing? From
  whence?

What wouldst ? Art thou indeed a form ? Or but
A fantasy, a wandering whim of brain,
That night and forest-glooms do paint on air,
Embodied only from the woof of thought ? "
At last it spoke ; and answer'd with a voice
Thin and attenuate, like whisp'ring reeds :
" Aurelia, human maiden, list to me ;
To those who mourn our race with ruth sincere,
It given is, at seasons rare and seld,
To see our forms appear—but ghostly now,
And all amort, bedwindl'd to a shade,
As I am : yet, grieve not ; though dead and gone,
We fairies still survive in other sphere ;
We still our dance and roundelay pursue ;
Still do we our pranksome feats enact ;
Still gambol merry in the forest glade ;
Still chase each other in the moonshine bright ;
Still frolic on the smooth brown sea-beach sands ;
Still, rainbow-rob'd, and clad in brightest tints,
We filch the honey-drops from op'ning flow'rs ;
But, as I said, 'tis in another sphere—
The poets' line ; there is our boundless realm,
Our endless reign, our never-dying life ;
Endue your sight with pow'r of vision strong
Deriv'd from them ; through them acquire the light
To rightly see our shapes ; instinct with fine
And vital beauty, then shall you behold
Us once again disporting in the woods
And fields as we were wont in times of yore
And not alone the fairy race and tribe
Of elves shall mortal eyesight still behold ;
The fauns, the dryads, and the sylvan gods,
The naiads, nereids, river deities,
The sea-born populace with sounding conchs,
And shrill-blown shells, and onward-rolling cars

O'er em'rald waves translucent with the shine
Of beamy rays from rising orient sun,
Cast slanting 'thwart the waters from some ridge
Of mountain-top that beetles o'er the main ;
All these shall once more rise to view for those
Who look with eyes that borrow keener sight
From poesy.   Study, then, its visual lore,
Its wisdom ocular, its guiding hints
To clear perceive in beauteous vivid trace
Things past and gone and dead to common eyes :
Learn thence, Aurelia, to behold us still ;
And mourn no more for what was erst our life :
We're living yet—in an immortal way—
To bless the sight poetically wrought :
Adieu !   Farewell, ye fairy-loving maid ! "
Another moment, and the voice had ceas'd ;
Another yet, and vanish'd was the tuft
Of silver film-clad flue from off the branch.
Aurelia rose, and thoughtfully retrac'd
Her steps tow'rd home ; and calmly slept that night.

THE EVENTFUL LIFE OF A BOY:

RECOUNTED BY HIMSELF IN FIVE STANZAS.

There was a time I cannot well remember ;
But I was born the middle of November :
My favourite food was chiefly milk and pap,
My usual seat was on my nurse's lap.
          'Twas when I was a baby boy.

There was a time when I was sent to school,
And though no genius, certainly no fool ;
I learnt by rote the whole of Eton grammar,
And through Cornelius Nepos I could hammer.
          'Twas when I was a biggish boy.

There was a time I went into the Army ;
The cannon balls flew round, but didn't harm me :
I winged a fellow in a duel once,
Who had the impudence to call me dunce.
          'Twas when I was a grown-up boy.

There came a time when I was still a beau,
And still could take my ride in Rotten Row ;
The ladies gave me still a favouring glance,
But didn't quite so often with me dance.
          'Twas when I was an oldish boy.

And now there comes a time when games of whist
Are all the battles won by my own fist ;
Yet even over those—'tis very odd—
I often find myself inclined to nod.
          Ah, well ! I'm now a worn-out boy.

ANSWER TO TWENTY QUESTIONS.

A trusting Patience is the virtue that I covet ;
It helps us bravely thro' Life's trials, and I love it ;
That "Time's the nurse and breeder of all good,"
    I've heard,
And as a motto I esteem it a good word.
The Rose, among the flowers, is my favourite :
The Oak, above all trees, doth most my fancy hit :
Grace Darling's noble courage gives her foremost
    place,
While Louis Nap. I hold the basest of the base.
My favourite diversion's reading pleasant books ;
And writing suits me best—I mean my own pot-
    hooks ;
I'm fond of needlework, but darning I detest ;
Of weaknesses, I own, I like the least the best.
Each season, in its turn, delights me most,
Since Spring and Summer, Autumn, even Winter,
    boast
The myriad charms of gracious Nature's bounteous
    hand,
And all as marvels of her endless power stand.
Of works of art I most prefer the most artistic ;
And violet's the hue that makes me eulogistic :
Motelli is the sculptor that straight won my heart
By group of " Paolo and Francesca"—true high art.
'Tis difficult to choose one painter 'bove the rest ;
But, perhaps, Murillo, altogether, I love best.
There's not a doubt that Shakespeare is my sove-
    reign poet :
I trust my faithful long devotion serves to show it.

Orlando is a hero greatly to my mind,
And worthy of his charming lady, Rosalind ;
While Imogen of heroines is surely queen,
So rich in woman's highest qualities she's seen.
Dear children more than please, they give me great
    delight ;
And I could wish to have them ever in my sight ;
With all their pretty looks, and all their winning
    ways,
They keep me always young, and lengthen out my
    days.
Of dark and bright—I shun the first and seek the
    last ;
Endeavouring a hopeful eye on all to cast.
The only solitude I like is that of two ;
The sociality I like is that of few.
I'm but responsive when I'm asked to give reply ;
And never give suggestions save when friends
    apply
For my advice : and as to whether I admire
An "animated No ;" why, yes, when I require
To give a most decided negative at once
In answer to a bore, a torment, or a dunce.
Now—not to keep you any longer in the dark—
I'll sign my name instanter, Mary Cowden Clarke.

WEDDING SONG.

Come, lovely June! Bring summer skies,
With cloudless blue benignant eyes,
To smile on Annie's Wedding-Day.

Come, lovely June, of blooming hue!
Bring roses freshly gemm'd with dew,
To deck sweet Annie's Wedding-Day.

Come, lovely June, thou month of joy!
Bring happiness without alloy,
To bless dear Annie's Wedding-Day.

AMY'S WEDDING-DAY.

Our Amy is to be a wife:
        How can we part with her?
She's portion of our daily life:
        We cannot part with her.

Our Amy's been our great delight:
        How shall we part with her?
She's been our cheer, our joy, our light:
        We will not part with her.

Yet Amy fain would be a wife,
        If we would part with her:
Shall we make sad her bright young life?
        We ought to part with her.

She still may form our great delight;
        We hardly part with her:
She still may cheer us with her light;
        We need not part with her.

Though Amy now becomes a wife,
        We shall not part with her:
She'll gladden still our daily life,
        We do not part with her.

Remember how we love her look:
        Don't make us part with her!
Oh, " think of that, good Master Brooke!"
        Don't let us part with her!

If she by marriage us forsook,
          Alas, to part with her!
We couldn't brook it, Master Brooke:
          We would not part with her.

. But, once our Amy's Mistress Brooke
          She'll be with you and us:
She'll ne'er forsake her parent nook;
          You *both* will be with us!

BIRTHDAY SONG.

DECEMBER 15, 1876.

Huzza for Eighty-nine!
An age so rare and fine,
When health and peace combine,
Is Heaven's gift divine.

What need is there of wine
To honour Eighty-nine?
Outpouring love is fine
Beyond the juice of vine!

With tapers seventeen
The cake is crown'd, I ween
With eight, for decades, green.
Nine white, for years, between.

A health to Uncle Charley!
To darling Uncle Charley!
May blessings be in store
For him for evermore!

A smile where'er he moves,
A kiss for all he loves,
He's loved by nephews, nieces,
With love that ne'er decreases.

The partner of his life,
His glad and happy wife,
Thus hails her Eighty-nine,
And proudly calls him " Mine! "

Additional Stanzas written next day.

To greet Charles Cowden Clarke
  On reaching Eighty-nine,
Come letters of high mark
  From friends in endless line.

From friends in England dear,
From distant friends and near,
They all one way incline,
Saluting Eighty-nine.

"God bless thee, dear old friend! '
'Tis thus they mostly end—
"God bless thee, Eighty-nine!
May happiness be thine!"

Old Time, with hand benign,
Has touch'd thee with his sign,
And made thee Eighty-nine
With gentleness condign.

    P.S.

To all, thus answers Eighty-nine:
"God bless you, dear ones mine!
May all who reach my years
Rejoice like me, my dears!"

THE 20TH OF JUNE, 1875.

These birthday lines are fondly penned
In hope that they will not offend,
Or even chance to weary her,
My darling niece, Valeria!

A cockney rhyme, it must be owned,
This *r* and *a* together toned;
But p'rhaps it may not weary her,
My darling niece, Valeria!

So partial to her Aunty she,
I hardly fear she'll censure me,
She will not let it weary her,
My charming niece, Valeria!

She'll make the best of aught I do.
She always does—that's nothing new!
She will not think I weary her,
My darling niece, Valeria!

And so I'll prose on farther still;
To prose in verse cannot be ill
Adapted to unweary her,
My darling niece, Valeria!

I wonder whether *yet* she's tired!
These lines must surely be admired!
There's nothing here *can* weary her,
My charming niece, Valeria!

So full of spirit and good sense,
Their merit ought to be immense ;
They cannot, cannot weary her,
My charming niece, Valeria !

No one can call them " very dull "
('Tis only slang that says " a mull ") ;
Impossible they weary her,
My charming niece, Valeria !

In fact, she'll find them full of fire,
Apollo's self might be their sire,
How can they then a-weary her,
My darling niece, Valeria ?

She's much too clever her own self
To put them by upon the shelf,
And frankly say they weary her,
My charming niece, Valeria !

She is so wise and witty both
That really I should be quite loth
To fancy they *could* weary her,
My charming niece, Valeria !

And since she hath both wisdom, wit,
That both are here she will admit,
And not allow I weary her,
My charming niece, Valeria !

Ill-natured folk might call this stuff,
And tell me I have penned enough
To thoroughly outweary her,
My charming niece, Valeria !

If such should be the case, suppose
I change the metre at the close
That that at least mayn't weary her,
My darling niece, Valeria !

If I could think my verse would weary her,
I would not write this to Valeria ;
But as I fancy it may cheery her,
I'll send this greeting to Valeria.

My heart with birthday wishes for her burns :
God bless my dear-loved niece, Valeria !
And send her many happy glad returns
Of this sweet day of June, Valeria !

HUMAN ENDEAVOUR.

Imperfect is the best that we can do;
Yet do our best our duty is to do,
Put all our heart in it with fervour true,
Just do our best and leave the rest to God.

Some trifling oversight in our own deed,
Or others misconducting doth mislead,
Producing imperfection's evil seed;
Still, do our best and leave the rest to God.

Ay, after all our carefullest attempt
And pains to make it from all faults exempt,
It brings us naught but scornfullest contempt;
Still, do our best, and leave the rest to God.

For, if we do our best, e'en though we fail,
Though in the sight of man 'tis no avail,
Yet in the sight of God it will prevail;
He knows we've done our best with faith in Him.

SYLVAN SINGERS.

At morn the soaring Skylark fills the air
With thrilling outpour of his hymnal rare :
Soft cooing in the wood, the whole day through,
The Dove croons low, so constant and so true.

At eve, the Blackbird's full and fluty note
Amid the stillness welcomely doth float :
When stars illume the copse with sparkling ray,
The Nightingale trills forth his tender lay.

In Spring, the Cuckoo and the sprightly Thrush
Make musical each leafy tree and bush :
In Summer, all the warblers seek the shade,
And chant their choral strains in forest glade,

In Autumn, fewest singing birds we hear,
This else abundant season of the year :
In Winter, Robin Redbreast in the croft
Sits carolling his notelets shrilly soft.

NOT YET.

I asked her when we should be wed,
  Besought her name an early day,
I knew no rest till then, I said :
  Her blushing cheek was turned away ;
    " Not yet," she softly said, " Not yet."

I asked her should I go to sea,
  And try if absence gave me rest :
She glanc'd up suddenly at me,
  Then hid her face upon my breast :
    " Not yet," she softly said, " Not yet."

Again I asked, " When shall it be
  You'll make me yours for evermore ?
When will you give yourself to me ? "
  She looked at me as ne'er before,
    And softly said, " Whene'er you will."

JUST THEN.

A HONEYMOON SONG.

Upon the grass, beneath a tree,
  My love and I sat happily ;
My cheek to hers drew near, more near,
I whispered something in her ear.
    Just then, a little bird began to sing.

Our honeymoon, beneath that tree,
  My love and I spent merrily ;
I told her she was not *amiss*,
And gave her many a laughing kiss.
    Just then, a ringdove coo'd above our heads.

Of married life, beneath that tree,
  My love and I talked cheerily ;
We counted endless joys to share,
And hoped for little cause of care,
    Just then, a raven flew across the path.

Up through the boughs of the old tree,
  My love and I looked trustfully ;
We gazed into the clear blue sky,
And thought of Him who dwells on high.
    Just then, the sun shone forth in glory bright.

MY VIOLET.

My love's a modest violet,
  Her eyes as blue, herself as sweet :
Oh, green the lane where first I met
My dainty woodland violet.

So timid is my violet,
  She still looks shyly when we meet ;
Though now I many times have met
My shrinking gentle violet.

So charming is my violet,
  She is my dearest, deepest joy ;
I fain would in my bosom set
My fragrant lovely violet.

But so reserved is violet,
  So bashful, maidenly, and coy,
I dare not whisper to her yet,
"I wish for wife my violet."

TRUE LOVE; OR, WOOING IN THE WOOD.

" Roo-coo, roo-coo," cooed dove to dove,
Among the leafy boughs above :
" Oh, love me true," said my true love,
        " Do love me true ! "

" I do, my Prue ; whom should I love
If 'tis not you, who are above
In love and truth the very dove ?
        I love you true."

Thus loves and doves each other wooed ;
And, musically mutual, cooed ;
Warmed 'mid the coolness of the wood,
        With love so true.

Our poet says, " 'Tis silly sooth " ;
In other words, " 'Tis simple truth " ;
Then who but feels some tender ruth
        For love when true ?

HOME KINDNESS.

What with kindness can compare?
Yet, alas, too often rare!
    Bluffly, thoughtlessly, withheld.

Angry thought and sudden wrath
Turn aside their bitter scath,
    Met by kindly spoken word.

Gentle glance, or mute caress,
Hand's soft reassuring press,
    Well sustain the fainting soul.

One kind word from those we love
Courage gives us far above
    Highest praise from others' mouth.

One kind look from those we love
Comfort gives us far above
    Loudest sympathy express'd.

Spare not, then, kind word or look,
Ye who live in Home's sweet nook!
    Balm and healing kindness brings.

Loving-kindness cures all ills;
Helps to cure, at least, and stills
    Aching hearts till strength they gain.

Chiefly, always bear in mind,
Let not one alone be kind,
  Mutual be forbearing love.

Patience, tenderness, and truth,
To each other shown, good sooth,
  Make of Home a Heaven on earth.

TO NERINA GIGLIUCCI.

Thy mother's crispy curls of jet,
Thy mother's eyes' dark brilliancy
Are mirror'd faithfully in thee,
    O rightly named Nerina !

Thy mother's title fondly given
In pleasant courtship days bygone
Is made for thee, sweet little one,
    O rightly named Nerina !

Thy father, when he calls thee thus
Will think of her whom thus he styled,
And love thee doubly well, dear child,
    O rightly named Nerina !

A maiden whom I called " Black Pearl "
Thy mother, darling babe, is now :
A pearl is she, a pearl art thou,
    O rightly named Nerina !

May Heaven appoint thy fate to be
Of diamond brightness, pearly clear !
And nothing black be thine, my dear,
    Except thy name, Nerina !

MADRIGAL.

My heart is stol'n away
By Love, sly rogue, at play.
  The theft I would forgive
  If for it he would give
Fair Chloe's heart to me
For ever mine to be.

MADRIGAL.

Why do I love my own true love?
  Because he's true as true can be:
Why does my own true love love me?
  Because I'm true, as true as he.

We to each other are so true,
  There's naught our two hearts may divide;
Lose what we may of worth beside,
  True love with us will aye abide.

MADRIGAL.

Alas, there's much amiss with me,
I am not as I used to be;
    With a fal lal la, heigh-ho!

Alas, my Phœbe's cold to me,
Most cruel and perverse is she;
    With a fal lal la, heigh-ho

She will not give her heart to me,
And says so with a mocking glee:
    With a fal lal la, heigh-ho!

The little gipsy cozens me,
She stole my heart yet keeps hers free;
    With a fal lal la, heigh-ho!

Alas, alas, this, this is why
I mope about and sadly sigh;
    With a fal lal la, heigh-ho!

GLEE.

A rustic little cot
Has fallen to our lot;
But in it love abides,
Worth all the world besides.

A simple home is ours;
But nested in by flowers,
And snugly holds us three—
My wife, and love, and me.

GLEE.

Keep your heart up bravely, boys !
Treat all trifles as but toys :
  When there comes a serious sorrow,
  Think a joy may come to-morrow.

Keep your heart up bravely, boys !
Weigh your sorrows with your joys :
  Though affliction's sometimes sent,
  Happiness is often lent.

Keep your heart up bravely, then !
Be prepared for all, like men :
  Bear whatever comes amiss,
  Gratefully enjoy your bliss.

SONG.

He gave me a fairing, that time ;
'Twas under the boughs of the lime :
  It chanced there was nobody by,
  Or maybe I might have felt shy :
    For something he gave me besides,
    And what should it be but a kiss ?

Full many a sweet thing he said,
When asking my promise to wed :
  I gave it him under the tree—
  'Twas well there was no one to see ;
    For something I gave him besides,
    And what should it be but a kiss ?

GIFTS.

A gift my love has given me;
Now pr'ythee guess what it can be :
 A dainty little posy neat,
 That looks so gay and smells so sweet.

Another gift he's given to me;
Now pr'ythee guess what it can be :
 A tender little cooing dove,
 That tells me of his perfect love.

A priceless gift he's given to me;
Now pr'ythee guess what it can be :'
 A little bright gold wedding ring,
 To me the very dearest thing.

FAITHFUL.

Oh, love me still, as I love thee,
  Though thou art gone, and I remain :
We cannot wholly be apart,
If we are faithful, heart to heart.
        Oh, love me still, as I love thee:
        I'm happy yet, if thou lov'st me.

Though we are sunder'd for a while,
  Our spirits can together be :
If faithfully we trust and love,
Eternal union's ours above.
        Then love me still, as I love thee :
        We're happy yet, if faithful we.

ACROSTIC.

A woman beautifully clear and bright,
M ade up of Nature's harmonies aright ;
E ndow'd with intellect and fine good sense :
L ive diamonds her eyes, with flash intense
I llumining her vivid speaking face,
A nd showing outwardly her inward grace.

THE STARS BEYOND THE CLOUD.

(FIRST AND TWO LAST STANZAS SET TO MUSIC BY
BERTHOLD TOURS.)

When dark the sky and louring all around
The night is gathering in 'mid threaten'd storm,
 When far from home we wander on in dread,
 Or anxious vigils keep on sleepless bed,
We still can firmly bid our fainting souls :
"Take heart! The stars are there beyond the cloud."

When faith is shaken in all human truth,
Most men seem false and women fickle prove,
 When trust in worth appears a folly weak,
 And we in vain for earthly comfort seek,
We still can whisper to our aching souls :
" Take heart ! the stars are there beyond the cloud."

When evil for a time rides rampantly,
Injustice reigns and innocence succumbs,
 When blind and wilful error gains apace,
 And virtue to prevailing vice gives place,
We refuge take in whispering to our souls :
"Wait, wait ! The stars are there beyond the cloud.

When mystery envelopes seeming wrong,
Mistake and calumny environ right,
 When purity's belied and merit veil'd,
 Unkindly judged or cruelly assail'd,
We patience gather, whispering to our souls :
" Await ! the stars are there beyond the cloud."

When, sore perplex'd, we cannot understand
The ways of God to man, and wondering see
   The wicked thrive and villainy succeed,
   The lilies droop, and flourishing the weed,
We can but whisper to our puzzled souls :
" Be sure, the stars are there beyond the cloud."

When, helpless, we behold the sobbing child
Or gentle age by illness stricken down,
   When near the bed of suffering we remain
   Unable to alleviate the pain,
Relief is in the simple thought our souls
Breathe low: "The stars are there beyond the
cloud."

When bowed beneath the load of care we sink,
And feel as crushed by burdens we must bear,
   When almost ceasing effort to be strong,
   And ready to exclaim "I've borne too long ! "
Then, brave, yet meek, we whisper to our souls :
" Look up ! the stars are there beyond the cloud."

When deep discouragement and self-distrust
Give way to hope and peaceful calm,
   When mists of earth grow clear, more clear,
   And light of Heaven draws near, more near,
Revivingly we bid our upraised souls :
" Behold ! the stars are there beyond the cloud,"

When life is fading from our feeble ken,
And scarce regretfully we watch it fade,
   So empty and bereft the world has grown
   Of those we best have loved and best have known,
'Tis then we gladly bid our trusting souls :
" Rejoice ! the stars are there beyond the cloud."

BODY AND SOUL.

The roses on thy grave are now breast high :
Keen as their thorns the thought that thou dost lie
Beneath, instead of in mine arms—and yet—
Thy spirit, like the fragrance of the rose,
Within my heart doth evermore repose.

VISIONS.

In bliss with God, with those we've loved and lost,
With universal Nature and her laws
All fully understood, is what my soul
Delights to picture thee, my own beloved,
Since now thou'rt gone from earth and art thyself
A spirit bless'd among th' immortal host!
Oh, dost thou, in thy new and higher life,
Still think of me as with thee, part of thee,
The half of thine own self, as when thou wast
Beside me here? I feel, I know, thou dost:
God puts assurance of it in my heart,
And makes me calm in the belief that now
Thou know'st the depth and truth of all my love
For thee: which, when thou wert but human like
Myself, thou could'st not fully know. The star,
Thy favourite of all the heavenly train,
Bright Sirius—now nightly visible,
Aglow with diamond sparkles red and green,
Intensest sudden darts of light, that shoot
Athwart the firmament to where I stand—
Seems sending vivid warranties of love
Undying, felt by thee for me, and felt
By thee from me. I watch with avid eye
These throbs scintillant, take them into my
Dejected heart, that beats responsive throbs,
And swells with upward yearning toward thee in
Thy blue abode serene, my Charles, my Charles!

"*ALL THOSE WE LOVE!*"

" All those we love!" my Father's fav'rite toast :
To them we drink, of them we think, when most
  Our souls are tuned to kindly mirth ;
  A toast embracing those we have on earth
And those we only have in heart and Heaven.

"All those we love!" Let's sing the hallow'd toast;
Including as it does a tender host
  Of living dear ones, blessed memories ;
  A starry circle of enduring ties
That crown our joys on earth and hopes of Heaven.

MAY THIRTEEN, 1880.

To please my darling little niece,
I fain would write a birthday piece—
Some merry, quaint, amusing verse:
And therefore I must first rehearse
The various freakish forms of rhyme
That suit to make harmonious chime
With both her pretty Christian names,
That might become the highest dames.

A Queen and Princess bear them now;
And certainly, we all know how
Distinguished those two ladies are!
Of course, I don't put on a par
With them my own grandniece for rank;
But setting rank aside, I thank
My stars she's not a whit less good,
Less dear to me; and they too would,
I know, be first to quite agree
With what I say, and think with me
That very good and very dear
She is; for that's a fact most clear.

Well, let's return to the main thing—
The anniversary that we sing,
The birthday which we celebrate
This month of May, the thirteenth date,
When seven years old my niece will be;
And many more, I trust, she'll see!

Now, shall I style her Beatrice
(The English way), and with a kiss
Invoke all blessings on her head?
Or (in Italian fashion said)
Pronounce her name as Beatrice,
And pat her cheek so fair, so peachy?

Or what if I should chance to fix }
On that rare form of Beatrix }
Implying that she's full of tricks ? }
Nay, p'rhaps it would be rather nice,
For fun, to call her Beatrice :
But then, I fear, Papa would wince,
And fancy I'd gone crazy, since
No person ever sounds it so
Except an ignoramus low.
   At one time, I have heard, they thought
Of calling her—it came to naught—
By her first name, Vittoria ;
Which would have been a glory, a
Remembrance of the lady-friend
Of Michael Angelo, and send
Our thoughts to fair Colonna's worth ;
Whose nobleness was less of birth
Than goodness, virtue, intellect.
Still, I am glad they did elect
To keep the title, Beatrice :
'Twould have been difficult to teach me
Use any other name than that
By which I knew her when she sat
A baby on my knee ; besides,
It well befits her, who resides
For most part on Italian land,
The land her ancestors had hand
In rendering illustrious,
Renowned, potential, glorious,
   Then here's to darling Beatrice !
Oh, may she live to gladly reach the
Extremest term of good old age ;
And be through life a happy sage,
Have cheerful wisdom, kindly ways,
And fond affection all her days !

A RIDDLE.

WRITTEN FOR BEATRICE ON HER SEVENTH BIRTHDAY.

My first is a second, by usual rule ;
My second's a first, recited at school ;
My third is a third, if an h you take ;
My whole is a darling, and no mistake.

TO MORICO GIGLIUCCI.

Dear new-born Lily-bud, oh, may'st thou prove
As branch of olive in the mouth of dove,
To herald lasting peace and joy and love
For parent stem ! Oh, may it be thy fate
To gloriously still perpetuate
The Lily name thou bear'st,* and renovate
With later honours all its old renown !
For this, sweet Lily-blossom, freshly blown,
We trust thou'rt sent by Heav'n our hopes to crown !
We hail thee gladly, gratefully, on earth ;
We hail thee at the moment of thy birth ;
We hail thee as our cherish'd flower of worth :
Oh, may'st thou live a life of noble deeds !
A life that scatters none but wholesome seeds,
And brings its own reward of happy meeds.

---

* The name " Gigliucci " is Italian for " little lilies."

TO MISS GUSCHL.

Dear Barbara, thy fingers fleet and fine,
That skim the keys like sea-bird hovering,
Light pois'd and air-borne on the level wing,
Pour out their music, touch'd with gift divine,
In memory's echo, to this brain of mine;
  And visionary strains they often sing
  Melodiously within me, murmuring
A faint delicious descant, soft, benign.
Endowments such as thine have double power:
  To charm the senses with their present spell;
  And soothe, when absent, with remember'd knell
Of sounds that lived in richly plenteous shower,
  Struck by the hand of masterfullest skill;
  Now sweet and low, now strong and firm as will.

TO MISS THORMANN.

Lady, from thy great kinsman, Mendelssohn,
  Thou dost derive a hand that grandly gives
  Its largess musical with a grace that lives,
In bounteous freedom, fulness, wealth of tone,
On listener's ear: gift that belongs alone
  To those whom Nature perfectly achieves,
  Bestowing on them choicest donatives—
Virtue, intellect, and genius, all in one.
'Tis privilege to hear the spirit rare
  Of masterful composer thus transfused
  Through living fingers admirably used
To rendering his works with nicest care:
  And so felicitously dost thou play his strain,
  That in thy felicity Felix lives again.

TO MRS. GREENAWAY.

Rose, my dear friend, whose modesty will shrink,
   I know, to find yourself addressed in verse;
   And wonder that some subject really worse
Had not been ta'en ; and diffidently think
Yourself the worst ; unless indeed love wink,
   As Shakespeare says it can (with eyes perverse)
   On homely object—as on negro nurse
A fair child smiles, when it to rest doth sink.
But you, dear Rose, need no such partial sight :
   The clearest and most candid mind can see
   Virtues to love and to revere in thee ;
A judgment true; unerring aim for right ;
   A constant loving heart ; unselfish views ;
   Worthy of better than thy friend's poor muse.

ON BARON POERIO.

Oft have I lain awake, and thought on one
   Whose night was made of days and years struck dark
   By tyrant's will : yet, latent, lurk'd a spark
No dungeon's damp could quench ; it bravely won
Self-light, self-glow, 'neath miseries would stun
   A less divinely kindred spirit : nor cark
   Nor care extinguish'd Hope ; like morning lark
Upborne by wings that shimmer in the sun,
It ever strove and strove to rise and rise,
And keep its heav'nward course, and reach the skies,
   There to derive new strength, new life, new fire.
   Now it flames free, a grand and lofty pyre,
As beacon to the world—that Hope of soul
Is far beyond a despot's brute control.

TO MRS. FREDERIC INMAN.

Mariel mine, that you chose me for friend,
  Despite my doubling your young years in age,
  Doth swell my heart with joy, and doth engage
A kind of modest pride which will attend
The thought of being loved for no one end
  But pure responsive liking ; appanage
  That rightfully belongs, as well-earned wage,
To true spontaneous love.   Thereon depend
A thousand grateful feelings ; therefrom spring
  A host of mutual sympathies, a world
  Of tastes reciprocal, held closely furled
In inmost heart for lavishment and sharing
  With her whose impulse has allied us both
  In happy, trustful, loving friendship-troth.

TO MISS PICKERING.

Dear Lucy, who, like Shakespeare's good old king,
  Hast ever " borne thy faculties so meek "—
Vers'd as thou art in Latin and in Greek,
Acquainted, too, with many another thing
Into a woman's province entering—
  It sets one's reason all abroad to seek
  The cause why you, with frame so fragile weak,
Should be so strong to master hard learning.
  The winged insect, that too rude a brush
  Deprives of life with instantaneous crush,
Hath learn'd to build his dainty waxen cell
Up-garnering the golden honey well :
  Fragility with high ability
  Can co-exist in strange affinity.

TO CECILIA SERLE.

Cecilia, younger sister mine, to you
  Who played Molière's "old woman" for me
  when
The years of neither reached six more than ten,
And bade me venture on the pathway new
Of authorship with such crude lines and few
  As I had tremblingly attempted then—
  Encouraging the efforts of my pen ;
To you especially a verse is due.
In gratitude I send you this poor sonnet :
  Receive it with the same indulgent scan
  You always gave to writing or to plan;
To essay, story, or to new-made bonnet
  Your elder sister's hand had tried to frame,
  Secure her young "old woman" ne'er would blame.

TO EMMA NOVELLO.

My sister Emma, most of all art thou
  Associate in my thought with him we lost;
  Dear Edward! whose bright promis'd path was
    cross'd
By Death's cold shadow: I remember how
'Twas you were always his companion most
  Preferr'd, while at the easel he'd endow
  With colour'd life the paintings we have now—
Surviv'd to form his glory and our boast.
'Twas you imbibed our brother's taste for Art—
  Adopting it, for his sake, as your own—
  When at his side you sat, and, studious grown,
Laid by the idler and the merrier part
  You played so long as mirth beguiled his hours,
  To gain a kindred portion of his powers.

TO CLARA GIGLIUCCI.

Clara, my sister, whose enchanting voice
　　Hath might to send out notes like soaring lark ;
　　Or vibrant sounds flung forth as at a mark,
Hurled like Discobolean throw of quoits ;
Plaintive or gay, severe or blithe, at choice ;
　　Next veiled in gloom, then bright as stricken
　　　　spark ;
　　But ever summoning the soul to hark
With thrilling ear—to hearken and rejoice
In that full stream of potent utterance
　　Which pours its liquid, pure, melodious flow,
　　Making each hearer's bosom throb and glow
Entranced ; now mournful, now in gladsome dance,
　　Now awe-struck at thy holy tones and strong ;
　　Anon uproused by Jacobitish song.

TO SABILLA NOVELLO.

Sabilla, youngest of my sisters four,
　　In you are blended gifts that well combine
　　Those that elsewhere conspicuously shine:
Cecilia's judgment ; Emma's pencil (more
Left-handed, you will say, than hers) ; a store
　　Of Clara's monarch tone and powers fine
　　In music ; skill to read the native line
Of Dante's, Goethe's, and Cervantes' lore,
Besides Molière's vivacious repartee ;
　　Accomplished, too, in language of your own—
　　Gay raillery, and sportive fancy shown
Whene'er occasion yields a playful plea
　　For manifesting wit, that ne'er out-bounds
　　The lady's tact to hit, yet give no wounds.

TO MARY SABILLA SERLE.

My niece and godchild, Mary, well hast thou
  The promise of thy childhood years fulfill'd :
  Then baby tones in baby accents trill'd
That Handel-Milton song—we scarce knew how—
Of " Let me wander not unseen " ; and now
  In singing and in playing thou art skill'd
  To such degree of polish as hath fill'd
The heart of those who love thee with o'erflow
Of gladness. Long may'st thou continue thus,
  My god-daughter, to proudly gladden us ;
Like full blown beauty of the open rose,
Where perfume, colour, form, and grace disclose
  Themselves perfected—bursting from the bud
  Which held them shrin'd beneath its close green
    hood.

TO PORTIA GIGLIUCCI.

Two Shakespeare women bear my niece's name:
  The Roman's " true and honourable wife " ;
  And lady lawyer, who from Shylock's knife
Redeem'd the Venice merchant, when he came
To pay the bond the wolfish Jew did frame
  With purpose to ensnare Antonio's life.
  Both these in goodly qualities are rife ;
Both these are Portias, nobly known to fame.
Be you, my Portia—though but known to those
  Who love you in your home and round of friends—
A living type of what the poet shows
  To woman's highest exaltation tends ;
A wifely truth and love unto the death,
Refinement, sense, and feeling in one breath.

TO VALERIA GIGLIUCCI.

(IRREGULAR SONNET.)

Valeria, my niece, whose Roman birth
  Becomes thee well; thy name on Shakespeare's
    page,
Doth shine effulgent; there, from age to age,
It beams—"The moon of Rome": that all the
  earth
May witness how a woman's modest worth,
  Recorded by a poet, doth engage
  Th' admiring gaze of reverent and sage
Beholders. History itself no dearth
Of praise awards; for Plutarch nobly tells
  The story of Valeria's timely thought;
With speech of wisest counsel, which impels
  Th' appeal that saves her country, and which
    wrought
Coriolanus to relent. May thou thus act,
My darling, when the time arrives to prove the fact
I augur from thy early promise—womanhood
Complete in all things lovely, gentle, wise, and good.

TO PORTIA AND VALERIA.

Your love, you darling nieces mine, has been
  A coronal among the wreaths made mine,
  By blest vouchsafement of the Hand Divine,
In bountifully rich and rarely seen
Abundance ; wreaths that blossom and keep green
  Themselves, while casting a perennial shine
  'Upon the lives they garland and entwine—
Enhancing happiness, relieving teen.
  True love has been my best of boons through life,
With parents, brothers, sisters, valued friends,
  And sacred-happy love 'tween man and wife,
That not the very grave itself e'er ends ;
  The love 'tween child and mother has been known
  To me through you, as dear as if mine own.

ON A RING OF LEIGH HUNT'S HAIR.

Nor coal, nor jet, nor raven's wing more black
  Than this small crispy plait of ebon hair :
  And well I can remember when the rare
Young poet-head, in eager thought thrown back,
Bore just such clusters ; ere the whitening rack
  Of years and toil, devoted to the care
  For human weal, had blanch'd and given an air
Of snow-bright halo to the mass once black.
In public service, in high contemplations,
  In poesy's excitement, in the earnest
Culture of divinest aspirations,
  Thy sable curls grew grey ; and now thou turnest
Them to radiant lustre, silver-golden,
Touch'd by that Light no eye hath yet beholden.

SONNETS ON HEARING OF THE DEATH OF LEIGH HUNT.

I.

The world grows empty : fadingly and fast
   The dear ones and the great ones of my life
   Melt forth, and leave me but the shadows rife
Of those who blissful made my peopled past ;
Shadows that in their numerousness cast
   A sense of desolation, sharp as knife,
   Upon the soul ; perplexing it with strife
Against the vacancy, the void, the vast
Unfruitful desert which the earth becomes
   To one who loses thus the cherish'd friends
   Of youth. The loss of each beloved sends
An aching consciousness of want that dumbs
The voice to silence—akin to the dead blank
All things became, when down the sad heart sank.

II.

And yet not so would'st thou thyself have view'd
   Affliction ; thy true poet-soul knew how
   The sorest thwartings patiently to bow
To wisest teachings ; that they still renew'd
In thee strong hope, firm trust, a faith imbued
   With cheerful spirit—constant to avow
   The good of e'en things evil, and allow
All ills to pass with courage unsubdued.
Philosophy like thine turns to pure gold   .
   Earth's dross : imprisonment assum'd a grace,
A dignity, as borne by thee in bold
   Defence of Liberty and Right ; thy face
Reflected thy heart's sun 'mid sickness, pain,
And grief ; nay, loss itself thou mad'st a gain.

SONNETS ON GODSENDS.

I.

Straight from the hand of God comes many a gift,
  Fraught with healing and with consolation
  For a world of toil and tribulation ;
And yet from which we blindly shrink and shift,
As from a burden onerous to lift.
  Work itself, hard, drudging occupation,
  Comes in shape of blessed dispensation
To those who wisely can perceive the drift
  Of such a boon to assuage the pangs of mind,
Sadness, suspense, anxiety, or worse,
  Rankle from wounding words and looks unkind,
The desolation of friends' eyes averse,
  Nay, e'en the anguish of a recent loss,
  Akin to that was felt beneath the Cross.

II.

Work is a Godsend most divine, direct :
  The call to active duty, the stern need
  For prompt alacrity and instant deed,
Teaches the soul its forces to collect,
Assists it still to raise itself erect
  When beaten prostrate like the wind-blown reed
  By stormy flaw ; it sows the fruitful seed
Of vigorous resolves, that will protect
  And grow around fresh shoots of budding hope,
Preserving them from frost of chill despair—
  Will keep them free from canker-slough, with
    scope
For spreads of tender leaflets, and prepare
  The way for future blossoms that may twine
  A garland for the brow no more supine.

III.

All the year round come Godsends evermore,
  Manifold and multiform, like wild flowers
  In summer-time, when warmth and genial showers
Have made the lanes and meads a broider'd floor,
Rainbow-hued, bright, and deep-ingrainèd more
  Than hall for dancers' footing, where the hours
  Bring speedy blur: proudly the foxglove towers,
Behung with white or purple bells, a store
  Of pyramided beauty; faintly blush
Dwarf mallows, lilac, veined with soft threading;
  Poppies, casting their vivid scarlet flush
Athwart the golden corn; umbel-spreading
  Hemlock; meek-eyed violets, amid the rank
  Tall rampant clamberers up hedge and bank.

IV.

Not more variety in wayside weeds
  Than in the Godsends lavishly bestow'd
  On man, who takes them often like a load
Of worthless or unvalued waifs; and heeds
No jot their purpose, nor discerning reads
  Their undevelop'd good; upon the road
  He lets them lie, trod like the toad
Beneath his foot; and, thoughtless, on proceeds.
  But, like the jewel in the reptile's head,
Or like the wholesome virtues in the herb,
  Latent, unnotic'd, dully left unread,
Cast by in carelessness, or mood acerb,
  The gem-bright eyes unseen, the healthful juice
    unsought,
  The Godsend's sacred lesson still remains un-
    taught.

V.

A stormy sky, with glimpse of promise fair ;
A trial bravely borne ; a sickness gone ;
An unexpected sob from heart of stone ;
A touch of magnanimity—too rare—
In one whose candour takes you unaware ;
The luxury of weeping when alone,
What time volition lies all prone
After stout will has done its best to bear
The tension of composure hard-sustain'd
Before the eyes of others ; a child's cry,
Where loud roaring ends in laughter gained ;
A smile from sadden'd heart, you scarce know why :
These sweets distill'd from bitterness of gall,
To my thought, are no less than Godsends all.

VI.

An old expressive simple word is this
Of Godsend, just a something sent from God,
The fountain of all good : an almost odd
And quaint directness—like a given kiss ;
Familiar-holy, pure in granted bliss.
Free and offhand, perhaps, as friendly nod ;
But dear and cherish'd as the grassy sod
That lies above the head we daily miss
From out our life, making that life a kind
Of death.   As special graces, treasure Godsends !
Oh, let us grateful-hearted bear in mind
The more inobvious, as the clearer ends
For which they are vouchsaf'd to those on whom
They fall, like stars, to brighten night and gloom.

ON RECEIVING A LOCK OF MRS. MARY SOMERVILLE'S HAIR.

That head—which long among the stars hath dwelt
   In thought sublime and speculation rare,
   In scientific knowledge past compare,
In deep research and questions that have dealt
With Nature's laws to make them seen and felt—
   That head now yields this tress of still dark hair,
   At sight of which, besprent with argent fair,
Methought my touched imagination knelt.
   It looks as though, communing with the stars,
It had received some beams of silv'ry light,
Some reflex of Diana's crescent white,
   Or steel-bright rays shorn from the crest of Mars.
A gift it is from one endowed with lore divine,
And proudly, gratefully, I treasure it as mine.

ON A LOCK OF
FLORENCE NIGHTINGALE'S HAIR.

Once smooth'd away upon that gentle head
Beneath the simple cap of snowy white ;
Which mov'd, in silence of each passing night,
Around the wounded soldier's pallet-bed,
And beams of blessed helpful promise shed,
Like far-seen beacon to the aching sight
Of seamen, straining for the hopeful light
Through blinding, bruising waves, sore spent,
half dead.
The very shadow of that head benign
Was reverently kiss'd, as by it past,
And on the pillow coolness, soothing, cast ;
A sense of healing watchful care ; a sign
Of one who, sleepless in devotion pure,
Brought with her presence comfort, aid, and cure.

ON A LOCK OF HAIR FROM GARIBALDI.

That brow which lifted up its dauntless look
   In front of old abuses, errors, wrongs,
   With energy that rightfully belongs
To patriot soul; and, sternly frowning, took
Its place to quell them down, and ne'er forsook
   Its steadfast gaze, amid their hostile throngs;
   But led his "thousand," with glad shouts and
      songs,
To conquest sure, like hero in a book:
   That brow so stern and yet so tranquil calm,
Those temples, with their furrow'd lines of care,
Yet wearing still a quiet, peaceful air,
   To foes so fierce, to friends so full of balm
That head, which ne'er to tyranny hath bent,
To me this hallow'd lock of hair hath sent.

TO ALEXANDER MAIN.

I.

How can I, on the nonce, compose a sonnet?
To gratify friend Alexander Main
My muse is, most assuredly, full fain :
But if I'm not in cue to write ?   Plague on it !
If only, now, 'twere just to make a bonnet,
   I might succeed, I might to that attain ;
   That asks but thread-and-needle skill, not brain :
Yet stay, I've writ eight lines, I've almost done it !
   I'll try to end ; yet he's a judge of verse,
And I'm afraid he'll say of mine, " What stuff! "
   But, then, though it is bad, he has read worse ;
Moreover he is partial, that's enough.
   He'll see, at least, I've sought to make him smile,
   By daring this strange sonnet to compile.

II.

You see I have endeavour'd to obey
   Your complimentarily kind request ;
   At any rate, my friend, I've done my best
To make you for a moment mirthful, gay,
By sending you this piece of scribbled play,
   This hasty trifle jotted down in jest
   That I might promptly follow your behest,
And not to any wish of yours say nay.
   You wish'd me to contribute to your book ;
And feeling that I could not now succeed
   In penning aught that's good, this way I took
To prove my readiness—by double deed :
   Since quality there lacks, 'tis quantity must do ;
   You ask'd me for a sonnet, and I send you two.

CONVALESCENCE.

I.

First, gratitude to God within the soul ;
  A lulling sense of comfort, trust, repose,
  As when on parent's breast a child doth close
Its tear-gemm'd eyes : then cheeringly console
The looks and voices of dear friends whose whole
    Device is dedicate to us in those
    Sweet offices of love, abating throes
Of pain, and smoothing on to healthful goal.
  Next, come contemplative soft musing hours
Of gazing from our window on the sky,
The garden ; where, beneath, around, on high,
  Are calming sights and hues : amid the flowers
We see for younger lives the hopes of future years.
In Heaven's blue our train of loved and lost appears.

II.

Receipt of letters from our absent friends
  Sheds double brightness o'er the cheerful meal
  Of breakfast : words of sympathy that heal
Our ills, while record of their welfare sends
A thrill of animating vigour, lends
    Reflected energy and strength : we feel
    As though, through them, we still take part and deal
With active life, its interests, its ends.
  'Tis almost worth the being ill, to prove
Th' extent of all our blessings, getting well ;
They multiply around us to dispel
  Ungrateful murmurs, and to raise above
Self-pitying plaints : God's gracious gift of renova-
    tion,
Friends' love, this simple verse — thanksgiving
    aspiration.

SONNETS ON LABOUR AND LEISURE.

I.

A Greek philosopher has wisely said,
 The end of labour's leisure: be it so ;
 But first, we ought to definitely know
What's meant by leisure. Is it to be dead
To active life, to be well clothed, well fed,
 And idle sit all day? I only know
 Such ease would hardship be to me, as though
Condemn'd to pass my every hour in bed.
 But if by leisure's meant to have full time
For thinking, acting, walking, resting, all
Without the sense of pressure—*that* I call
 Blest privilege : well worth our while to climb
The steepest path, with labour's closest strain,
The height serene of Leisure Work to gain.

II.

Enforced inaction is as hard to some
 As hardest work to others : the dull weight
 Of doing nothing when the mind's elate,
Alert, and eager to fulfil the dumb
Yet urgent inward impulses that come
 In throngs, doth burdensomely grind and grate
 Upon the spirit with the stress of fate,
And hold the faculties in deadly numb.
 But strenuous exertion, at a pinch,
When needful cause exists for extra moil;
 An effort made to the extremest inch
Of possibility, or long calm toil
 Sustained with trusting patience to the end,
 Are positive enjoyments, I contend.

III.

Then, after Labour in our strength and youth,
  With energy and perseverance firm,
  Comes Leisure—as *I* understand the term—
Sweet Leisure, in its plentitude and truth ;
The leisure to be free from the uncouth
  Necessity of letting John affirm
  We're "not at home" to friends, or else confirm
His words by being "absent" when his ruth
  Permits them to come in and talk with us.
  The leisure for a chat without the fuss
Of saying "we're engaged," or feeling so ;
The leisure for a drive, a quiet row
  Upon the river ; leisure for a host
  Of pleasant things that formerly would cost
The sacrifice of more momentous tasks ;
The leisure for enjoying Art, which asks
  Attention in its due delight ; or rhymes,
  For which we had "no time" in busy times ;
The leisure to peruse the last new book,
Or through the magazines to cast a look ;
  The leisure to arrange in vase or glasses
  Fresh flowers, leafy ferns, or drooping grasses ;
The leisure for dear needlework—that best
Of all resources for a woman's rest,
  When, tired with too much headwork at a stretch,
  Her brains repose while fingers nimbly stitch ;
The leisure to make up no end of "lovely bonnets,"
Or time to pen (like this!) long-ending playful
  sonnets.

NOVEMBER EIGHT, 1871.

Still-born! The little being upon whom
  So many hopes were fixed has ne'er drawn
    breath;
  Borne tenderly away at once by Death,
As though to save it consciousness of doom.
Upon her couch, within the soft-hush'd room,
  The gentle mother lies, resign'd beneath
  God's will; but weepingly unweaves the wreath
Of buds 'mid which her blossom ne'er must bloom.
  O buds of promis'd joy! O blossom lost!
Gone from among the flowers of our life!
Your fragrance will be miss'd, however rife
  Our other sweets henceforth may be: yet most
Meantime remains our comfort to revive,
The parent Rose is spared to live and thrive.

AT MIDNIGHT OF ALL SOULS.

I hear the rushing of the Sea of Time ;
   Whose mighty waters, in their pauseless whelm,
   Suck down, resistless, nation, race, and realm,
Like rotting seaweed, drench'd in ooze and slime.
Ocean ! incarnardin'd with countless crime ;
Green with drown'd hopes, and wreck of joyous
     prime ;
   Salt with the myriad tears of human woes ;
   Toss'd with the surge and tumult of earth's
     throes ;
We note thy shifting sands, and pace thy shore ;
We watch thy ebbing tides, and list thy roar,
   Heark'ning, with awe, th' innumerable things
   Told in thy billowy thunderings ;
Until, by the coming of our one appointed wave,
We're swept into th' eddy of that universal grave.

SICK-BED REFLECTION.

From angle of the bed whereon I lie—
White-curtained, softly, shroudingly, from glare
Of southern sunlight that doth broadly stare—
I see a patch of welcome clear blue sky
Reflected in a picture-sketch close by,
Of Child and Virgin, called " Riposo," where
The Mother, seated on the ground, with bare
Tired feet, gives from her breast the bland supply
Of Nature's earliest, sweetest food to Him
Who lived to help the way-worn, sick, and sad.
The patch of heavenly blue, the sketch half dim
'Neath glassy surface-reflex, render glad
My illness-wearied heart, inspire fresh strength
To bear, in hope of health again at length.

ON A DEAFNESS.

I.

As one shut out in cold and darkness drear,
  Beyond the strains of minstrelsy within,
  Beyond the reach of talking's pleasant din,
When eager voices ring their changes clear,
In conversation full of welcome cheer—
  As one whose senses only murmurs win
  Of muffled nothingness, dim, sparse, and thin—
Thus feel I with this cruel deafened ear.

From me, who whilom heard the slightest sound,
From me, who revelled in the finest tones
  Of music-notes or speaking-voice around
My happy life, nigh forceth heavy groans
  This torture of dull numbness in my head
  That almost seems as if already dead.

II.

Yet I will cheerfully indulge the hope
  That this affliction may soon pass away,
  Like drifting storm-cloud on a summer day:
Its suddenness of advent gives good scope
To trust it may as suddenly elope;
  It came upon me in a whelming way,
  As though besmothered by a load of hay;
Believing this may lift, I will not mope.

A swelt'ring heap of pillows, feather-bed,
And quilt of eider-down in thick brocade,
  A wadded hood lined heavily with lead,
A hundred-weight of flannel stuffing laid
  Around my nape, suggest the dreadful numbness
  That strikes attempt to speak it into dumbness.

SONNET,

The spirits of our dear lost Dead are oft
Around us : in our moments of distress,
Of doubt, of self-mistrust, they're near to bless
Us with a sense of subtle presence, soft,
Invisible, but felt; they raise aloft ˙
The fainting soul from out its worst excess
Of weary sadness and dejectedness,
In sympathy for what themselves have doff'd.
With shining wings, aye free from mortal dust
They hover o'er to shield us and enfold ;
They comfort us with yearning love that must
Prevail to help and steadfastly uphold ;
They bid us take fresh heart, and firmly trust
In HIM they now for evermore behold.

EXPECTATION.

As when the sea lies grey and smooth and still,
  With long-stretch'd level lines of leaden sky
  That either burst to tempest tossing high
And all the air with dread confusion fill—
Or gently break into dispersion till
  Blue rifts of heaven's depth between them lie
  In soft assurance of serenity,
And one bright gleam illumes the distant hill:
  So wait I in apparent calm for those
Expected news the post will surely bring;
  When all my soul's horizon in will close
With darkest storm-clouds, surging, clamouring—
  Or open tranquilly to hope and peace,
  Cerulean, golden, setting heart at ease,

RENOVATION.

The softened glow of sunset in the West,
  The glimmer of the planet in the sky,
  The murmur of the Baby voice close by
That talks itself unconsciously to rest,
Like the low prattle of young birds in nest—
  As I sit watching at the door a-nigh,
  In case the little one should sudden cry—
A sense of rapturous quiet fills my breast.
  Ay, quiet and the deepest gratitude
That sunset, starlight, Baby's voice are sent
  In God's own gift of blessed latitude
To renovate the spirit with content
  When, bruised by late anxiety and dread,
  It drooped, and sickened, and was all but dead.

ON A DESIRABLE RESIDENCE.

I.

To live within the view of open space
  Of sky, and sea, and far outstretching land,
  Is privilege and hourly blessing grand:
As age advances, double is the case
Of benefit derived from Nature's face
    Thus constantly beheld : while doomed to stand
    Inactive, frame and limbs worn out, a bland
Activity of soul may now take place.
    In sight of boundless firmament, and wide
    Extent of rolling Ocean's ceaseless tide,
Of woods, and fields, and undulating hills,
A sense of liberty and power fills
    The soul; and, leaning back in our arm-chair,
    We range with ease through realms of earth,
      sea, air.

II.

The buoyant motion and resistless force
  Of aye-succeeding waves, that tumble each
  O'er each in race to whelm the sandy beach,
Or break against hard rocks that in the course
Of time they fret and wear, or fill with hoarse
    And thund'rous roars vast caves that inward reach,
    Is gifted with an eloquence like speech
To urge idea of action as resource
    For feeble and infirm beholders : thus,
    The sweep of upland, vale, or meadow fair,
Suggests fertility and growth and care
    To cultivate ; long walks, hard rides, to us
Familiar once : 'bove all, the ordered speed
Of planets satisfies our mental need.

TO HENRY LITTLETON.

Kind Friend—who in thy boyhood won the firm
   Regard of him whose judgment clearly knew
   How to award the estimation due,
Ay, even then, to virtues in their germ,
That since have shone conspicuous in their term
   Of full matureness—virtues giv'n to few
   In stronger excellence of sterling, true
Perfection ; one who would not hurt a worm,
   And yet, though gentle-natured, can be stern
To wrong ; and who by ceaseless energy,
By diligence, by noble industry,
   Hast master'd fortune only these could earn—
Accept my lines for sake of him who's gone,
Whose mind and mine, thou know'st, were always
   one.

TO MAJOR-GENERAL SIR VINCENT EYRE:

ON RECEIVING FROM HIM A SONNET IN MEMORY OF

JOHN KEATS.

The gallant brow once crown'd by the red hand
Of Mars amid Cabul's rebellious strife
With laurels blood-besprent, near costing life,
Now wears a laurel-wreath that well may stand
Beside the first, since placed by bright command
Of Phœbus' self, the Poet-god : thus rife
In bays the man who wielded erst the knife
Of War, and now the pen's more potent wand.
That breast on which was set as its due right
The Star of India's ruddy blaze of light,
Recording martial deeds, has shown of late
How gently it can mourn th' untimely fate
Of early-stricken Keats in moving strain,
Lamenting tenderly his death and pain.

TO SAMUEL TIMMINS.

I.

The house where Shakespeare first saw light
  Is sent to me in effigy by one
  Whom I have never seen, but who hath done
Repeated kindnesses, nor few nor slight,
But make me feel I know him well by sight
  Of grateful friendship, shining like the sun
  That Shakespeare's baby eyes first look'd upon,
To make all vivified and clear and bright.
  It shows to those whom distance keeps apart,
And e'en to those who ne'er have known or seen
  Each other, that within their mutual heart
Which serves to manifest with purest sheen
  The constancy and faithfulness that gain
  Undying love to countervail all pain.

II.

One morn, in Birmingham, a stranger sat
  At breakfast, feeling somewhat lonely there;
  As not a soul, for aught he knew, did care
One jot about his coming : so he ate
With rueful downcast looks upon his plate,
  And thought but little of his tempting fare
  While thinking much upon the dramas rare
He came to lecture on and highly rate.
  But all at once there beam'd into the room
A face of frankest welcome that dispell'd
  The previous sense of solitary gloom,
A voice of friendliness, a hand outheld,
  That since has been unceasing in its acts
  Of friendship, speaking fervently in facts.

Y

ON RECEIVING "A TREASURY OF ENGLISH SONNETS."

John Mills, dear valued friend of him we've lost,
  Accept my thanks for this Aladdin gift
  Of priceless fruit-like gems, with careful sift
Stored up and garnered in unsparing cost
Of labour-love, to yield at will a host
  Of richest thought-suggestions that uplift
  The soul when sadly it inclines to drift
Away down-cast, like scatter'd weeds wind-toss'd.
  In the joint names of us who cannot be
Disjoin'd—no, not by even Death itself—
  Take loving earnest thanks for giving me
A book that henceforth rests upon our shelf
  In company with those we used to cherish
  And read together—books that ne'er will perish.

ON READING GEORGE H. CALVERT'S "SHAKESPEARE: A BIOGRAPHICAL AND ÆSTHETIC STUDY."

Oh, that my Charles had lived to read this book
  With me ; to revel in its fervent praise
  Of him who wore supreme Apollo's bays,
Who straight in Nature's sun-bright face could look,
Transcribing faithfully what thence he took,
  With eagle might of firm undazzled gaze ;
  His page the reflex of her golden rays,
Himself liege-lord of her he ne'er forsook.
  We both—as now but one, alas ! can do—
Would from our heart have thanked the man whose
    part
  Has been to bring distinctly into view
The essence beauty of our Poet's art,
  And show with strength of finest eloquence
  The source divine of Shakespeare's excellence.

MOODS.

A sense of awe at all that doth surround
Us mortals in this universal frame
Of sky, and sea, and mountains all a-flame
With sunrise, noontide, sunset, in a round
Supremely order'd, strikes us with profound
  Humility, discouragement, self-blame,
  To feel we know so little of these same
Grand patent miracles that thus abound.
  At times comes this : at others comes a sense
Of ecstasy, of comfort, deep delight,
  Beatitude and gratitude intense
To merely live within this wondrous sight.
  When either mood of mind doth most prevail,
  Trust, simple trust, is all that can avail.

WIDOWED.

A torn half-sheet of writing thrown away,
  Disfigured, crumpled, meaningless, and blurr'd,
  With scarce one clear intelligible word—
A poor, fragmentary, disjointed stray,
That naught coherent or worth heed doth say—
  A thing devoid of sense, inane, absurd—
  A script inscrutable, a song unheard,
A remnant given over to decay.
  Such, such am I, asunder rent from him
Who made my life harmonious, smooth, distinct
  In purpose and felicity: the dim,
Defacèd lines, the syllables dislink'd,
  God's own good time, in patient trust await,
  For firm reunion set for ever straight.

SOLACE.

Unspeakable the comfort in the thought
   Of tendernesses interchanged long, long
   Ago: a gentle word, a look, a throng
Of then scarce-heeded loving trifles wrought
Their sounds for future melody, and brought
   The murmur'd music of their memory-song
   To soften pangs of anguish, bitter, strong,
With consolation sweet, else vainly sought.
   O lips of balmy touch! that never breathed
A word but kind, a tone but fond! O eyes!
   That ne'er met mine but with a look of love!
The grief to know ye gone for aye from earth
   Is strangely solaced by the consciousness
   Ye never gave me aught but blessedness:
And hope to find ye still unchanged in Heaven
Makes hope of Heaven dearer yet to me.

THANKSGIVING.

O Thou—Thyself the Infinite of Love—
Who hast with bounteous hand bestow'd on me
Through life full measure of the ecstasy
Of love, who from Thine azure heights above
Hast sent upon the pinions of thy dove
Continued waftage of benignity,
Through Mother's blessed care and ministry;
Through Father's strong affection, naught could
    move;
Through Husband's tenderness, from first to last
A lover's love and constancy maintain'd—
For all this love that made existence past
So happy and so bright, enjoyed, attain'd,
Accept my fervent thanks, O God! And now
Its mem'ry even is comfort, well know'st Thou!

DECEMBER SIXTEEN, 1878.

" A girl—both child and mother doing well!"
  The joyful news comes bounding o'er the sea
  And land, to bring us blissful certainty.
O longed-for little one!   Let this verse tell
How welcome is thy birth : a fairy spell
    Thou art, enhancing all our Christmas glee,
    Enriching our New Year by having thee,
A fairer sprite than Spenser's Florimel.
    Fond friends in England, friends in Italy,
Thy birth, dear child, exultingly will greet ;
    And many a winter hearth will brighter be
By reason of thy coming, Baby sweet !
    To Him who sent this priceless Christmas gift
    In fervent gratitude our hearts we lift.

NEW YEAR'S EVE.

Upon the threshold of another year
I stand : to-morrow's sun will open wide
Its portals.   What within them may betide?
What new, or unexpected, may appear?
What solemn chance, or what event to cheer?
A range of veilèd shapes, set side by side,
I dimly see awaiting there to glide
Each one upon us, in its turn, more near.
Shall I be still on earth, to see unveil'd
These shapes ?   Shall I behold them clearly then
As now I vision-like descry them, paled
By distance ?   Will they come within my ken
Of living sight ?   Or shall I view them, passing,
   past,
With sense immortal—seeing, knowing all at last?

BEQUEST.

Each tender-sacred blessing and caress
   He gave me in our bygone wedded years
   Its own especial hallowing appears
To have bequeathed, with an immortal stress
Upon my heart and lips, intense impress :
   They help to calm despairing fears
   And chase away those sternly held-back tears
That heavily the drooping heart oppress.
Oh, Love, that in thy gentle-potent might
   Art stronger than the ruthless giant, Death !
   Oh, Love, that with thy vital balmy breath
Hast power to fan into a radiant light
   The spark within the darkness of the grave,
   I thank Him who to me thy fulness gave !

DOUBLE EXISTENCE.

Two lives are lived by many a living soul,
 An outer and an inner life : the one,
 In sympathy with friends, in open tone
Express'd, and frankly patent to the whole
Community 'midst whom our days do roll
 Their course. The other, secret, mute, alone
 With God and our own thoughts, laid bare and
 prone
Before His eye—their judge and witness sole.
 A crowd of musings, hopes, high aspirations,
Of penitential tears, sharp agonies,
 Of earnest strivings, conscious aberrations,
We pass among and through without surmise
 By those who, from our cradle to our grave
 Can mark how staidly, calmly, we behave.

ON RE-READING MY DEAR MOTHER'S LAST-WRITTEN LETTERS TO ME.

I.

Oh, Mother! past all mothers good and kind!
   I take into the inmost of my heart
   Thy words of love and confidence, a part
Of thine own being interfused and twined
With mine to elevate and make refined
   Its essence; thus thy spirit to impart,
   As once thou gav'st, with throes of willing smart,
Corporeal frame to body and to mind.
   'Tis more than quarter-century since thou
These letters penned, since thou didst leave this
      earth ;
   I read them with the hallowed feeling now
That they are sent to me from where thy worth
   Receives its heavenly reward for all
   It was to us on whom thy blessings fall.

II.

This morning, as I reperused thy lines
  Of Mother love and care, the nightingale
  Poured forth its early song amid the pale
Grey-golden light aslant between the pines
And belt of gayer trees that round confines
  This pleasant house. Such sounds and sights
    avail
  To typify thy words, which never fail
To raise the soul when sadly it repines.
  Oh, thou, who wrote such helpful words to thy
E'er grateful daughter, look upon her still,
  Behold her soothed beneath the soft spring sky
By letters that her eyes and heart upfill
  By thought of thee, surviving e'en thy loss
And aiding her to bear whate'er may cross.

OUR TERRACE.

I.

I pace the Terrace up and down where thou
   And I were wont to walk together when
   Thou wert on earth beside me. Then, oh, then,
I had thy hand in mine, I saw thee bow
Thy head down towards me with a gesture how
   Confiding, earnest, fond! Dear, best of men!
   I listened to thy voice the while the wren
Her small shrill note chirped near to us. But now,
   Thy tones, thy presence, thy corporeal self
Are gone from me! Their memory alone
   Are blended with the chirp of that bird-elf,
With gracious sounds and sights that thus have
     grown
   To be embodiments of thee, my love,
   Who watchest me from yonder blue above!

II.

Such "gracious sounds and sights" are rife around
   This pleasant spot, Italian in its grace,
   Its richly coloured amplitude of space,
Its wealth of blossoms that superb abound,
Its blue expanse of sky and sea and ground
   Of distant mountains, with deep azure trace—
   Distinguishable scarcely is the place
Where strictly the horizon may be found.
   The sails, bright snowy flecks upon the wave,
Reflections seem of those white clouds that sail
   Through æther: all is peaceful silence, save
When notes of feathered warblers tell their tale
   Of happiness with their outpouring song,
   As now alone, alas, I pace along.

III.

Oh, well may " gracious sounds and sights " bring
   thee
To mind, who wert all gracious, all benign !
Who never uttered word, or made a sign
That was not gracious, when thou spok'st to me!
Not once, through all the happy years that we
   Together were, didst thou the least repine
When we were poor; but with a courage fine
Thou cheerful wert, and blithe as blithe could be.
   No syllable impatient or cross word,
No pettish movement, not one peevish tone,
   Can I recall that e'er I saw or heard :
In health, all brightness; ill, no single moan ;
   But, ever patient, hopeful, hearty, kind—
As excellent in heart and soul as mind.

IV.

And thus, my love, my Charles, doth God permit
   Thee to be with me still as here I walk ;
   To hear thy gentle elevating talk
In Nature's gracious sounds that soothing flit
Around me ; to behold thee as I sit
   In one of those two seats wherein we'd balk
   Our pacing and take rest ; no slender stalk,
Or spray, or blade of grass, but brings with it
   Thine image ; so sufficing in its form,
Consummate in its character create,
   Containing latent virtues multiform
For those allowed to know their good innate,
   As I, thank God, was granted thus to con
   By heart thyself and have thee, though thou'rt
   gone.

v.

When erst I paced our Terrace to and fro
   Alone, I kept thee with me by a look
   Each time I passed the window where, with book
In hand, thou sat'st and never fail'dst to throw
An answering glance and smile at me. But no
   Bent head or quick responsive glance, that took
   Me to thee then, now makes the window nook
A magnet for my eyes: the subtle glow
   Of memory is all remains to mark
The spot and fill it with thine image there.
   Instead, my gaze seeks higher for the spark
Divine, thy spirit, yonder in the air,
   The universal all-embracing span
   Of heaven's blue, thou best-belovèd man !

ON RE-READING SOME LETTERS OF MY CHARLES TO HIS SISTER ISABELLA, WHICH WERE RETURNED TO US WHEN SHE DIED.

As one who, searching in a drawer for some
  Laid-by apparel, encountereth the sweet
  Enduring scent of lavender—so greet
Me in these long-uphoarded words a sum
Of countless comforts, cordial strengths, that come
  With perfume of undying love to meet
  My famished senses and pour out a treat
Fit to revive them from their faintness numb.
  Dear sister Bell! To thee of me he writes
In full outspoken warmth and fervour fond,
  And dwells upon our wedded life's delights
With happy unreserve. Thou from beyond
  The grave hath sent this fragrant solace. Take
My heartfelt thanks for his and thine own sake.

A REMONSTRANCE.

My soul—that birdlike beat'st thy wings in vain
  Against perplexing bars—with ceaseless bruise
  Of spirit and with efforts that contuse
Thy feebleness, thou mak'st perpetual strain
To pierce the veil of mystery and pain
  That cramps thee in : oh, fluttering soul ! Why
    use
  Such constant futile struggles, which confuse
Thy sense, and nothing but defeat can gain ?
  A restless longing to behold again
My lost Beloved, to penetrate the haze
  Of time and space and distance that retain
Us from each other's love-contented gaze,
  Is mine. Yet learn, my soul, from this my rhyme
  To closely furl thy wings and wait God's time.

TWILIGHT.

At dusk I often slip away and creep
 To our own whilom room—now mine alone !—
And listen to the inward undertone
Of my heart's memories, the while I weep—
And watch the fitful firelight glinting sweep
 O'er statuettes and pictures, thickly sown
 With old associations, forcing moan
But half suppress'd, as when we restless sleep.
 Oh, quiet shadowy room, so dear to him,
So dear to me—the scene of so much peace
 And joy to both—within thy twilight dim
On bygone days I muse without surcease :
 I live again our happy wedded life
 And feel I am my own Beloved's wife.

WOUNDS.

Some wounds there are we know will ne'er be
　　healed ;
　　Nor do we care to have them cured or set
　　Aside, or put beyond our inward fret :
We only strive to keep them well concealed,
And by no murmur let them be revealed.
　　Why cause our friends one fruitless sad regret ?
　　Why suffer them to see our eyes are wet
With tears that courage teaches may be sealed
　　Beneath resolvèd patience to endure ?
God sends such courage and the mental strength
　　To use it, if we trust His mercy pure.
He wisely judges what shall be the length
　　Of time we have to bear : oh, may it be,
　　That pain borne bravely wins joy heavenly !

A MORNING MOON.

(IRREGULAR SONNET.)

I.

The faintest thread of silvery bow is there,
Discernible in golden azure sky,
'Mid which the rosy cloudlets sail on high—
The morning moon, the waning moon, so fair
Yet slender in its beauty, that mine eye,
If straying for a moment, has to try
Afresh to find the spot in heaven where
The Cynthian gem maintains its coy repair—
This lovely sight—but one of myriad more
That Nature prodigally spreads around
In bountiful, benign, abundant store,
To comfort hearts forlorn upon Earth's ground—
Thou, thou, my love in Heaven, surely see'st,
Enjoyest, from the largest to the least;
Behold'st them with a comprehending sight,
The sight of souls endowed with final light.

To think that thou and I, my Charles, still gaze
   Together on the glories of the vast
   Grand universal frame by Nature cast
Around to fill man's soul with glad amaze,
Methinks assuages pain, and helps to raise
   My drooping heart when brooding over past
   Delights, in trusting that until at last
We're reunited evermore, our ways
   Remain the same—adoring God-sent sights,
Beholding Him in them, receiving as
   His boon direct the tender soothing lights
Of sunshine, moonbeam, star-ray, when it has
   Touched lucently the surface of the rippled sea
   And made a seeming pathway to eternity.

VARIED FROM SHAKESPEARE'S 144TH SONNET.

Three loves I've had of comfort through my life
 Which like good spirits did suggest me still:
My father, mother, him who called me wife,
 Allaying by affection ev'ry ill.
They vied with one another who should bless
 Me most, evolving all was best within
My nature, teaching it the loveliness
 And bliss of virtue, misery of sin.
These angels upon earth were given to me
 By God Himself as nearest dearest friends
And guardian spirits of my soul to be
 (Such spirits He beneficently sends),
Three loves supreme to be my heart's best food
And bring to me chief happiness and good.

VARIED FROM SHAKESPEARE'S 105TH
SONNET.

Let not my love be called idolatry,
　Nor my belovèd as an idol show,
Since all alike my thoughts and praises be
　Of one, but one, still such and ever so.
Kind was my love to me, and always kind,
　Still constant in a wondrous excellence ;
Therefore my verse, to constancy confin'd,
　One thing expressing, leaves out difference.
Dear, kind, and true is all my argument—
　Dear, kind, and true, varying to other words ;
And in this change is my invention spent,
　Three themes in one, which wondrous scope
　　affords.
Dear, kind, and true, have often lived alone,
Which three, in mine own Charles, were found in
　one.

TO C. C. C.

I.

It fills my heart with joy to think of thee :
Thou art so altogether real and good,
So genuine in thy every mood ;
Whether in mirth's exuberance of glee
Thou laugh'st a ringing laugh right heartily,
Or when on man's injustice thou dost brood--
Sad meditation's bitterest food—
With face sincere in mournful gravity.
My Charles, from youth my guide and my best
friend !
The thought of thee brings gladness to my heart,
Full bliss when near, a comfort when apart ;
And thus 'twill be, I feel, until life's end :
For thou art manly-soul'd and truest of the true,
Worthy of all love—e'en the love I bear to you.

II.

So one we are, to praise thee seems self-praise :
Yet we are one but by the might of love ;
Since thy fine essence sets thee far above
Her whom thou chosest sharer of thy days,
Esteeming her thine equal in all ways.
To this thy generous nature did thee move,
More than desert in her thou e'er could'st prove :
'Twas thine own excellence that help'd to raise.
For—genial, full of warmest sympathies,
Large-hearted, bounteous, greatly tolerant,
Poetic-minded, spirits high-buoyant,
Most gentle, kindly, humorous, and wise—
Thy varied goodness wrought unconsciously,
And stirr'd an emulative good in me.

III.

What well inclin'd thou found'st, that didst thou
    cherish,
    Asserting no superior will or might,
    Assuming no prerogative from clearer light:
What ill defect there was, thou mad'st it perish,
Exacting no observance blindly slavish;
    But mildly taught by dint of purest right
    Made evident, unurg'd, to reason's sight:
Prescribing no jot, thou ruled'st by a wish.
Thy ways make children treat thee as their own:
    With thee the young Valeria prates apace,
    Sits on thy knee; persuasive, smoothes thy face,
And—patronisingly familiar grown—
    Oft kissing it, calls thee her " dearest boy,"
    And makes thy silver'd hair her fav'rite toy.

IV.

(DECEMBER FIFTEEN, 1869.)

Thy eighty-second birthday sees thee still
    The same, my Charles! Some natures ne'er
    grow old:
· Their essence is so vital and uncold
That no advance of shadowy years may chill
The innate sunshine: there it lies to fill
    The daily homes of those around with gold
    Glad warmth, to cheer and genially enfold
With constant comfort whomsoe'er it will.
    Thy loving friends, thy proud and happy wife,
Have basked beneath its ever-shining ray,
Have felt the bright benignant influence play
    Upon their onward course of passing life
To help them ever trustfully sustain
Their God-sent share of mingled bliss and pain.

V.

(DECEMBER FIFTEEN, 1875.)

And thou hast reached to eighty-eight, my love!
And forty-seven of those years have seen
Our wedded happiness in life serene
Of mutual comfort, help, and joy above
The share most mortals are ordained to prove;
   Our way has lain through pleasant paths and
   green,
Full of contentment has existence been:
All this our deepest gratitude doth move.
   Together, hand-in-hand, we've been allowed
To work, to write, to read, to pass through life
With thanks perpetual, heartfelt, not loud,
To Him who made us happy man and wife.
   Together, hand-in-hand, may we be still
Throughout Eternity, by God's good will.

VI.

Sometimes when I sit quietly and muse
   On bygone times and long-departed joys,
   I hear with startling clearness thy loved voice
In sudden ringing laugh, that still renews
An echo of my then delight to use
   Whatever wile might win that pleasant noise
   Of heartfelt mirth from thee: the veriest toys
Of fancy served to please us and amuse.
   Our own old favourite books read o'er and o'er
Ne'er failed to charm again and yet again:
   We freshly savoured all the pith and core
Of jests from Sheridan's or Molière's brain;
   Jack Falstaff's racy wit ne'er lost its zest,
   And Shakespeare's fun we always found the best.

VII.

A bright true spirit hadst thou, Charles, my own !
" Touch'd to fine issues " certainly it was ;
And, kindled warmly to a noble cause
For sympathy, with fire responsive shone.
Sometimes, from mere apparent nothings grown—
A witty thought, a droll suggestive pause—
Would clear crow forth thy jubilant Ha-has !
With sparkles of the eye and cheery tone.
Anon some grave injustice, cruel wrong,
Would force from thee indignant protest, strong,
Poured forth in many a fierce vehement word.
How present to my mental eye appears
Thy sympathetic nature, promptly stirred
To cordial laughter or to earnest tears.

VIII.

(NEW YEAR'S DAY.)

Although thou art in Heaven, I on earth,
My greeting I must give thee, as of old,
Whene'er another year hath past us roll'd,
Whene'er another year hath its new birth.
That which hath made the years supremely worth
Is our affection to each other told
With firm conviction that 'twill constant hold
'Gainst Time, 'gainst Death itself, and know no
dearth
Or diminution. Mine is more intense
Than ever : thine, I feel as sure, is just
The love it always was—in truest sense
A perfect love and full of perfect trust—
The dearest love that ever blessed the life
Of woman, and thy happy, happy wife.

IX.

If, coming into our own quiet room,
    I were to see thy figure standing there,
    How would my soul sustain or even dare
Believe the blinding light amid the gloom ?
How bear the mingled awe and joy would bloom
    Within me ?   Should I paralysedly stare
    Upon thy semblance, hardly yet aware
If it meant bliss restored or instant doom ?
    I know that I should fling me on thy breast,
Instinctively should clasp thee in mine arms,
    Should feel that all my cares were set at rest,
Myself securely haven'd from all harms :
        My lips would seek from thine the rapturous
            breath,
        Or bid thee take me to delicious death.

X.

At times a longing so acute doth seize
    Me for thee, dearest, I can scarce refrain
    From uttering a wild sharp cry of pain ;
A hungry craving naught can e'er appease,
Or bring my heart its old accustomed ease,
    To see thee, hear thee, touch thee yet again,
    And so dissolve away in softest rain
Of tears upon thy breast, attaining peace
    Eternal, blended once for all with thee.
Imperishable love between us two
    Has been our gift from God : the power to see
This gift supreme lends courage to renew
        My patient trust, and set my heart at rest,
        Submissive ever to His great behest.

XI.

ON A PROSPECT OF SEEING PUBLISHED THE SECOND SERIES OF " SHAKESPEARE-CHARACTERS."

Small rosy clouds endapple morning's blue ;
  Then bars of gold, that broaden more and more,
  Bespread the East, uplighting sea and shore :
So rise within my soul glad thoughts of you,
My Charles, and of your love so deep, so true.
  And with these thoughts arise to-day a store
  Of sunny hopes that only dawned before
In twilight held obscure ; but now renew
  Their brightness, and assume substantial shape.
Oh, may I live to witness your desire
  Fulfilled, and, rescued from all chance of 'scape,
These written words of yours, instinct with fire
  Shakespearianly kindled, put in print,
  Completing your intention without stint.

XII.

(DECEMBER FIFTEEN, 1880.)

Communing thus with thee in verse, I seem
  To still hold converse with thee face to face,
  Although between us two th' abysm of space
Hath drawn its veil of blue expanse : a beam
Direct from central sunlight sheds a gleam,
  Methinks, upon thee in thy hallowed place
  Among the blessed bright immortal race
Of spirits whom we see in blissful dream.
  This day, which gave thee birth, I greet with these
Poor lines ; that I may feel as though I spoke
  Them to thyself, my Charles, my love, and please
My fancy with believing I invoke
  Some still supremer touch of joy to thee,
  E'en where thou art, bethinking thee of me.

XIII.

At night, when I am thinking of thee, dear,
  With more than usual energy of thought,
  Meseems as though it actually brought
Thy spirit in its vital presence near ;
Ay, in this very room, where without fear
  I lie and listen if there may be caught
  Some slightest rustle, faintest sound, or aught
That may assure me thou art truly here.
  So earnestly my thoughts go forth to meet
With thine, methinks it cannot be but both
Our spirits meet at moments thus, in troth,
  In close conjunction, mystical, yet sweet ;
As when, of old, we mingled thoughts and soul
In one transcendent undivided whole.

XIV.

(ON COMPLETING MY COLLECTED VOLUME OF
VERSES.)

This book—like all I've done since childhood years—
  Is dedicate to thee, my Charles ; for thou,
  As when thou wert on earth, in Heaven now,
Regardest, with fond interest that cheers
Attempt, e'en trifle such as this appears,
  Except to eyes that lovingly endow
With grace small seedling efforts which do bow
Their heads and wither amid trembling fears,
  If winds severe of criticism " shake
Their buds from growing." Thou, therefore, and all
  Who've loved and love us both, I think, will take
This handful of verse-blossoms, simple, small,
  Yet from the garden of my heart, where grow
Perpetual flowers of love, deep set, down low.